I found that we could relate to any one of the characters in this book. The White Room of Darkness, puts into perspective that no matter who we are or think we are and how wealthy we might be, that in the end if we don't know Jesus we will be eternally lost. This book was a great read!

I found the book hard to put down the further along I got into it. I was glad that everyone came to accept God in their lives. I loved how it unfolded for each of them. It was interesting to see how all the characters had parts in being where God placed them to bring His plan about. It makes you realize that while we see what happens now, overall God sees the big picture.

"Imaginative and inspiring! Thanks, Lorne, for your creative story that once again confirms the authority and supremacy of God and His plan of salvation for each of us! Keep writing!"

"Like Bart, it is easy to follow the wrong paths in life, but with the love and forgiveness of God and family, there is never a time to doubt the miracles the Lord can do in ones life. While reading The White Room of Darkness, I was left wanting to know more about Bart's life and the paths he chose for himself and his future."

Gwyn Robertson ... School Bus Trainer/
Driver ... N. Battleford, SK, Canada

"The White Room of Darkness is an amazing novel. You start reading it and it is very hard to put down. It made me feel that with the love of my children and family, a person can overcome anything and we all need is God in our lives."

Jacqueline Dionne Cook /Baker ... Fort St James BC, Canada

"We all struggle and strive for answers to life questions. In The White Room of Darkness you find a family who are in different places as far as finding their own answers; some have theirs, some have found one part, and some not. Their discoveries will be surprising and thought provoking as you consider if you have found your own answers and the truth we all want and need to know."

Karen Harrison ... Legal Assistant ...
Black Diamond, AB, Canada

THE WHITE ROOM OF DARKNESS

LORNE SPENCER HRABIA

WESTBOW
PRESS®
A DIVISION OF THOMAS NELSON
& ZONDERVAN

WestBow Press books may be ordered through booksellers or by contacting:

WestBow Press
A Division of Thomas Nelson & Zondervan
1663 Liberty Drive
Bloomington, IN 47403
www.westbowpress.com
1 (866) 928-1240

ISBN: 978-1-5127-4826-0 (sc)
ISBN: 978-1-5127-4827-7 (hc)
ISBN: 978-1-5127-4825-3 (e)

Library of Congress Control Number: 2016910426

Print information available on the last page.

WestBow Press rev. date: 7/6/2016

To my son, Bradley Joseph Hrabia, who has been a tremendous inspiration in my life, even though we don't always see eye to eye. My son looks at life with open eyes and no fear of the what-if that we all seem to face and fear in our walk. To me, he is the best son a father could ever have; the best husband to his wife, Shandra; and the best father to their beautiful daughters, Bella and Zoey. They are active in their church and are training up their children in the Lord.

Start children off on the way they should go,
and even when they are old they will not turn from it.
—Proverbs 22:6

INTRODUCTION

Through our lives, we have all faced the trials and temptations that the characters in *The White Room of Darkness* face in their day-to-day lives. It matters not if we are financially rich or very poor in the eyes of the world. What really matters is what we do with what we have.

Bart is a spoiled, rich young man, living off the hard-earned wealth of his father, whom he hates—and he makes no bones about it either. He is angry that his older brother left home, because of their father's lack of attention towards both of them, so he embraces a lifestyle of riding on the wild edge of life with money, women, and pleasure, while still living at home. His anger rages on, gaining strength, but in the midst of it all, there is something eating away at the very center of his being.

Within all of Bart's anger live Earnest Bartholomew Woodsworth, his father; Katherine Sylvia Woodsworth, his mother; Caroline, his sister; and Franklin, his brother who left home. Also thrown into the mix are Thomas Hillman, Earnest's best friend and business partner; his wife, Shelly; and Winter Rose.

Just like these people, we all face the chores of day-to-day living, working and surviving in a world that really doesn't care who we are, but there is *hope* for each of us. The quest we are on is to seek out that hope and use it to change our lives for the good, whether that be to better ourselves or those around us who come and go in our everyday lives.

The White Room of Darkness is a book that turns anger to peace, hatred to love and hurt to forgiveness once hope is found along with the real reason we are all alive and well on planet earth!

CHAPTER ONE

Roadside gravel shot out 30 to 40 feet over the edge of the cliff as the glossy jet-black Jaguar XJ Saloon drifted along the harrowing edge, eventually turning in a neat, tight 35-foot circle until its tires regripped the security of the pavement. The 100,000-dollar luxury sports car quickly accelerated to a speed of 200 miles per hour along a straightaway for only a few seconds before decelerating into an upcoming hairpin corner. The driver was now travelling in the center of the road, making a tight right-hand turn when suddenly the Jag encountered a semi coming from the opposite direction, carrying a large construction excavator in the outside lane as it was attempting to make the same curve. The fast-moving Jag cut hard back into its lane but not without overcompensating, causing the black, bullet-like convertible to partially climb the sloped wall of rock to its right.

Once again, rocks flew out in all directions as the driver's young hands tried to correct the out-of-control car before it plunged over the cliff to certain death at 500 feet below. The car passed so close to the cab of the semi that its driver could see into the terrified green eyes of the female passenger, her long blond hair streaking out in all directions, before they quickly lost that brief moment of contact. He also heard the tail end of her screams and another puzzling sound just before the driver of the car managed to get it under control. The moment was so quick that he wasn't exactly sure, but the semi driver thought he heard the sound of the driver laughing.

"Bart, you scared me so much that I almost peed my pants!"

"Hey, babe, you only live once, you know!" Bart said as he brought the expensive car to a stop just outside of her apartment complex in the heart of the city.

"That is true, but I like to think that it will last a little longer."

"Hey, if you can't handle the heat, babe, then feel free to leave."

"Leave? What do you mean by that?"

"You're a big girl. You know exactly what that means."

"Bart, we have been together for almost a year now. I thought you loved me," she said as reality began to sink in and tears formed in the corners of her amazing green eyes.

"Loved you? What are you talking about? Sure, we have had a great time, but love? No way!"

She burst into tears, there in his 100,000-dollar luxury car.

"Be careful there. Try not to get any tears on this upholstery," he said as he ran his hand lovingly over the finely crafted leather.

With that, she was out the door, slamming it shut as she turned. She ran towards her apartment building, sobbing all the way.

"Hey! You don't ... have to ... slam the door," was all he had to say, just before he floored it and left the imprint of tire tread marks there on the pavement in front of his most recent girlfriend's apartment building.

Woodsworth Industries International prided itself on its worldwide achievements that helped to improve the lives of hundreds of millions, if not billions, of people. At the helm of the company sat the CEO and founder, Earnest Bartholomew Woodsworth, a man of character, integrity and morals, something he would often refer to as a lost cause in today's society.

Earnest was a man who started at the bottom in a furniture-manufacturing plant and through dedication, hard work and perseverance, eventually became the manager until he bought out the company some years later. At that time, many others like him were buying up such companies and then selling them off piece by piece. Earnest, however, wanted to own something when it would finally be time to retire, so he went against the flow and began to look for smaller companies that he felt could be turned around and made profitable once more to purchase.

From that point on, the rest was history—that is, until he met his wife, Katie. They had two boys and one daughter and a very happy beginning, but as the company grew, it required more and more of Earnest's time, which inevitably cut into the family time. His lack of time at home also affected his marriage and his relationship with his children.

He was not a greedy man, but he had a burning passion to see to each and every company he purchased, restructured and turned around until it was making money hand over fist, as the saying goes. But his children, the boys in particular, resented the fact that the company was more family to their father than they were. His eldest son, Franklin, was hurt the most and left home as soon as he graduated from high school. He wanted nothing of his father or his fortune and was bound and determined to make it on his own. Bart, on the other hand, lived for the wealth and all its pleasures. He hated the fact that his older brother had left home and that they rarely talked; he blamed it all on his father and made sure that his father knew the only reason he stayed was for the wealth.

Caroline, their only daughter, was very close to both parents, and she, unlike her brothers, understood her father entirely. She loved them both and towed the line, no matter what was requested of her. Katie and Caroline were like two peas in a pod and spent a lot of time shopping, doing lunch or redecorating the house. They also hosted parties at their summer home in the country and occasionally at the main house in the city as well.

Earnest Woodsworth was a man on a mission and always had an eye out for something new and innovative in the line of manufacturing or electronics. He always had to be the first one to have something new. When they first were released, he was the one to own a Polaroid camera, a video camera, a new remote car starter and even a new computer.

It was a warm summer day that found Earnest in his corporate office, high above the rest of the city beneath him. He was lounging out on his private deck, which jutted out from his office. It even came complete with a hot tub; lounging furniture; floral plants in large, ornate planters and a private barbecue, as he loved to cook for himself on those occasions when he spent the entire day working in his large office suite.

He sat in his favorite wicker lounge chair with his legs stretched out and his head supported by a soft pillow. As he lay there, taking a break from the everyday demanding workload, his mind began to wander back to simpler days and Thomas Hillman, his best friend.

Earnest's thoughts flashed back to the first time he had met Thomas. He was checking out a new product at a local welding shop that was promoting it as the next great thing in rural heating units. Earnest had just met the welding shop owner, who was giving him a quick tour through his business. Welding projects were this company's priority, but the owner, just like Earnest, was always on the lookout for something new, just breaking into the marketplace. He had given Earnest's company a call, knowing they were always looking for some new technology, when he heard about this new heating system. As the two men moved through the building, Earnest was finally introduced to Thomas Hillman, the contract designer for the welding shop.

The manager and Thomas then set about explaining to Mr. Woodsworth the concept and details of this easy-to-build heating wonder. Earnest could see right off that Thomas was a man worth getting to know, based on his design and creative skills. He was able to talk circles around his boss about details, innovative ideas and even the simplest construction plans.

"So you really do believe this idea of yours will work?" Earnest asked of this bright young man before him.

"Yes, sir, and even more exciting than that is the fact that it can be mass-produced at a relatively low price at three different usage levels."

"Price is definitely a major factor in production as well as sales. Have you had any outside interest in this project at all to date?" Earnest asked the two men.

"Well, I am mostly out of this project," the welding shop owner said. "Other than my willingness to produce the units. So I will leave you two gentlemen to discuss the nitty-gritty details," he added as he turned and left the room.

"So," Earnest started, "do you work for him?"

"Actually no. I only work under contract. That way, I have more say in any of my designs and the construction details."

"Smart move," Earnest said, liking this fellow even more as they talked. "So please give me some more details about how it works and any test results you have come up with so far."

"Okay, I would love to do that. Frank there, the owner of this shop, is okay to talk to, but he really doesn't understand the simple concept I am proposing."

"Well, my friend, this is the type of project I love hearing about, so go ahead and just explain it all to me. I won't interrupt until you're finished."

"I appreciate that. Okay then. This concept, which I have named 'Green Heat,' is a heating unit that uses no fossil fuels, solar power, electricity, or any type of conventional power source. It does require a conventional furnace to tie into but only to circulate the heat being generated by it. A fan powered by a gas generator would work as well.

"The unit could also be marketed to work in conjunction with a furnace, with the furnace being the backup unit, just in case problems ever arise. It also can be sold as three different types, but before we get into that, let me explain to you just how it works."

Earnest just nodded his head as Thomas continued with his explanation.

"It took a few prototypes before I finally got the system right, and we actually have an installed unit that is heating this building right now, so maybe I will show you the unit and explain its working components ... if that is okay with you?"

"Yes, that would be great. You just lead the way, and I will follow."

With that said, the two men began to weave their way through the large welding business; they went out a door on the south side and finally over to the heating unit.

"This is it," Thomas said as he pointed to what looked like the roof of a building sticking up out of the ground by about a foot.

"Well, I must say that this is quiet unusual and I have never seen anything like it before."

"Yes, it can be quite confusing when a person first sees it, but as I explain the components, I'm sure you will see how it all works," Thomas said as he went to one side where he released some sort of latch before walking to the opposing side and releasing the same type of latch. Then he leaned into the top center of the roof and pulled out a snap-pin, before returning to a standing position beside the heating unit.

"Can you give me a hand with this? You will see a hand grip on your side. Just hold onto it as we both pull it up. It is hinged on the side just behind us and will flip up as we lift."

Together the two men began to lift up on the roof of the structure, and Earnest was very surprised at just how easily it lifted up until they both heard a *click* that notified them that it was full height now and locked into place so that it wouldn't fall back down.

"Wow! Now there's a sight you don't see every day," Earnest said as he leaned in close for a better look at the inner workings on the heating unit. "I never in a million years would have ever thought of using that material to heat a building, but before you say anything, I think I know how this works. Once the furnace kicks in and begins to draw air into the building that is being heated, the air is sucked in through the vent in the roof," he said as he stood up and pointed to the separated vent in the center of the roof. "When you pulled out the snap-pin, it separated the vent from the end of the copper tubing we see just sitting there. The air being drawn in then circles down into the coiled copper tubing in the culvert, there in the middle of the unit." This time, he pointed to the galvanized culvert in the middle of the heating unit. "All the vegetation and plants surrounding the culvert give off heat, which is heating the air passing through the tubing until it gets to the bottom and is sucked into the building you are heating. Ingenious!"

"Well, thank you, and yes, you did get it right. This invention is a win-win situation. What that means is that after about two years of use, the plant material will decompose into soil. At that time, it will be removed before new plant materials are added. This soil can be used to fertilize the garden so the cycle is complete."

"You certainly know your stuff," Earnest said with a big smile on his face.

"Do you remember me saying that these units could be sold on three levels?"

"Yes, I do. Please explain."

"Okay, my pleasure. Well, as you see, with this unit here, when it is time to clean out the soil that will be the by-product, we will use a backhoe to scoop it out; therefore the walls of this unit must be very strong and durable, reinforced with a grid pattern of rebar to handle the bumping and scraping. But if we were to sell this unit to a third-world country, where they would have to clean it out using shovels, then the unit could have thinner walls with just a bare minimum of reinforcement in the walls. Also, it could use plastic tubing instead of copper, which would help with the overall cost," Thomas said as he looked down at the unit before them, which was giving off a lot of heat on the cool day while the two men stood there.

"Amazing, simply amazing, but you mentioned three levels; what would the second level be then, assuming that the third-world sales would be the bottom level?"

"You're right on that," Thomas said as he looked up at Earnest again. "The second level would be more for smaller-scale units that could be sold for cabins, hot tubs, and items that require heat on a more limited scale. I guess it would be for more seasonal heat."

"Is there anything else I would have to know?" Earnest asked.

"Funny you should ask that, because anyone else who has seen this unit almost always asks about the smell."

"I did notice it, but then it is from the decomposing process, I would assume?"

"Precisely, but even more than that, it is methane gas. In the beginning, I thought that it would be a fire hazard, but we have fixed that problem by placing vents all around the underside of the roofline as you can see here," Thomas said as he pointed here and there on all four sides of the roof that showed a series of predrilled vent holes. "With the proper amount of ventilation, the gas just dispels into the air as soon as it leaves the structure. There is also a series of such holes at the top, just under the vent that comes up through the roof."

"So then, if I read you right here, these units could be placed in a person's backyard even?"

"Yes. I finally got approval from the city, based on our tests that prove that once the gas hits the open air there is no danger of premature ignition due to an open flame, cigarette, lightning or even a spark from something like a lawnmower blade striking a rock."

"Thomas, you do realize that this could revolutionize the home and business heating industry. You also will face tremendous pressure from the big companies dealing in conventional heating practices."

"Yes and that does concern me, as I want this system made available to anyone who wants to buy one. It could be shipped as a complete package that would include everything needed to assemble and install the unit at a very low cost. I have even played with a *deluxe* version of the unit."

"A deluxe unit?"

"Yes. It would cost more, but there will always be those who don't have money issues when it comes to expensive items that can improve their lifestyles. Basically the culvert we see here in the middle would be sealed on both ends, and along with the coiled copper tubing, the chamber would be filled with antifreeze. The benefit of this is that the liquid would remain warm even when the unit is not in use, pretty much ensuring instant warm air at a moment's notice."

Earnest Woodsworth could not believe his good fortune in being offered the opportunity to invest in this heating-unit wonder. This was the type of innovation that he lived for, but there he was, standing at the threshold of something that could change humankind and he wanted in—no, he wanted it all.

"Where do I sign?" he asked, full of excitement at the possibilities.

"Uh ... well, there is nothing to sign, other than a cheque maybe?"

"Okay, Thomas, let me put it to you this way. I would like everything involved in this project—all the plans, ideas, test results, city consultations, and such. Also, I want you to join me on this venture. I would like you to be the project manager overall and your name will be on each and every unit produced and sold. You will be in charge of all the manufacturing and design details, whereas I will take on the marketing and pricing. What do you say?"

As Earnest lay in his lounge chair on that bright sunny day, he recounted that conversation, all the details and more than that, Thomas's excitement and passion for the project. This was the type of person he needed in his own business. Together the two of them had hit it off and became immediate friends from that first meeting to this very day. The rest was history, as they say.

Earnest bought the Green Heat project, fully funding the operation, which was now bringing in approximately 10.5 million dollars annually after costs. But there were even more projects to come besides the heating units, seeing that Thomas was most definitely an inventor who liked to think outside of the box. Both of them had become very wealthy over the past 15 years because of this creative genius.

CHAPTER TWO

"Are you at least going to give me a chance to win this time?" Nathan Brooks was asking Bart Woodsworth as the two of them prepared for a game of racquetball in the gym facility of Woodsworth Industries International headquarters in the heart of Vancouver, Canada.

"Hey, man, I give you a chance to win every single time we play," Bart said with a snort in his voice.

"Yeah right!" Nathan shot back. "For about the first 10 minutes after which you totally decimate me and not within the scope of the rules, I must say."

"Oh, whatever do you mean?" Bart retorted, his hand over his mouth in mock surprise.

"C'mon, Bart; you know exactly what I mean, and it's the reason that most people won't play against you anymore. I'm reaching that point myself."

Bart said not a word to that statement as he quickly reflected back over his racquetball career, if one could even call it that. He had been introduced to the sport shortly after his father's headquarters skyscraper was completed. One of his father's cronies had taken him into the facility and after showing him around, asked if he would like to try a game.

Being naive at such a young age, he accepted and the man proceeded to explain some of the rules of the game to him before they began. Of course, the older man beat him badly, even

11

peppering him with the ball a time or two, which left Bart with some bruises and sore muscles in the days that followed.

Bart never said a word about that encounter to his father but made himself a promise that he would become the best racquetball player he could and would one day return the punishment he had received during his first game.

Over the following months, Bart would find himself at the courts until the wee hours of the morning, perfecting his skills until he became confident enough in his game to take on an opponent. Once again, he lost the game, but this time, the score was closer and his confidence rose that much higher. Word soon got out in the corporate circles within his father's empire that anyone could take on the boss's son without retribution from the man upstairs.

In the course of six months, Bart was beginning to win some games, much to the surprise of those he beat, and the desire for the game rose higher and higher within the young man. He began to enter singles tournaments and started winning. As his love for the game increased, so did the burning fire within him to be the best—even unbeatable.

Bart soon gave up all other activities, including dates and time with the family, something he never really enjoyed in the first place, as he was expected to be on his best behaviour in the midst of people he neither knew nor enjoyed. His winnings began to include city-sponsored tournaments and provincial tournaments, and at one point, he even had his eye on a national tournament, but that never worked out because of the injury.

After about two years of being the best of the best at the sport, he felt the excitement of winning begin to wear thin and he looked for other ways to increase his lust for the game. That was when he came up with a plan to beat opponents into submission with outrageous scores. It was during one of these games that he unintentionally hurt another player. The ball had bounced off the wall in front of the two of them so hard that his opponent missed the return and the ball ricocheted off the glass walls behind them and struck his opponent on the back of the head. The force was so great that it actually knocked the grown man out cold, and Bart was amazed that he could actually do such a thing with a small rubber ball.

From that point on, the thrill of the win was replaced by the thrill of doing physical harm to each and every one of his racquetball opponents. Many of them threatened to sue before the game even started, if he intentionally tried to hurt them, but to Bart, it was all about his protection through money. *If they get hurt and threatened to sue, I will just buy them off with my father's fortune,* he thought, and for the longest time, it worked, but eventually, he found it harder and harder to find worthy opponents to play—at least ones who were worthy of his impeccable skills.

Finally the day came when there was no one who would take his challenge seriously anymore. He was so overcome with the lust and power of winning at no cost that he even tried bribing people with money to play him, still with no takers. Eventually, that rejection turned to anger, which in turn got him kicked out of college, until he finally just walked away from any kind of an education.

"Bartholomew William Woodsworth," Bart heard in his father's headquarters café one day when he was sulking over a cappuccino at the lack of action in a sport that he obviously dominated. "I hear you are looking to take anyone on in a game of racquetball, and I am your man."

"Wha?" he said as he spun around to see who was speaking to him.

"Yes, you heard me right. I will take you on in a game," the man said, looking down at the seated young man before him.

Bart was surprised to see a very good-looking man with a

slightly darker skin tone, jet-black curly hair, and the most amazing eyes he had ever seen, standing before him.

"Don't you ever call ..." Bart started to say in a very demanding way, but he was promptly cut off by the stranger.

"What? Call you by your actual name?"

"Yes!" Bart said, intending it to be more forceful, but it came out rather weakly.

"So are you up to a game, young man?"

"Yeah, but are you any good?" Bart spouted off.

"Better than you, I bet."

"Wha?" Bart said again. "Who are you anyway? I've never seen you here before. Do you work for my father?"

"In a roundabout way, I guess."

Just what does that mean? Bart thought as he just stared up at the stranger.

"Just let me know when and where," the man said, and then he quickly turned and walked away from the table and Bart.

It took him a few moments to realize that he didn't know how to contact this man about a game, so Bart bolted from his table and rushed in the man's direction just as he exited from the cafeteria through the double doors into the foyer. Bart was right behind him as he burst through the doors, scaring an older woman who was just about to enter from the other side.

"Where is he?" Bart shouted at the startled woman.

"W-where is who?" she finally managed to say.

"That guy with the black, curly hair. He just came through these doors!" Bart continued to shout, pointing at the slowly swinging doors.

"I-I am sorry, young man, but you were the only one who came through those doors, at least since I came down to this floor."

"Wha?" Bart said for the third time.

14

It was an early morning in June. The birds were singing their songs of praise to the God who had created them. The sun was shining its warmth on the earth as Earnest Woodsworth and his wife, Katie, were enjoying a rare breakfast together on the stone patio just outside of their stately upscale home on the city's east side.

"Don't you have to get to the office?" Katie asked, surprised that he was still home.

"Yes, I do, sometime today, but I know that I have been neglecting you and the kids lately, so I thought maybe you would enjoy having breakfast with me today. Ha! ..." he said, leaning way back in his chair as it balanced precariously on its back two metal legs. "It's kind of funny thinking of Bart and Caroline as kids now. Guess I need to start treating them as adults."

"They will always be our kids," Katie said with a smile. "But yes, they should be treated as adults now that they are grown up and out of school."

"That would be great if Bart would have actually finished college in the normal way instead of being asked to leave—again," Earnest said as he turned away and looked over the huge swimming pool directly behind them.

He marvelled at all they had acquired over the years with the tennis courts, hot tubs, gardens, acres of fruit trees, and neatly trimmed shrubs, along with statues and fountains discreetly placed here and there throughout the property."

"Is everything okay?" Katie asked softly as she reached for his hand.

Her touch startled him slightly, even though he showed no sign of it. He loved the feel of her soft hand on his and realized that he had gotten away from simple hugs and even kisses in his hectic schedule.

"I-I just wish ..." His voice trailed off in sadness.

Katie knew exactly what he meant.

"Yes, I too wish that Franklin were here with us, together as a family."

Earnest turned his head to face her, tears streaming down his face. He knew he had the love of both his wife and their daughter, Caroline, but still, he greatly missed the love of Bart and the company of his eldest son, Franklin.

"You could give him a call and just tell him how you are really feeling. All he ever wanted was for you and him to be closer."

"Yes, I know," Earnest said with a heavy sigh as his shoulders slumped downwards. "But you and I both know that he won't talk to me."

"Would you like me to give him a call and set it up so that the two of you can talk? Maybe you could schedule a golf game for two at the club?"

Earnest said nothing as his mind began to wander back to when Franklin was born and the great joy he and his wife shared. In those days, he was busy for sure, making a name for himself in the business world, but he made sure to take some time to help raise the child. He even managed to change his diapers a time or two and feed him as well, but it was those special times he missed most, when they would wrestle on the living room floor or just sit on the sofa watching a movie together.

Where did those days go? he thought to himself.

"Well, you can try," he answered. "But we both know what the answer will be. He hasn't talked to me in over eight years, and I am not expecting any miracles now."

One of the housemaids came out on the patio and after clearing off the breakfast dishes, offered to pour them both more tea, but Earnest said he would take care of it and thanked the woman as she hurried off. He then stood and poured Katie a cup of hot Earl Grey tea before he poured one for himself.

The two of them just sat and chatted about the lovely weather, the backyard grounds, and other small-talk topics as they sipped their tea, both of them lost in their thoughts about earlier days as a family. When they were finished with their tea, Katie figured that Earnest would head off to his office and was very surprised at what he had to say next.

"Mrs. Woodsworth, would you care to take a walk with me?" Earnest said as he stood, pushed his chair back, and walked to her side of the table, extending his hand to her.

Wow! What's gotten into him today? she wondered as she gracefully extended her hand, and as he took it, she rose to join him.

Katherine Sylvia Woodsworth had not grown up with money. She had come from the other side of the tracks, as it was called in her younger days. Even though they didn't have a lot of money, her parents and her siblings most definitely had love.

Her parents were devout Christians and attended church each and every Sunday. Work was not allowed in their home on Sundays, except for the cooking of meals and washing of the dishes.

As she and her husband walked along, hand in hand, throughout their many acres of manicured lawns, shrubberies, fountains, and pools, her mind flashed back to those years as a child living with her parents and four siblings.

She recalled how they would all sit at the table and play board games, like Monopoly or Sorry!, a game she usually dominated. They would snack on freshly popped popcorn while they laughed and groaned as they won or lost within the game they were playing.

Then she recalled the times when she would sit on her father's knee as they watched television. *Those were the days*, she thought. *Only two channels to choose from and no remotes.* Her three favorite shows to watch on the weekends were the *Bugs Bunny Show*, *The Ed Sullivan Show*, and *Bonanza*.

"Ha!" she said out loud as she recalled an episode of *Bonanza* where Hoss and Little Joe were running around in the bush, trying to catch leprechauns.

"What has you so happy, my dear?" Earnest asked as they walked.

"Oh, just remembering back to when I was a kid and the television shows we used to watch," she answered as she squeezed his hand a little harder.

"Yes, it would be nice to go back to those days," he said with a slight sigh in his voice.

They came to a secluded bench surrounded on three sides by manicured shrubbery and sat down together, still holding hands. She snuggled in close to him, cherishing this rare time together.

"So tell me some things of your youth that you miss?" Earnest asked, lounging back on the bench with his love close to him.

"Well, that could be quite a list." She laughed lightly.

"I am all ears, my dear."

Katie hesitated for a moment as she thought back to the things she still missed from days gone by.

"I'm sure you'll find this funny, but I really do miss Fudgesicles."

"Fudgesicles? Really?" he said in a surprised tone.

"Yes. Well, I know one can still buy them today, but back when I was a youth, they were made from real cream milk and not the ice milk they now use. And they were oh so creamy back then." She turned her head to look at his reaction, and all she saw was a big smirk on his face. "Oh you!" she said as she jabbed him in the side with her elbow.

"What? I never said anything."

"You said it with that smirk on your face."

"Oh really. You think you know what all my facial expressions are saying these days?"

"I know you, mister. After all, I have lived with you all these years and a woman knows certain things," she said with the smirk on her face this time.

"Yes, one can't argue that fact," he said as he bent low and placed a soft kiss on her cheek.

"Mmmmmmmm," she responded.

"So is there anything else?"

"What do you mean?"

"Are there any other things you miss from your youth?"

"Yes. There is another food item that comes to mind. There were these soft chewy suckers that were pink in color, and they too were oh so good as well. Every so often, I will smell a certain air freshener being used here and there that reminds me of the taste of those suckers."

"I used to love suckers too when I was a kid, so maybe we both loved the same kind."

"Maybe!" she said with a smile, still luxuriating in their time together on the secluded bench.

"Anything else?" he asked again.

"Oh, there were certainly the toys, dolls and such, but I think those were just items of the times, and if one still wants them, one can find them on eBay or places like Kijiji if they have the money. I will tell you one thing though that I see guys doing that looks really out of place."

"What's that?" he asked, eyebrows raised in a questioning manner.

"It's just that when guys are in their teens and twenties, they all want to drive the latest sporty cars, like the Ford Mustang GT, let's say. The problem at that age though is that most of them couldn't afford a car like that. So here they are now, in their fifties, and they now have the money to buy those dream cars. But a 50- or 60-year-old man driving a Mustang GT looks really stupid and way out of place."

"Hmmmm, yes. I agree with you there, my dear. About a year ago, when I was driving to a meeting, I was passed by just such a car, definitely sporty and made for a younger generation. As they passed me on the highway, I had to laugh at the sight of this older gentleman driving the car with the convertible roof down and a woman in the passenger seat. She was wearing this long scarf, complete with sunglasses, and it looked as if the two of them were reliving the past, but it just looked oh so wrong."

With that said, Earnest and Katie had a good, long laugh, until they finally both sat upright on the bench side by side. They said not a word as they looked deeply into each other's eyes before falling into each other's arms with a long, passionate kiss.

It had now been over three weeks since Bart's encounter with the dark-haired man in the corporate café, and Bart had become even angrier at his lack of action in trying to find out just who the man was or how to get a hold of him. He began to lash out at anyone who was tried to calm him down, especially his mother.

"Bart, dear, you will have to tell me what is going on in order for me to help you," she said one morning at the breakfast table when it was just the two of them there. "I really want to help you with whatever it is that has been bothering you for the past few weeks."

"Just leave me alone!" Bart rudely blurted out as he tried to eat his breakfast. "I don't need your or anyone else's help."

Katie sat there, stunned that her son had become so demanding and very rude at the same time. She had taken great steps to raise the kids properly, taking them to church every Sunday possible. She also read to them from a Bible storybook every night before she tucked all of them in for the night with a kiss and "I love you." But for some reason, Bart always seemed to pull away, maybe not physically but definitely emotionally. She had far fewer problems raising Franklin and Caroline, who seemed to understand her desire for them to know the Lord, and the two of them had embraced his love at a very early age in their lives. Though Franklin wasn't *saved* and was gone from their lives now, Katie knew that he still loved those Bible stories, even though he wouldn't admit it to anyone.

"You need someone to talk to about whatever it is that is bothering you, Bart; otherwise, it is just going to consume you from the inside out. Please, just let me help you somehow," Katie said with tears now forming as her love for her son overwhelmed her.

Bart jumped up, pushing hard on the chair behind him until it flipped over and clanged loudly against the cobblestone deck as he reacted to her words.

"I don't need any help, and I most certainly don't want any help from you or some shrink that you would surely try to set me up with!" he said loudly as he stormed off to his room.

About 10 minutes later, Katie heard him slam his bedroom door and stomp out of the house and then to his car. He roared out of the five-bay garage in his bright-yellow Viper SPSCC, fishtailing wildly on the long paved drive from the lavish house to the streets of the city.

"Mr. Woodsworth, you have a lunch meeting with Thomas Hillman in 30 minutes at the Evergreen Club," came the voice of Earnest Woodsworth's secretary on his office intercom.

"Thank you, Hillary," he answered.

"Would you like to have the car waiting for you at the main entrance?" she asked.

"Yes, that would be much appreciated," he said over the intercom.

"Consider it done, sir."

Earnest sat back into his black-leather executive chair as his mind began to wander, something that seemed to be happening a lot lately. He was fighting an inward battle of his thoughts and wasn't sure just how to approach the subject of this battle. Finally he made a decision and picked up his desk phone. Quietly he made a call, sure of how it would go; still he made it anyway. The phone rang about four times before it was answered.

"Hello, Franklin here," he heard on his end.

There was silence for a few moments as Earnest built up the courage to talk to his eldest son.

"Hello, Franklin," he said.

Again there was silence for a few moments, and Earnest was glad that his son hadn't simply hung up on him.

"Before you hang up on me, son, may I ask if you would be at all willing to meet me for lunch sometime this week?" Earnest asked.

The silence was still there, yet he knew his son was listening on the other end of the call. He might not be talking to his father these days, but he did have manners.

"Okay, I take it that your silence is a no, but will you at least come home for my fiftieth birthday coming up soon? You can phone your mother for the details."

The conversation continued to be one-sided with only Earnest talking and his son merely listening.

"Okay, Franklin, I appreciate that you didn't hang up on me. I-I know ..." he continued as his emotions began to rise to the surface in his deep longing to once again connect with his son. "I know how difficult it has been for you over the years, but I want you to believe me when I say that I love you so much and miss you even more." Earnest paused a few moments before continuing. "Y-your presence at my party would be the best gift this man could ever want, so please give your mother a call. Good-bye, son," he said as he hung up the phone, and with his head in his hands on his glass-covered desktop, he cried.

CHAPTER THREE

"So good to see you again, Thomas," Earnest said as the two friends met, shook hands, and sat at their table in the large dining room of the Evergreen Country Club.

"The feeling is mutual," Thomas responded.

The waitress then handed them a menu and asked what each of them would like to drink. After that, she then left them to decide what they would like to order for their meal, while she went to get them their drink choices.

The two friends sat quietly as they made their choices from the menu until the waitress returned with their drinks and took their orders.

"So what are you working on today?" Earnest asked as he slowly sipped his coffee.

"Actually I have a new project in mind that I thought I would run past you," Thomas said.

"Great! I am always interested in new things, especially when they come from that brilliant mind of yours," Earnest said with a slight chuckle.

"Well, thank you, but you haven't heard the details yet," Thomas countered with a smirk.

"Okay, go for it. Impress me."

"Well, you know what it takes to build a new home or commercial space, not skyscrapers mind you, but the smaller independent business locations, like on the city's outskirts. Construction is at a rapid pace right now as our economy continues its growth," Thomas started off and then had a drink of his coffee.

"Yes, there is no doubt that we are experiencing a building boom as the city continues to grow because of the renewable resources sector in this part of the country," Earnest said.

"It is the construction industry that is the focus of my newest creation. What would you say is the number-one problem in having any construction job completed on time?"

Earnest sat back and thought about the question for a few moments before offering his answer. "Well, I would have to say it is the weather."

"You have hit the nail on the head with that answer, my friend. Most job sites simply do not have the money or resources to tackle this problem, but I believe I have come up with the answer," Thomas said, now on a roll. "In the bigger projects, such as hotels, banks and schools, they use tarps to cover exposed areas, but overall such materials are very expensive and either they are written into the cost of the project or it is an expense that the construction company can handle. I have a concept in mind that is both inexpensive and very portable. It would be very easy to set up and also would be a great rental unit."

"So are you saying that this concept could both be utilized by contractors themselves or they could get the items from rental locations too?" Earnest asked as the wheels in his mind began to roll with the possibilities.

"Yes, exactly, to both of them," Earnest said, just before their meals arrived.

This new concept would take a lot of explaining and understanding on the part of Earnest Woodsworth, so with that in mind, Thomas decided to wait until they had finished their meals before going on with his idea. The two men ate in silence.

When the dishes were cleared away and their coffees were refilled, Thomas pulled out some drawings from his carry case and placed copies in front of his friend.

"What you see before you are the beginning sketches of this new construction tool that will revolutionize building construction and help to speed up that process as well."

Earnest's eyes scanned all the details, as his mind processed all the possibilities of just what this project would mean monetarily for both men. He knew that it could take months for Thomas to come up with new ideas, but when he did, he never disappointed him.

"Wow, Thomas! I can clearly see what you are proposing with these drawings, and I know that these units will be a big success, just like the Green Heat units. So can you please share with me what you see in these units, all the details and your plan on how we should proceed from this point on?" Earnest said, eager to hear all about it.

The two friends then delved into the inner workings of this newest innovative idea that involved the casing for the roll-out units, their dimensions, the joiner units and the supporting systems to get the units up off the ground.

"So basically, it works like this," Thomas said. "The workers lay out the units in the center of the proposed building after the hole has been dug or piles have been drilled. The units are all joined together using the connection boxes. Then the lift support stands are set up at the joints and the entire box unit is lifted onto the support stands, much like a beam resting on tele posts. When all is ready, they begin to crank up the support stands, which lift the cover units into the air. When they get to a height of six feet, they stop cranking and pull out the cover sections complete with the Velcro joining strips until the entire cover is pulled out to the edges of the proposed building outline.

"Next, the anchors are placed through the cover into the earth at all the ringed slots on the very outer edge of the cover. Once this is completed, then the cover is cranked up another two to four feet and locked in place. After that is done, then the inside supports are set up and pushed into place against the cover, raising it to a height of six to eight feet at the outer edges of the proposed building, depending on the angle of the cover that the contractor desires for runoff purposes.

"The two ends of the housing units and stands are then anchored to the ground, using connecting rods, so it is anchored in a triangular pattern. After that, the contractors can go ahead with any construction, free of rain interference. At any time, they can have the lifters unlocked to raise or lower the units above.

"When the building gets to the stage of the floor being finished, then the contractors can install new lifters on the floor and transfer the cover units to the next phase of construction until the rafters are in place. Then with the roof almost sheeted in, they can install lifters on the roof and use the covering until the shingles are installed, and then the entire unit can be taken down and removed," Thomas explained.

"Wow!" was Earnest's initial reaction. "You certainly have covered all the bases based on what I have seen and heard here. What would be the next step then?"

"I think we will have to come up with some trial test boxes to determine what material would be best suited for them, in order that the units are lightweight yet durable as they will be handled roughly in various construction sites."

"Yes, you are right about that. So can any of our companies handle that, or will we need to source it out?" Earnest asked, accepting another refill of coffee from a passing waitress.

"Source it out, I think, makes more sense for this one. We are going to have to look at such materials as aluminum, plastic or even carbon composite for the housing boxes. The stands and all other attachments can be made of aluminum or a lightweight steel, but the housing boxes will be the priority when it comes to testing them," Thomas said as he sat back, letting it all sink in.

"So what other attachments are there other than the ones you mentioned?"

"I have given that a lot of thought and come up with quite a few; that is why I think that these units will be a great sell to rental companies. For example, there could be outer roof supports for shingling companies. The cover would then only be supported by the roof alone and not interfere with siding installers and the like. Also there could be other roof supports that would run the cover from the roof's edge to the ground for siding installers or those installing windows.

"These cover units could be used in a host of other settings as well, like to cover outdoor weddings in case of rain or outdoor events, such as yard sales or barbecues. The list could get quite long. I have even thought of marketing it to cover gardens in overly extreme rainy seasons," Thomas said as the excitement of the project began to grip him.

For the next 30 minutes, the two friends and business associates shared all the details of how they would market the product, what the name of the units should be and just which trades would benefit the most from this new innovation.

"Well, my friend, I have to go, as I have a meeting with some officials from TXBG," Earnest said as they began to put away all the design drawings and other paperwork.

"TXBG? Isn't that the big oil conglomerate in Texas?" Thomas asked with a puzzled look on his face.

"Yes, it is."

"I thought you stayed clear of any dealings to do with oil?"

"Yes, I know I have told you that in the past, but this one is different."

"How can it be different if it deals with oil? You have told me that you want all your employees to be working all the time with no layoffs or down times and that is why you have stayed away from the oil patch."

"That is true, very true. I believe that a man is worth his wages. That is something I picked up from Katie. She says it's in the Bible somewhere, but I like the logic in the statement. The problem with the oil patch is that it is too unpredictable, jumping up and down with the market. When it's up and running, it is a great investment, but when it's at a standstill, well, then nobody makes any money."

"You have told me all that in the past. So what makes this deal any different?"

"TXBG has stakes in a huge oil field recently discovered in Midwest Saskatchewan. They started off with a temporary offloading system near a small town right in the middle of this oil field. Then they built a more permanent facility that can load 40 tanker railcars at a time. But the oil is coming in so fast by tanker trucks that they now want to increase that facility to load 100 tanker railcars at a time, and they are looking for investors, preferably Canadian investors, which gives them a better tax break."

"So are you going to invest with them?"

"I'm really not sure. I am really set in my ways when it comes to oil, so I am just going to meet with them, see what their strategy is, what amount they are looking for in an investment, and then I will go from there. Would you like to be in the process, my friend?" Earnest asked Thomas.

"It's not what I want to invest in. I am happy with what I make these days, and life is good, but I feel a check in my spirit and I would just like you to let me know what happens after that meeting? Please do not sign anything until we have talked about it again—please?"

"Okay, okay," Earnest said with a chuckle. "You sure you and my wife haven't been talking, because she basically said the same thing to me this morning before I left for the office?"

"Really?"

"Yes, almost word for word."

"Hummmmm," Thomas said as he sat upright in his chair now, which caught the attention of his friend across from him.

"What is it?"

"I am not sure, but I will pray about it that the Lord would give me more wisdom in this new venture of yours."

"Well, it's not a done deal yet; I am just going to hear what they have to say, remember?"

"Yes, I do, but be very careful, my friend, as I feel that the Lord almost wants to warn you of something, but of what, I am not sure."

"Okay, but I must get back to the office," Earnest said as he rose from his chair, gathering his light overcoat and briefcase.

Thomas paid for the meal this time, while Earnest left the waitress a very generous tip and then the two men left the restaurant. Just before they parted for their separate vehicles, Thomas stopped, like he just remembered something.

"Oh. I almost forgot. Shelly and I would love to have you and Katie over for a barbecue supper one Saturday evening this month. Do you think that would be possible?"

"I will have to check my schedule and get back to you sometime later today, if that's okay with you?"

"Yes, please do."

The two men turned, and Thomas walked to his truck while Earnest climbed into his waiting Limo.

Katie was flying and loving it as she did barrel roles, loops along with twists and turns at every chance she had. She would fly straight up as high as she could go before zooming back towards the ground below at alarming speeds. On her way down, she found herself thinking, *Stop one inch before the ground*, and that was what her body did, actually stopping one inch from the ground and just floated in the air.

From there, she flew over to a two long rows of trees that flanked either side of a quiet dusty country road. On either side of the road were wide-open green fields with beautiful horses grazing on its greenery. As she flew over the rolling green hills and trees, she spotted a beautiful aqua-colored lake, but what really caught her attention were the flowers around the lake. It was like a full field of flowers, and their colors were so vivid, so bright, almost as if they were electric or florescent in nature. Katie looked around at her surroundings as she slowly and lightly set down on a grassy hill. She immediately felt the soft long grass caressing her bare feet, and it felt exhilarating. As she looked up, she saw that same electric-like blue sky, far brighter and more vivid than she had ever remembered in her life before.

It was then that she realized she was dreaming. It was the kind of dream that no one wanted to wake up from, but inevitably she did wake up.

"Noooo!" she said as she rolled around in bed, wanting to fall back asleep and go back to the dream, but such was not the case.

Katie sat up in her large bed and stretched her arms upward and wide.

"Thank you, Lord, for such a wonderful dream," she said out loud. She did not understand it, but Katie felt wildly alive, even in her spirit, like something totally amazing was going to happen today.

She washed and got dressed for the day, picking out a yellow dress she loved to wear on happy occasions. Today was definitely one of those days. As she bounced out of her room, she felt light and happy all mixed in with a sense of excitement.

Walking out into the beautiful morning air, Katie again thanked the Lord for the gorgeous weather. She began to walk through the manicured gardens at the back of her home, which covered 20 acres of land. Earnest had also loved the location when they first saw it and pictured in his head all the gardens, streams, foot bridges, fountains, walking paths, benches, and so much more. She walked for a while, stopping here and there to breathe in the aromatic fragrances of various flowers along the way. Finally she came to the bench that she and Earnest had shared recently. She sat down and stretched out as the expectancy she had felt earlier began to flood her very being once again.

"What is it, Lord?" she asked as she sat in the Lord's presence, there in her garden, but all was silent and she wondered why the Lord had her feeling this way while he remained silent. Slowly she lowered her head and spent the next 20 minutes in prayer.

Later on that morning, Katie was lounging on the patio, having tea and thinking about what to wear to Shelly and Thomas's place for supper later that evening. As she took a few minutes to play with her two dogs, Ginger and Roger, her personal cell phone began to chirp. When she looked at the name display, all time seemed to stop, right then and there. Her hand immediately went to her mouth in disbelief before she answered the call.

"F-Franklin, is ... it really you?" she said, answering her phone as tears filled her eyes at the joy she felt. She always yearned to hear her oldest son's voice after he had left home and cut all of them out of his life it seemed.

There was a short pause on the other end before he spoke.

"Hello, Mom."

"Oh, Franklin, it is you!" she said in utter happiness.

"Yes, Mom, it's me."

"I-I really don't know what to say, and what kind of a mother am I, not knowing what to say to her own son?"

"Mom, it's okay. Let me do the talking ... well ... asking too, I guess."

"Okay," was all that Katie could get out as she fished around in her purse for a hanky or a tissue at least.

"As you probably already know, Dad called me a couple of weeks ago and invited me to his birthday party coming up."

Earnest phoned him? she thought. *Oh no, Lord, please don't let him say that he won't be attending. We both need to see him so badly.*

"I gave it a lot of thought, and it has been well over eight years since I have been home," Franklin said as his mother's hopes began to rise. "So ... I guess ... I will be coming home, Mom."

Katie broke down; she just couldn't hold back any longer, and at the same time, Franklin's heart was breaking as he heard his mother's sobs on the other end.

"Mom?" he asked quietly, wanting to get her attention for what he had to say next, but Katie continued to cry.

"Mom ... Please listen to me." He tried again, and this time, he heard her settle down a bit before she answered.

"Y-yes, what is it?"

"I just wanted to let you know that I won't be alone when I come home."

"What do you mean, dear?"

"I have met someone, and she will be with me."

There was a pause on the other end, which had Franklin wondering.

"Y-you have a girlfriend?" Katie said hesitantly.

"Yes, Mom, and ... we are engaged."

"Engaged?"

"Yes, Mom."

"So that means ..." Katie paused.

"Yes, Mom, it means we are going to be married."

"M-married? When?"

"That hasn't been decided yet, but we both wanted to talk to you about it first."

"To me?" Katie asked, unable to hide her curiosity now.

"Yes, Mom, and there is one other very important thing you must know about her that I have waited one full year to tell you."

Katie couldn't say anything now as her mind raced with good and bad thoughts, at all the possibilities of what he might say.

"Mom?"

"Yes?" she finally said very quietly.

"Julie is a born-again Christian!" He paused momentarily as he mustered the strength to continue on. "And so am I."

Katie's mind instantly flashed back to the three children and herself sitting in church together with the pastor sharing a children's story from the Bible storybook for children. She could remember exactly what each child was wearing and what their reactions were to the story as well.

She saw Bart playing with a toy race car, not really too interested in what was being shared. Caroline was playing with her favorite doll and would occasionally stop and listen to the pastor before going back to her play. But it was Franklin she remembered the most as he sat there almost in a state of awe at what he was hearing.

As Katie sat there, listening to her son's voice, she had always wondered just where her children stood with the Lord, and she had just heard the best words any Christian mother could ever hope to hear from any of her children.

"A ... Christian ... You are a Christian?" she managed to force out of her mouth.

"Yes, Mom, thanks to Julie and the Lord, of course."

"Praise the Lord! Oh thank you, Lord Jesus!" Katie said out loud in thanksgiving to her Lord at the fact that another one of her children who was lost now was found.

Franklin knew that this would be a long phone call, and out of love and respect for his mother, he never cut her off, but let her thank the Lord for the news he had just shared with her. Finally she seemed to settle down as Franklin continued.

"Mom, there is one more thing."

"There's more?" she asked, surprised, not sure she could handle any more news.

"Yes, Mom, it's about Dad. When he phoned me awhile back, it took all I had in me not to tell him, but I just couldn't share the news with him—not yet."

"Oh, I have to tell him, Franklin," Katie said, her voice now filled with excitement and joy.

"No, Mom, please ... but I have a plan."

For the next 40 minutes, Katie and her son Franklin talked about his plan, his father's birthday, his fiancée, Julie, and their upcoming visit home.

CHAPTER FOUR

"You are so lucky," Jenn said to Caroline as the two friends sat in a local coffee shop, drinking their mocha latte beverages and chatting it up as most friends do over a drink or a meal.

"What do you mean 'lucky'?" Caroline asked between sips.

"Just look at the lifestyle you live, with money, cars, clothes and just about anything a girl could ever want in life."

"Oh, believe me, girlfriend, it is not all glamorous like you make it sound. We still have to eat, sleep and live just like everyone else, you know?"

"Okay but you do all that in luxury is what I am getting at."

"I know what you are saying, and okay, yes, my father makes good money—no doubt about that, but he had to work hard to get where we are at today and therefore he is entitled to what he has ... and us too."

"Still, it must be nice."

"Oh, c'mon, Jenn, you aren't exactly living in poverty. Your parents are doing okay, and you are living a good life too. It isn't the dollars you should be fixated on; it's your family."

"See, that's something I don't understand about you. You have it all—the huge mansion, the swimming pool, tennis court, hot tubs, cars, clothes and everything else and still all you talk about is family. You should be out having wild parties, living the good life and shopping till you drop, girl!"

"Those are all just superficial and really don't describe who I am."

"Okay, and just who are you then?"

Caroline knew that answer straight up and did not even hesitate to answer. "Why a child of the King!"

"Here we go again," Jenn chided.

"Jenn, can I ask you a question?" Caroline asked in a way that had Jenn wondering if she should say yes.

"Why?" was all she said back.

"C'mon, Jenn; it won't hurt."

"Okay ... yes, you may ask then."

"You and I have been friends since we were kids—right?"

"Yes."

"We have shared a lot of ups and downs, and I consider you to be my best friend."

"You are my best friend too."

"You know that I am a Christian and that the Lord is a big part of my life, right?"

Jenn hesitated a few moments.

"Yeah, I know."

"Obviously you know that we are fairly well off."

"Fairly? More like excessively, I would say," Jenn said with a smirk across the coffee-shop table.

"Okay, call it what you like. It is what it is, but my question to you in light of all I have just said and asked is why do you stay with me? Why are you still my friend? You are a very popular girl in school. Lots of guys would die to have a date with you or girls to be your best friend, so why are you still in my life?"

There was a long, awkward pause, as Jenn didn't know how to answer the question. The truth be told, she really didn't know why they were still friends. They had just hit it off as friends at a young age, when such superficial outward things don't usually matter, but now they were both in high school where it seemed that such things should matter and she didn't know what to say.

"I ... uh, ummm ... I ..."

"It's okay, Jenn; I know why, but I think you should take some time to figure it out for yourself," Caroline said as she rose, picking up the empty mugs and carrying them to the tray set out for them by the waste containers. "Gotta go, girl. Catch up with you later ... Text me!" And with that said, she was out the door before Jenn could say another word.

Why? Why? Why? Jenn said in her mind over and over as she just sat at the table, ignoring the constant stream of texts that she received each and every day from her male admirers and other female friends.

Shelly and Katie were chatting in the kitchen, while Thomas and Earnest were out on the deck, talking and keeping an eye on the steaks cooking on the barbecue.

"This is a rare event, you know," Thomas said to his friend Earnest.

"Oh really, what's that?" Earnest asked back.

"Me cooking. We usually have the chef do all of this for us, but once in a blue moon, we like to do it ourselves, maybe just to remind us that we can still cook."

The two men had a good laugh at that as they sat at the bar table.

"Yes, well, at my age, young man, I have earned the right to have someone else cook it for me, and the best part is that they cook it right the first time."

Again the two friends burst out into laughter.

"Well, the boys are certainly enjoying their time out there," Shelly said to Katie as the two women were preparing the salads, baked potatoes, corn on the cob, and all the other small things that would make up the meal they would soon all be sharing.

"It was so nice to hear from Earnest that you had invited us over," Katie said to her friend as she busily unwrapped the hot baked potatoes and placed them in a glass bowl.

"Oh, Katie, it seems like it has been so long since we last got together and it is much more enjoyable here in our home than out in a restaurant."

"Yes, we have both missed your company since ... ummm ... when was the last time we actually got together?"

"Last November actually, just before the Christmas rush began."

"Okay, yes, I do remember now. We met at Charlie's Grill over on the west side. Come to think of it, the meal wasn't all that great."

"You've got that right, and that is the main reason Thomas is cooking tonight," Shelly said as the two of them howled in laughter.

"Sounds like the girls are having a good time in the kitchen," Earnest said, nodding in that direction.

"Yes, they do get along well. Maybe someday when we both retire we can live close to each other in some retirement villa or condo and spend a lot more quality time together."

"Retire? Are you kidding? I have no plans of retiring. I plan to keep working until I drop at my desk," Earnest said with a chuckle.

"I have heard of 'shop till you drop,' and now with you, it's 'work till you drop,' eh?" Thomas said with a sly smile on his face.

"You got that right, buddy," Earnest said as the two men again had a good laugh.

The meal was great as the four friends sat around the dining room table, laughing and sharing memories of good times gone by—that is until the subject of the kids came up. Earnest became sombre at the thought of talking about his children, and even though they were grown up, he still had a hard time breaking away from the thought of them as his children.

"So how is Nathan doing?" Katie asked Shelly.

"He is finding university a bit of a challenge, but he is the kind of a man to face his challenges head-on, and we are sure that he will do well. It is only his first year, and university is so much different than high school."

"Yes, I know it is, and we went through the same types of things when Franklin was in university too," Katie said, and as soon as the words had left her lips, she turned to look at Earnest, knowing that just the mention of their eldest son's name brought out a host of emotions in him.

She could see the turmoil in his eyes, so she changed the direction of the conversation for her husband's sake; besides, she knew that one day soon his sadness would be turned to joy.

"Caroline, on the other hand, is acing grade 12 and I just know that university will be a breeze for her, simply because she applies herself wholeheartedly to any task she takes on."

"Does she have any idea what field she wants to go into yet?"

"She has mentioned something in the business field, but she still has time to decide."

"Like father, like daughter, eh?" Thomas had to say as he looked at Earnest.

"Yep, I guess some of me has rubbed off on her," was all he had to say.

"How about we all go into the living room, as it is more comfortable there?" Shelly said as she began to rise from the table. "Just leave everything here and we will clean it up later."

"Oh, so then the maid will be doing the cleaning?" Earnest asked with a chuckle.

"Actually, my friend," Thomas cut in. "It will be Shelly and I clearing them away later."

"Really?" Katie asked.

"Yes. We clear the table off, and together we wash and dry the dishes," Thomas said.

"Isn't that what the hired help are for?" Earnest asked, as the four of them made their way into the living room.

Shelly and Thomas sat on the love seat side by side. Katie sat on the opposite sofa, hoping Earnest would join her, but he chose to sit in the large leather armchair.

"Yes, that is what they are for, but we have found a closeness in doing the dishes together. You should try it, Earnest. You will find a closeness to Katie that will remind you of when the two of you were younger—at least that's the way we found it for us," Thomas continued.

"Oh yes, I love it when we do the dishes together. I know that we don't have to, but it is almost a fun adventure," Shelly said as she snuggled close into her husband's side on the love seat. "There are times when we are both feeling frisky that it turns into a suds fight with water and soap suds flying everywhere, but then there are times where we just stand side by side, one washing while the other dries. We will get some love song in our heads and will start singing as we sway from side to side. Believe me; you must try it. It is very therapeutic and can do wonders for one's love life too," she continued with a wide smile on her face as she gave Thomas a mild nudge in his side, which brought on a smile too as the two of them just looked into each other's eyes, full of love for a brief moment.

Then there was silence for a few moments in the living room.

"Well, I think that at my age, washing the dishes is way down on my list of things to do," Earnest responded with a small chuckle.

Katie just sat there, saying nothing, but her mind was thinking hard and fast. *Why won't he wash the dishes with me? I would love that!*

"So, my friend," Thomas said, directing his words towards Earnest, "there is a reason that Shelly and I asked the two of you here tonight."

Earnest turned slightly in order that he could fully take in what his friend was going to say, but Katie continued to just sit there, not saying a word as she was trying to think of a way to get Earnest interested in doing the dishes with her, even if it were just for one evening.

■

"The both of you know where we stand when it comes to our religious convictions," Thomas started off, immediately catching Katie's attention.

Earnest, however, just sat there, thinking that he didn't want to get into it or any other Christian discussions for that matter.

"Yes, we do," Katie said with a big smile. She loved the fact that their best friends were Christians, just as she was, and she always welcomed any talk pertaining to that fact.

"You also know that the four of us are very well off and that we really don't have to work as hard as we have been doing these past few years," Thomas continued. "Shelly and I have been seriously looking at our options in life as we move forward in our faith and have come to the conclusion that we want to give back the blessings we have received."

Again the room was silent as Thomas just let those words settle in. He knew that this would be a very touchy subject to talk about, but there was more.

"Earnest," Thomas said, looking directly at his best friend and business partner, "have you ever wondered why the Lord brought us together?"

"The Lord?" Earnest shot back, so loudly that it startled the others, especially his wife. "Our meeting was just one of chance. I heard about a possible business venture, and I went to check it out. I was introduced to you, and we just hit it off, plain and simple."

"Do you really think that it was just by chance that we met?" Thomas said, his eyebrows raised in mock surprise.

Earnest was a bit hesitant in his response, not wanting to offend his friend.

"Please don't get me wrong, Thomas. We are very good friends, but to say that there is a God who controls all the actions of our lives is a bit of a stretch, wouldn't you say?"

"Actually there was a time in my life when I would have agreed with you on that, but that was before I had an angel encounter that changed my life forevermore."

"An angel encounter?" Earnest said, this time with his eyebrows raised in surprise.

"Please tell us about it," Katie asked. "We would love to hear the story," she continued as she looked over at Earnest, who was indicating with his facial expressions that he wasn't so interested. "Well, at least I am," she said.

"Okay, I would be glad to share the story," Thomas said as he pulled Shelly even closer to his side. "I was 16 years old and was out snowmobiling with my brothers and my father on the family farm. We didn't live out there but went out often in the winter to fire up the sleds and have some fun." His face lit up with a smile at the recollection.

"Dad had a Golden Ghost Snow Cruiser, and those machines were almost indestructible. We loved using it for pulling a tractor tube behind, because you could swing out really far with no worries of ever tipping the snowmobile over. Yeah ... I sure can remember riding on that tube with six or seven of our friends, and Dad would swing towards the edge of a slough we were on. This would cause the tube to swing around and away from the machine and into the banks of snow and cattails on the outer edges of the slough. We would plow into the soft banked snow, causing a cloud of snow mixed with cattails and bodies flying everywhere as we desperately tried to hang on." Thomas laughed out loud at the recollection. "Man, those were the days! And when the tube finally swung back out onto the ice of the slough, it would be empty. Dad would swing around in a huge circle to see how we all were, and we would be clambering to get back on the tube and do it all over again—and again and again."

"Sounds like you had a lot of fun," Katie said enthralled by the story so far.

"Yeah, it was lots of fun, so what's the point?" Earnest asked, more perturbed now than really interested.

"Well, one day, we were out again, but this time, it was just me, dad, and my brothers. My brother Peter was towing me behind his snowmobile with a rope that was about 20 feet long. We had done the cattails, but so far, he couldn't shake me, so he pulled me into the yard site. This yard site was set up so that all of the buildings and bins were on the west side. The little house we had out there was on the south side, and the combines were on the east side of the yard. The road was plowed from the main road to the yard. Then in the yard, the road did a large loop around past the front of the buildings and bins and then the house and finally past the front of the combines before it joined again at the entrance to the yard site. The snow on either side of the road was up about three feet all around and down the road.

"As my brother entered the yard site, he was going wide open on the snowmobile's throttle. So as we rounded the curve in the road, close to the house, Peter was going really fast. He knew that the machine would not tip over, and he was bound and determined to shake me off the tube he was towing behind. So with a 20-foot rope, we later figured out that I would have been doing about 80 miles an hour when I rounded the curve."

"Oh my!" Katie said.

"Yes, it definitely was an '*oh my*' moment for sure," Thomas continued, while Earnest just sat there, looking bored.

"As the tube hit the banked snow on the east side of the road, it went airborne, as did I." Thomas stopped talking as tears welled up in his eyes at the recollection of that event.

Earnest had never seen his friend get so emotional, and he settled down a bit in his doubting demeanour.

"I-I flew off the tube at a height of about 10 feet in the air, heading headfirst for a combine. I was like a bullet. I wasn't rolling or tumbling at all. Suddenly ..." Thomas hesitated when his voice quivered with emotion.

"It's okay, hon," Shelly said, holding him tightly to her side. "Take your time."

"I-it ... was then that I felt something or someone take my body and flip it end for end. Just one complete turn and nothing more." Thomas stopped talking as sobs began to rack his body.

"Are you okay?" Katie asked, becoming very concerned.

"It's okay, Katie. Really, it is. It's just that when he tells this story, he becomes like this. No matter how many times he has told it; he always has this reaction," Shelly said, passing a tissue box to her husband from a side table.

"Is it the recollection of his collision with the machinery?" Earnest asked as he slid forward to the edge of his seat.

"N-no!" Thomas said through the tears. "It was the angel."

"Did you see an angel?" Katie asked as excitement began to course through her spirit.

"Y ... yes."

"Where was it?"

Regaining his composure somewhat, Thomas continued, "As I ... was travelling through the air towards ... the combine, I opened my eyes for a brief moment and there ... he was."

"Where?" Earnest asked, surprised at his own interest now.

"He was right above me."

"Was he like standing in the air above you?" Earnest asked.

"No, he was lying the same direction as I was but directly above me."

"How high above you?" Katie asked.

"About six inches."

"Wow!" Katie said, almost bouncing on her seat.

"What did he look like?" Earnest asked.

"Well, all I could see was his face and his head, but he was male with the darkest and thickest black, curly hair I have ever seen, and as I looked closely, I could see what looked like thousands of miniature diamonds and jewels embedded in his hair—like it was part of his hair, but there was something else."

"What?" Both Katie and Earnest asked at the same time. They gave each other a look before looking back expectantly at Thomas.

"His face was glowing like a very bright Coppertone tan."

"Glowing?" Earnest asked.

"Yes, all around the outer edges of his face and the glow made the diamonds and jewels sparkle. It is a sight I shall never forget."

"Tell them what he said," Shelly urged Thomas.

"He spoke to you?" Katie almost shouted as the joy rose in her soul.

"Yes, he most certainly did," Thomas said with a big smile on his face.

"What did he say?" Earnest asked, sitting on the very edge of the armchair, unsure of just how he was feeling about all of this or if he even believed any of it at all.

"Fear not, for I am with thee!"

"Oh!" Katie exclaimed. "And then what happened?"

Again Thomas paused, thinking about that day, not wanting the images in his mind to leave but knowing that as he went on with the recollection that they would. "The next thing I remember was waking up in the hospital, and I was obviously in pretty bad shape, but I was still alive."

"How bad was it?" Earnest asked.

"I had broken both my legs, cracked my right knee cap, and removed a lot of skin, along with a few other problems."

"What happened to the angel?" Katie asked.

"He was gone after his purpose was done."

"What purpose could that be?" Earnest asked, feeling the doubt beginning to surface once again.

45

"To protect me from death."

"Yeah, okay, but you still got all broken up," Earnest said with a smug look.

"God has never said that he will protect us from such things."

"Well, why would I want to serve a God like that then? What's the purpose?"

"I would hope that in time you would find the answer to that, my friend," Thomas said as he looked his friend directly in the eyes. "Anyway, I just wanted to tell you about my encounter with that particular angel, and how from that moment on, I knew that there was really a God who was protecting me. From that day on, I set my eyes on him and dedicated my life to him as my Lord and Saviour."

"Wait just a minute there, buddy," Earnest said loudly. "You said 'that particular angel.' Are you leading us to believe that you have actually seen more than just one angel?"

"Yes, I have, and Shelly has seen one—actually, we both saw him together."

"Okay, so just how many have you seen?" Earnest asked rising to his feet, feeling the sudden need to actually walk around.

"Three ... no, actually it was four!"

"Yes, four," Shelly said, agreeing with her husband.

"Wow! You two have actually seen angels," Katie said. "Please tell me about them."

"Katie, I would love to tell you about them, but it is getting late and they will be a story for another time."

"Awwwww!" Katie said in mock complaint as she made a pouting with her lips.

"If we have the time to really talk about it some other day, I might even tell you about the demon I saw as well."

Katie said nothing but turned to her husband who could see the excitement and fear mixed in her eyes.

All Earnest had to say was "Oh brother!"

CHAPTER FIVE

t was 3:00 a.m. at the Woodsworth Industries International headquarters building in the heart of the city's business community. Normally at this time of the day, only the security staff were on hand, but today was not a normal day for Bartholomew William Woodsworth. He could not sleep, as aggravation and anger kept him awake most nights now.

Bart, as he liked to be called, could not find the mystery man who had earlier challenged him to a game of racquetball, claiming that he was worthy of taking him on. Other than using women for his eye candy and spending his father's money recklessly, racquetball was Bart's burning passion—not that he actually loved the game. At first, it was the thrill of winning each game, but soon it progressed to decimating his opponents. After that thrill wore off, he learned to love physically hurting his opponents by his mastery over the small rubber ball. Eventually no one would take him on in a game anymore, not even when they were offered money to play him in a game. Then the stranger came on the scene that day in the headquarters café, not that long ago, but he left in a hurry with no mention of his name, where he lived, or how Bart could get a hold of him. With this frustration eating away at him, Bart found himself alone in the lower level of his father's corporate build at this ungodly hour, blasting away on the racquetball court. As he slammed the ball wildly, he ranted in his anger.

"Where *are* you? You said you would play, so c'mon 'n' show me your face, you coward! I will pulverize you into the floor, just as I have all the others, 'cause I am a racquetball god, don't you know?"

Bart was running wildly now, just hitting the ball any chance he got, no matter if it was within the rules of the game he had perfected. Sweat was coating most of his body by this point, and it ran down from his forehead into his eyes and mouth. He was panting loudly as he grunted with each and every swing at the small rubber ball. He was dangerously close to collapsing from exhaustion, but he would never quit, never give up. They would have to pick him up from the hardwood floor.

"C'mon!" Bart yelled at the top of his lungs. "Where are you?"

Suddenly Bart was startled by a strange cool breeze that swept through the court. In all the years of playing the game, it was the first time he had ever felt such an occurrence and it almost frightened him.

"W-what was that?" he said out loud, even though he knew there was no one listening or even there for that matter. He stopped his frantic motions and just stood in the middle of the court, trying to figure out just what had happened. He was facing the glass viewing wall where normally people could just sit or stand and watch a game being played without fear of being hit by the ball or the players as well.

"I am ready!" Bart heard behind him, and he was on his knees before he realized that someone was actually standing behind him.

As Bart struggled to stand up, fear still coursing through his body, he slowly twisted his head around to see just who it was that had spoken to him. He froze at the sight of the stranger standing about six feet over from him.

"W-wha ...?" Bart managed to stammer out. "H-how did y-you get in here?" he said as the anger began to re-emerge within his innermost being.

"The door was open," the stranger said simply.

"I was looking that direction, and I never saw you enter," Bart said as the level of his voice began to increase.

"Maybe so, maybe not."

"Huh? What does that mean? And how did you even get into this building at this time of the night?"

"Like I said, I kind of work for your father."

"Yes, I remember you saying that, and just what does that mean?"

The stranger just stood there for a few moments, and Bart took the time to really check him out. His outfit looked very expensive, and if anyone knew anything about racquetball fashion, it was Bart. The stranger had the proper eye guard, wrist tether, and footwear required for the game. He had jet-black curly hair that almost seemed to sparkle. He looked to be in very good physical shape and stood at least six feet tall. But there was just something about him that didn't quite feel or even look right, and try as he did, Bart just couldn't put his finger on it.

"Well, let's just say that I watch out for your father's best interests," the stranger said with a smile that almost seemed to light up the court they were both standing on. "I am very good when it comes to protection," he continued with a slight chuckle in his voice.

"Protect—" Bart started to say, but the stranger cut him off.

"Well, we could spend a lot of time just chatting, but that will come soon enough. So let's play this game that you claim you are the god of."

Come soon enough? Bart thought to himself. *What does that mean? And just when did he hear me say that I am a racquetball god?*

"Bart?" He heard the stranger say his name, which brought him back to reality. "You okay there, buddy?"

"Uh ... ya ... okay so let's start this game," Bart finally got out.

"By the way, my name is Michael and it has been my pleasure to know you."

Again, Bart was flooded with questions in his mind. *Your pleasure to know me? I don't know this guy at all. Is he saying these things to just throw me off my game because he knows just how good I am?*

"Earth to Bart," Michael said as he looked at his opponent with some doubt in his expression. "You okay there? Maybe we should just leave this for another day?"

"*No!*" Bart shouted. "We are going to have it out right here, right now!"

Racquetball was a game of precision, thinking ahead like the game of chess, always trying to be one move ahead of one's opponent, and both players were thinking this way in any given game. Bart had taught himself to think two moves ahead, but here on the court in his father's complex, he was playing solely by rage, not determination. It was his goal to decimate this strange man to the point just short of killing him, and these thoughts were clouding his judgement when it came to the game.

The game started off fast and furious with both men hitting hard and moving fast on their feet. The screeching sounds of rubber soles on the hardwood court soon filled the entire room, along with the sounds of Bart grunting and ranting at the same time.

Michael showed no signs of exhaustion or even breaking a sweat. Bart, on the other hand, was drenched already.

"You ... are a ... dead man!" Bart was yelling as he turned and twisted, jumped forwards, and quickly backed up, following the small rubber ball and it's every move.

Michael, however, never said a word, and his silence continued to fuel Bart's rage as the pace quickened, but try as hard as he might, Bart could not make that ball hit his opponent.

The game was so intense, played by two men who obviously knew the game well, that it took a full 15 minutes before Bart was the first to score from his serve, when Michael apparently was unable to hit the ball on the return.

"Ha! There ya go, loser. This is just the beginning, so ya better get used to it!" Bart grunted out as the game continued.

Conventional rules were thrown to the wind as the game went on and on, both men moving like well-oiled machines, making all the right moves with no scoring other than Bart's first point, or hinder as it is referred to in the game. The ball never hit another wall other than the one directly in front of the two men, nor did it ever hit the ceiling. Finally the game had gone on nonstop for almost an hour, and Bart was beginning to feel its effects as he began to tire out.

"You getting tired there, young man?" Michael finally asked.

"Not before you will, old man!" Bart shouted back sarcastically.

"Oh, you think so, do you?" And with that said, suddenly Michael seemed to shift into high gear and began to almost fly around the court.

Then Michael scored a hinder, then another and another, never stopping for the win, but on and on, he continued to a now bewildered Bart. *How can he move like that?* Bart thought. *We have been playing nonstop for over an hour, and he seems to have even more steam now than when we started?*

As Bart was thinking these thoughts, he momentarily lost contact with the small rubber ball and felt it suddenly make contact with his right arm, just above the elbow.

"Ahhhhhh!" Bart cried out as he spun around, holding his right arm. His mind was in turmoil now with the fact that he was the one in pain. *This is not part of the plan*, he thought, but soon, the throbbing pain in his arm drowned out all such thoughts in his head.

Michael approached Bart to make sure he was going to be okay. "Are you all right?" he asked as he reached out and touched Bart's right arm, placing his index finger on the exact location of the impact the small rubber ball made.

Bart started to say something as Michael approached him, but the instant the stranger's finger touched his arm, an electrical-type shock of some sort coursed through his arm, up his right side, and through his head where it seemed to exit. Then Bart collapsed on the floor and passed out.

He felt as if he were floating but could make no sense of where he was or just what was going on. Finally Bart felt as if the floating and spinning sensations he was feeling slowed down until they finally stopped, and he opened his eyes.

W-what? He thought as he found himself sort of up in the air looking down at himself, lying sprawled out on the racquetball court. *A-am I dead?* Another thought came as he just floated in the air of the room. As he looked down on the still body beneath him, he could see that the racquet he had been using was untethered from his wrist and was lying about three feet from his body, as if it had been tossed over there.

Suddenly Bart felt a very weird sensation begin to coarse through his body, and he never even had a chance to say a word before he shot up straight through the ceiling, picking up speed as he seemingly flew through floor after floor of the 80-story skyscraper. He could see floors flying by, complete with cubicles, stairways, copy machines, desks, and so much more as he continued speeding faster and faster upwards. Then suddenly he slowed down as he approached the very top floor of the Woodsworth Industries International building, which held his father's private office, complete with a small gym, steam room, large private washroom, kitchenette, and patio gardens. All of it had been designed by his father alone.

Bart now found himself standing on the floor, able to walk and move around, even though he knew he wasn't in his own body. As he looked around the huge office with all its ornate decorations, fine paintings and expensive archeological objects from various parts of the world, his eyes finally came to rest on the vault.

The vault! He thought, the one room that he had never been inside. He, his sister and his mother had the entire run of the skyscraper, except for this room—no one but Father was allowed within its walls.

This is where his treasure is hidden, Bart was thinking. *And I can now just walk through its walls and finally see what's inside.* Slowly and cautiously, Bart approached the solid steel door with its detailed locking mechanism. He had never seen his father open the door, much less go in, but that wouldn't be a problem now.

Why am I feeling cautious? No one knows I am here or can even see me, Bart thought as he strode right up to the massive door. *Now, Father of mine, I shall finally see the treasures you have hidden from my eyes,* he thought as he easily passed through the door.

Bart wasn't surprised to find that the room was pitch-black, but he couldn't find a way to turn on any lights so he just stood there, in the room, he presumed. Slowly the room just seemed to illuminate above him, and he was surprised to see a single old-style wooden swivel office chair in the middle of the room, directly beneath the illumination above him. He moved to the chair and felt compelled to sit in it, which he did.

The chair felt very comfortable and well-worn at the same time as his hands gripped the arms and slid along the length of the fine wood. Suddenly the whole room seemed to illuminate to reveal pictures, hundreds of finely framed photographs on all the walls of the room, and nothing more. There were no piles of gold bars or stacks of cash and precious jewels, as Bart assumed he would find; instead there were just photographs. What startled Bart even more, as he swivelled around in the chair, taking in everything he could see, was the fact that the photographs were of his brother, Franklin; himself; his sister, Carolyn; and his mother too.

"What is all this stuff?" Bart said out loud, not sure if he had actually said it or just thought it. "Photographs? That's his treasure?" he said, as the enormity of this secret room still hadn't permeated his brain. Then he began to hear sounds being piped in from speakers somewhere, even though he could not see them. "That sounds like a baby," Bart said as more and more sounds began to fill the room. There were sounds of a baby crying and then people fussing over the baby sounds. Next there was laughter and joy at what he assumed were the parents playing with the baby. Then there was another baby's cry and the same scenario again, even though the parents seemed to be a little bit older. Then finally he heard yet another's baby's cry all mixed in with the sounds of laughter, playing, and joyful talking.

Bart just sat there, dumbfounded, even though he had still not made the connection—until he heard his brother, Franklin, talking, followed by his own voice and then that of his younger sister. It was when he heard the voices of his mother and his father, saying prayers with the three of them in their beds, the one year when they all shared a bedroom in their smaller home on the west side of the city. Bart had forgotten about all those times, the good times, before Franklin had left home once and for all, and as he heard the voices and the prayers, he suddenly felt an emptiness deep inside.

He wanted to leave, to get up from the chair and just run from that room of memories, but he could also feel something way down inside of his being. It was something he hadn't felt since his brother and best friend had left home.

"No!" he cried out as anger began to slowly rise to the surface once again, but deny it as he tried, the feeling rose as well, until it overwhelmed Bart as he sat alone in that chair, in that treasured room of memories past. Bart knew that if he were in his body right then, tears would be gushing forth as the feelings of love washed over him.

Suddenly it all made sense to him.

"My father's treasure is love—not just the word or feeling of love but love missed and love of days gone by, family and closeness, prayers at night and fun times during the day. It was love as it was meant to be."

Bart didn't know how long he had been sitting there, but he finally realized he was again sitting in the dark, all alone, with not a single word or sound to be heard. It was the feeling of being totally and utterly alone. *Is this how my father feels?* he wondered, but before he could think another thought, Bart found himself on the roof of the 80-story skyscraper.

As he spun around slowly in the brightness of early morning light, his eyes came to rest on someone resting on their elbows, looking over the edge of the building.

"W-who are you?" he asked hesitantly, not sure whether he should approach or not. Suddenly he was moving towards the person, but not of his own will; it was as if he were being softly pushed in that direction. Then something caught his attention. It was a smell, a very pleasant smell, like cotton candy, meadow flowers, and the first rain of spring all mixed together. Oh how he loved that fragrance and just wanted to breathe it in deeply and forever. Then he was standing right beside the person, who was still looking over the edge.

Bart took in all the details of the person's attire, which seemed very strange to him. It looked like a coat of many colors, but not just ordinary colors, for they seemed to be alive and bursting forth, almost florescent, if that was the term to use. More than that though, Bart saw what looked like feathers mixed in with the colors, and as his eyes made their way upwards, he caught sight of the hair. It was jet-black in color with thick curls, just like the stranger's hair, but there was something else there too. He had to lean even closer towards the person as he took in thousands upon thousands of small jewels within the dark curls, almost as if they were a part of the hair itself.

Suddenly Bart stood straight up as another smell began to waft through the air, and as he turned to his right side, he saw a sight that frightened him right from the top of his head to the very toes in his feet. He was now looking into the eyes of sheer terror and that smell.

What is that ungodly smell? he managed to think. *It is like rotting garbage, mixed with the smell of death, like one smells in a vehicle that has a dead animal in it somewhere, all mixed in with the smells of sulfur, smoke and fire.* But it was the eyes that scared him the most. His own eyes were riveted to those eyes, which looked like molten metal mixed with red-hot coals.

Just when he thought he could stand it no longer, Bart had that feeling again, just like when he was floating above his body on the racquetball court, and suddenly he shot straight up into the air, passing through the clouds and the light of the earth's glow at breakneck speeds. Looking up, he could see the stars coming into view in a brilliance he could never have even imagined. He could see the moon as a huge bright ball of light before his eyes, and off in the distance, beyond that, he could see star clusters of various bright colors, much like what he had just seen in the person's jet-black hair. Then he simply stopped!

He was floating once again, but this time in outer space, and as he turned to look back where he had just come from, he gasped at the sight of the earth far beneath him; still, he was not afraid and had a strange peace about him.

It is amazing! Bart thought as he looked at the earth in all its fullness. He had seen pictures of earth taken from the International Space Station and satellites, but none of them even came close to the greatness of what his eyes were now seeing. As he looked down on the earth, his eyes suddenly picked up on an object just coming around the far side, floating it would seem, just as he was. As it got closer and closer, he started to figure out just what it was. It was a very large cube, a pure black cube.

"Mr. Woodsworth?" Bart could hear as if someone were calling his name from far off.

"Mr. Woodsworth, can you hear me?" the voice continued.

"W-what?" Bart finally stammered out as he slowly came to.

"Mr. Woodsworth, can you open your eyes please?"

Slowly Bart began to feel the fact that he was lying on the floor somewhere as he hesitantly tried opening his eyes. He could finally see a uniformed pant leg, and as his eyes travelled upwards, he realized he was looking at one of the security guards of his father's complex.

"W-where am I?" Bart finally managed to say.

"Sir, thank God you are okay," the guard said with a sigh.

"What time is it?" Bart asked as everything came rushing back to his mind.

"It is 9:15 a.m., sir."

Then a second security guard showed up, and the two of them helped Bart to his feet and over to a nearby bench. Bart sat down, trying to make sense of why he was on the floor in the first place when it all came rushing back into his mind—being alone on the court when the stranger mysteriously showed up, the words that they shared, the intense game that ensued, the pain in his arm, the unreal out-of-body experiences, and then that cube.

"Where is the cube?" Bart suddenly asked as he startled to two security guards, standing just in front of him.

"W-what, sir?" one asked.

"Uhhh ... Okay, forget that. Where is Michael?" Bart spat out, flustered at the guard's inability to understand what he was asking.

"Who, sir?"

"That guy with the curly black hair ... who was playing a game of racquetball with me here last night?"

The two security guards just looked at each other and shrugged their shoulders before one of them answered, "I'm ... sorry ... Mr. Woodsworth, but you were the only person allowed into the building last night."

"No, he was here. We played a game, a very long game, until I got hit by the ..." Bart stopped talking as he realized just what he had said. It wasn't the words that he said, but the fact that he almost admitted to someone that he had actually been hurt by the small rubber ball for a change.

"We're sorry, sir, but there was no one in this building but you," the one guard said.

"Excuse me, sir, but you were about to say you were hit by the ball. Are you okay, sir? Do you need some medical attention?" the other guard cut in.

Bart instinctively reached for his right arm but found no pain or any mark at all that would have indicated that he had even been struck by the racquetball as he remembered. But he did feel a very slight tingling that felt almost like a small shock.

"Uh ... no, I ... I am okay," was all Bart said.

After a few more minutes of assuring the guards he was all right, Bart stood and made his way to the change room for a much-needed hot shower, as he seemed to be caked in dry sweat. As he stood under the hot spray of the shower, Bart tried to figure out if he had actually played a game with the stranger and had the out-of-body experience or if it all was just some weird dream.

Once he was showered and dressed, he made his way out of the building and over to his Jaguar in his personal private parking spot. As he slid into the expensive leather seat, he suddenly felt a twinge in his right arm, just above the elbow. He reached for it, but as quickly as it came, the pain just seemed to disappear, so he just shrugged his shoulders, started the car and roared out of the adjacent parking facility, almost running over a homeless man, pushing his overloaded shopping cart across the entranceway of the facility.

"Hey! Watch it with that cart, old man! Don't scratch the car!" Bart yelled back as he swerved out onto the street. He fishtailed wildly as he sped down the street and away from one very wild dream and a night he hoped to soon forget. As he sped away down the street before him, the homeless man could hear the driver laughing loudly until the sounds of the city in the early morning drowned it out.

It was now only one month away from Earnest Woodsworth's fiftieth birthday bash, which had Katie and Caroline in the midst of preparations for the big event that would see well over 200 guests and business associates. The party would be held at the house in the city, which made it easier for the guests who would be flying in for the event.

The caterers were all lined up and given the menu choices for the event, as was the company that would be supplying the alcohol and other beverages. Katie was not in favor of this but knew that in her husband's business dealings, alcohol played a big part and so rather than fight about it with Earnest, she just gave in to the fact that it would be a part of the party.

Caroline had taken on the task of lining up the music for the evening; that also included the construction of the huge covered dance floor that would also be part of the outdoor festivities.

Katie had talked to Thomas, who agreed to be the master of ceremonies for the birthday bash at the meal and short program to follow.

"So how are things progressing on your end?" Katie asked Caroline.

"They are right on schedule, and unless something major happens in this city, everything should be a go."

"That's great, sweetie, and have you invited any of your friends?"

Caroline hesitated a moment at her mom's question, which caused a bit of concern with Katie for her daughter.

"Is everything okay, Caroline?"

Again Caroline hesitated, so Katie got up from her seat at the table and walked around to her daughter's side. She never said anything but just placed her hand on her daughter's shoulder in a show of love and support. Then Caroline began to sob. Tears rolled down her cheeks.

Quickly Katie knelt at her daughter's side and wrapped her arms around her as she pulled Caroline tightly to her side.

"What is it?" she whispered into her daughter's ear.

"I ... it's Jenn," Caroline finally managed to whisper through her tears. "She's not coming."

"Is there something wrong with Jenn? Is she sick or have another engagement?" Katie asked, finding it hard to believe that Jenn, Caroline's best friend, would not be attending the party.

"No ... it's nothing like that, and it's not just that she won't be attending the party; s-she is no longer ... my friend." With that said, she broke down again.

Katie got Caroline to stand up and led her over to the large leather sofa in the corner of the room. Together they sat down, and Katie took her daughter into her loving arms and simply comforted her. She said not a word but knew that in time Caroline would tell her all the details. Katie just held her grown daughter in her arms and slowly rocked with her for about 20 minutes until Caroline had completely settled down.

Caroline finally pulled herself away from her mother's arms, accepted a tissue from her, and then sat back in the sofa as she started to explain the situation.

"A while ago, Jenn and I were out for a light lunch in the city. She got talking, like she always does, about our wealth and the fact that she doesn't understand why I am not a party girl or into fashion like she is. So I asked her a question that she could not answer ... at least she didn't then."

"What was the question, dear?" Katie asked, still concerned about her daughter's breakdown.

"I asked her why she stuck with me as my best friend, knowing that I am a Christian and am not into the lifestyle she figures I should be, and she just stuttered a bit, not being able to give me an answer. We were just batting the subject around, Mom. I never thought she would seriously end it just for that reason." With that said, Caroline broke down again as her mother simply cradled her in her arms again and comforted her once more.

"Hushhhh!" Katie whispered into her daughter's ear. "It will be okay. The Lord knows what is happening, and I know he has a wondrous plan for your life from here on in. Caroline, you need to begin to pray that the Lord will bring some very good Christian friends into your life and get away from those at your school who are not so."

For the next 10 minutes or so, the two women never said a word. Caroline just let her mother comfort her as she lay in the safety and love of her arms.

"Caroline?" Katie finally said, as she softly pushed her daughter back into a sitting position. "I have one last thing I want to know about Jenn before we move forward to better things ahead."

"Okay," Caroline said quietly.

"In all the time that you knew Jenn, did you ever talk to her about the Lord?"

"Do you mean like salvation?"

"Yes."

"Yes, actually I did once when we were both in grade 10. We had gone on that field trip to Dino Land—remember?"

"Was that the trip that Bart's class went as well?" Katie asked.

"Yes, unfortunately!" Caroline said sarcastically, rolling her eyes at the memory of that trip.

Katie burst out laughing. "Oh yes, then I remember that event quite well. Bart thought that the big dinosaur beside the tar pit display was a slide."

Caroline was doing her best to hold a straight face, but the memory of Bart covered in tar oil as he fought to stand up after sliding down the dinosaur was just too much to bear and she too burst out laughing.

When the two women finally calmed down, Caroline was the first to speak.

"That actually felt good, you know—laughing, I mean. It kinda makes me feel good, considering the situation with Jenn."

"Yes, well, a good belly laugh now and then can work wonders," Katie said as she patted her daughter's leg. "Now please continue what you were saying about you and Jenn talking about salvation. I really would like to know."

"Okay. Well, we had gone on the trip and found it very boring."

"With the exception of Bart," Katie interjected with a wide grin.

"Yes, with the exception of Bart, Mother. Jenn and I found a nice grassy area beside a creek that flows through the property. We had our lunch with us so we decided we would just eat our lunch and talk, something that we had done a lot all through our friendship." Caroline hesitated as the seriousness of her lost friendship overwhelmed her for moment.

"It's okay, hon. Take your time," Katie said.

"I-I'll be okay," Caroline said as she began to talk once more. "We talked about the Dino Land Park and how boring it was. Then we talked about a few of the boys on the trip and how they all wanted to sit close to Jenn, as per usual."

"Oh really now?" Katie cut in. "And just what kind of things were you discussing about boys at that age?"

"Oh, Mother!" Caroline said with a slight chuckle. "Getting back to our talk ... things eventually got around to my faith. She wanted to know how it felt to be a Christian and what I had to give up. I told her it wasn't like that at all, that Jesus was everything to me, that he helped me so many times and answered my prayers many times as well.

"She was captivated and searching for answers herself, so I just felt the moment was right and went for it. I shared some personal experiences I had felt with the Lord in times when I felt alone or afraid. Then I basically shared the love of Jesus with her, telling her how he could take her life and change her from the inside out, how she would have a joy and a peace that the world could never give her, and by that time, she had tears in her eyes.

"Taking a chance, I asked her if she wanted Jesus in her life. I explained how she could get it and how easy it was to accept the Lord ..." Caroline abruptly stopped talking and just sat there, her head now hung low as she struggled to go on.

Katie said not a word. It was her daughter's story, and she didn't want to push her for details in any way, so she just sat and waited.

Caroline was grateful that her mother wasn't probing her with questions; it was one of the many reasons why she loved her so. She just sat there recalling that day on the grass by the slow-moving creek. She could still remember the sounds of the birds chirping and the smells in the air, but the one thing she wished and had prayed that she could forget were the words from her best friend, Jenn.

"Jenn just sat back on her hands and said to me, 'Hey, you are pretty good at all that stuff.'

"'What are you talking about?' I asked.

"'All that Jesus stuff, you almost had me believing you, girl.' I was stunned, because I thought she really was coming around but realized that it was just a game to her and we have never talked about it since."

Even Katie was stunned that Jenn would act in such a way, but she knew that human nature was very unpredictable at the best of times.

"It's okay, hon. You said and did all the right things, but I feel in my spirit that Jenn may never know the truth, at least not from our side of the family. Her god is not your God."

Caroline let out a little laugh, but it was a sad laugh just the same.

"What?" Katie asked.

"It's just funny that you said it that way."

"Said what?"

"That her god is not my God."

"Why do you find that funny?"

"Because the very last thing that Jenn said to me the last time we talked was that she didn't need my God, because fashion was her god!"

"So how did that meeting go with the Texas oil executives you were telling me about the last time we had lunch at the Evergreen Country Club?" Thomas asked Earnest as the two men met in Thomas's office to confer on the latest designs for the new construction covering project.

"Well, they pitched their ideas to me, and I must say it was very convincing," Earnest said before pausing.

"But?" Thomas continued.

"Yes, well, I am still mulling it around in my head."

"Obviously there is something that is troubling you about it, seeing you are a man who tends not to wait on investments. I have known you for some time, my friend, and I do know that you do all your homework first, then you make up your mind before you talk to anyone about the final details. Still here you are, uncertain of what to do, and that is not at all like you."

"I know, but I have a lot on my mind these days and they are trying to get me to make a rush decision. I understand that they want to get going on the project, and I am confident they will, with or without me, still ..." Earnest paused again, his mind going somewhere else.

"Okay then, let's just concentrate on this project for now, if that is okay with you? We can leave it to a later date, but I really would like to push forward on this in order that we can have a working prototype in place within a month or two," Thomas said, turning back to the plans on the table before them.

"What?" Earnest said, coming back to reality. "Oh! Yes ... sorry about that."

"No problem, my friend, no problem," Thomas said, giving his friend a big smile of reassurance.

"So where are we?" Earnest said, returning his attention to the project.

"Everything is going smoothly so far. We have determined that the outer case of the main unit needs to be made of either lightweight plate steel or composite materials. Aluminum is just too light and will not stand up to the wear and tear of most construction sites."

"That makes sense, but what are the cost differences?"

"Therein lies the problem. If we go with the steel plate case, it will be cheaper for sure, but composite materials can take a real beating in most cases," Thomas said and then had a sip of his coffee.

"Can you give me some cost figures?" Earnest asked.

"Yes. A welded steel case at cost would run us in the neighbourhood of 50 dollars, but that is based on at least 1,000 units. The composite cost for the same unit would be around 75 dollars; however, if we place a minimum order of 5,000 units, that price would drop to 50 dollars as well."

"Ah, the old Catch-22, I see. Basically, the supplier gets more for less or we get less for more," Earnest said with a chuckle. "Are these units going to be sold strictly to individual construction companies, or do you have other possibilities in mind?"

"Actually I have thought long and hard on that very subject, and I think to start off with, we should focus our attention on construction and equipment rental companies."

"Okay then, why can't we go for both materials? We could sell the plate steel cases to construction companies and the composite units to the rental companies. Rental units would take more abuse, I would think, seeing that they will be used over and over, more than the ones owned by construction companies," Earnest said.

"Yes, that is very true, and I think we could come up with a final cost that would make both sectors of the construction industry happy. I think that rental companies would also be more interested in all the additional pieces that will accompany these units," Thomas said as he sat back in his chair.

"How many additional pieces would there be?"

"Considering the possibilities of the various scenarios that these units could be used in, I think we are going to be looking at 10 to 15 extras, but there could be more in the future as the units are used more and requests come in from rental companies."

"What are some of the other possibilities?"

"The basic idea for these units is to use them for the construction of buildings from the footings to the finished roof. However, there are brackets that would make the units easier to use for the roofers, window installers, those companies installing siding, stonemasons, and even those doing parging. But it can even go farther than that. They could be used for outdoor venues, such as weddings, funerals, parties, or even as far as to cover gardens. There is quite a list of possibilities!" Thomas said with an obvious excitement in his eyes and voice.

"I am sure there is, and knowing that mind of yours, I am sure you will come up with even more uses for this product. Have you come up with a name for the units yet?" Earnest asked of his friend and partner.

"Not a final name actually, but I have been tossing around ideas, like The Roof in a Can and Canned Roof and things like that, but just give me time and I will have just the right name, I am sure."

"Oh, that I am sure of, my friend, that I am very sure of!"

The two men began to wind down their meeting with small talk about the everyday things of life, family and the upcoming fiftieth birthday bash for Earnest.

"Do you have any idea yet if your entire family will be there?"

Thomas asked, knowing that family could sometimes be a touchy issue with the man.

Earnest looked away and out a window before he answered the question, not wanting to look his friend in the eyes.

"No, sadly I don't. Oh I am sure Katie and Caroline will be there, seeing they are doing all the planning for it, but Bart I am unsure about and …" He paused, as it was even difficult to say his eldest son's name. "I am unsure about … Franklin …" Earnest said in barely a whisper, his voice full of emotion, and Thomas knew the deep love he had for his son, who had forsaken his father.

A thought came to Thomas. *Maybe this is the way to reach Earnest?* He pondered that thought for a moment as the two of them rose from their seats and began to depart.

"Earnest, before you go, I was wondering if we could schedule in a game at the club one day next week?"

Earnest wasted not a moment in replying. "Yes, a round of golf is just what I need these days. I love golf, as it is a great way to get away from all the hustle and bustle and relax. Okay, I will check with my secretary and get back to you later in the day. Is there any day in particular you prefer?"

"Nope. I am free anytime you are, my friend."

"Great. I will get back to you later."

With that, the two men moved to shake hands, but Thomas stepped in quickly and gave Earnest a big hug. When it was done, both men stepped back to leave.

"Thomas?" Earnest suddenly asked.

"Yes?" Thomas said as he turned to look at his friend.

"You will never know just how much I needed that hug. Thank you!"

CHAPTER SIX

It had now been a few weeks since Bart had played a wild game of racquetball with the stranger at his father's downtown corporate office building, and he still didn't know if it had really taken place or not. Bart and his newest girlfriend, Bubbles, as he liked to call her, were swimming in the family's large outdoor pool. Bubbles had exited the pool much to the delight of Bart as he watched her climb the pool ladder and then walk over to a lounge chair. He was always amazed at how the female body looked and moved when walking either towards him or away, especially in a bikini.

Bart stayed in the pool for a few minutes more as he just relaxed and floated on an air mattress in the center of the massive stone-faced pool.

"Bart, honey, could you please come and put some suntan lotion on my back?" Bubbles asked, lowering her dark sunglasses as she batted her eyes in his direction before she rose and lay down on the lounge chair, making sure that Bart saw her undo the back of her bikini top.

Not wanting to say no to this very lovely buxom woman, Bart made his way over to the pool ladder, where he slid off the air mattress, intending to climb out of the pool. He placed his hands on the railing on either side of the steps, but when he began to pull himself upward and the muscles in his right arm began to do their work, Bart experienced a sharp, burning pain just above the elbow that hurt so much he had to let go of the railing and fell backwards into the pool.

"Ahhhhh!" Bart cried out in pain as he rose to his feet in the shallow water, clutching his right arm.

"Bart? Are you okay?" Bubbles called out as she suddenly rose from the lounge chair, forgetting that her top was undone, but Bart was in so much pain that he didn't even notice. She quickly did it up again.

"My arm! My arm!" Bart cried out as unbelievable pain radiated from that one specific spot.

"Bart, what do you want me to do?" Bubbles asked as she quickly made her way over to the pool ladder.

Bart tried to think for a moment on how he was going to get out of the pool, but the searing pain was blocking out all reasoning, and then he felt a touch on his arm and spun around. He was surprised to see that Bubbles was in the water with him.

"Here, let's go this way, over to the steps," she said to him as she guided him, making sure not to touch his right arm in any way.

Bart used his left hand to grip the railing, but even that was hard to do, seeing he wanted to hold his right arm with his left hand in hopes that it would somehow ease the shooting pain. Partway up the steps, he suddenly slipped when trying to support his right arm with his left hand. Instinctively he reached for the railing with his right hand and gripped it solidly.

"What the ...?" He shouted as he realized that the searing pain was gone completely.

Bubbles was almost in a state of shock as she saw him slip and reach out for the railing with his hurting arm.

"Ohhhh, Bart!" she yelled out as she instinctively tried to grab him to support him, but then she was amazed that he was standing straight up with no expression of pain at all. "What?" was all she could get out.

"It's gone! It is actually gone!" Bart said loudly as he gripped his right arm here and there, almost trying to make the pain reappear.

"How did that happen?" Bubbles asked. "You sure looked like you were in pain to me, babe. Are you sure you weren't just kidding me?"

"*No!*" Bart yelled in a way that almost scared her. "If I said I was in pain, then I was in pain, you idiot!"

Bubbles didn't know what to say. Bart had never talked to her like this before. Yes, he was a playboy of sorts and she knew it, but he had always treated her well—at least until this.

"Leave me alone!" Bart shouted at her as she moved towards him. He brushed right past her, up the stairs, across the patio, and into the house.

"I-I ... was just trying ... to help," she whispered as tears began to run down her cheeks.

Finally she exited the pool and after drying herself off, went to the change room just off the main house, where she got dressed and composed herself before stepping out. As she stepped out into the hot afternoon sun, she was startled to see Mrs. Woodsworth sitting at one of the patio tables, playing with her dogs.

"Oh excuse me," she said as she walked in that direction with the intention of leaving. "I didn't realize that there was anyone else here."

"That's okay, my dear. I just came out onto the patio to have a cup of tea before heading back in," Katie said. As she looked at the young woman, she could tell that she had been crying and saw that she had a very sad look on her face, even though she was trying to hide it and be polite.

"My name is Katie," she said as she rose and greeted the young woman with a polite handshake.

"Uh, my name is Bubb ..." she started to say. "No, actually, my name is Winter ... Winter Rose," she said as she extended her hand as well.

"Would you care to join me for some tea?" Katie asked as she sat back down.

"N-no, but thank you. I probably should get going."

"Please, I insist. It would be good to have some company today. Just have a tea with me, and then you can go. Besides it is you who look like you need some company today."

Winter just stood there, unable to grasp the fact that this wealthy woman really seemed to want her to visit with her over a cup of tea. This was not just any woman; she was Bart's mother and with all of that in mind, Winter slowly pulled out a chair and sat down.

"Winter Rose! Now that is a very lovely name, my dear. Does it have any special meaning?" Katie asked as she reached for another cup off the tableside tea cart and began pouring the tea for the both of them.

"Well, not really, other than the fact that my parents always liked the name *Winter*, and when I was born, they naturally gave me the name, along with the name *Rose*, which they thought went well with *Winter*."

"Okay, well, it is a very lovely name, and I think it suits you well."

Winter actually felt herself blush somewhat.

"Thank you," she said as she accepted the cup of tea.

"So how has my son been treating you?" Katie asked, looking directly at Winter across the small decorative wrought-iron table.

Winter didn't know what to say. He had treated her very well up until the incident in the pool just a few minutes earlier.

"Okay, I guess!" was all she could come up with.

"I do know he made you cry recently," Katie said as she placed her hand on the young woman's hand, which was resting on the table. "And I want to know why, as I raised him better than that. I know that he has a reputation as a ladies' man, but even so, he must be respectful, at least here at home."

Winter could feel the tears beginning to well up in her eyes again at the kind words of this woman before her. *I would love to have a mother-in-law like this one day*, she thought to herself as Katie handed her a napkin for her eyes.

"I am not making excuses for my son, but lately he seems to be very preoccupied with something, at least he was until a few weeks ago, when all of a sudden, he seemed to come around again."

"Y-yes ... I noticed that too. He was very angry at some guy, even though he had just met him briefly in his father's building—the cafeteria, I believe he said. Then one afternoon when I saw him, he seemed very happy ... at least until ..." And her voice trailed off as she lowered her head, not looking at Katie now.

"At least until today? Is that what you were trying to say?"

"Y-yes," Winter said in barely a whisper.

Bart walked out of the house after having a shower and getting dressed. He figured that Bubbles would be long gone by now and was startled to find her having tea with his mother of all people.

"Mother, I didn't realize that you were home. I hope Bubbles here hasn't been telling you horrid tales about me?" he said as he walked over to the two women.

"She has told me enough," Katie said as Bart came up to the table. "Bart?" she suddenly said in a questioning voice.

"Uh, yeah?" he answered, wondering just where this conversation was about to go.

"I have just had a lovely talk with your friend here," Katie said as she took Winter's hand in her own. "Do you know what her name is?" she asked her son with her eyebrows raised.

"Yes, her name is Bubbles," Bart said, matter-of-factly.

"Is that her real name, or is it the name you want to call her?"

Bart looked at Winter and then back at his mother, feeling somewhat like a rat in a cage at that moment.

"Uh ... well, her name ... is ... uh ..." But hard as he tried, Bart could not think of her name and he just stood there with a blank look on his face.

"I figured so," Katie said as she looked away from her son and over at Winter. "Her real name is Winter Rose. Now why on earth would you ever think that *Bubbles* is nicer than that?"

Bart just stood there. He could feel anger rising up inside him again, and even though he would love to just tell her off right then, he also knew that he had to hold his tongue in the presence of his mother and his toy girlfriend.

"Okay, Bart, and, Winter, too, it is not my intention to overstep my bounds as mother in this case. You are both grown people and know how to conduct yourselves, but sometimes a mother just has to have the last word. Bart, I want you to start using Winter's name from this point on, and I want you to apologize to her right now for treating her so rudely today when all she was trying to do was help you out of the pool."

Now Bart had a real problem as the anger rose quickly to the surface, yet at the same time, he knew that she was right. A battle began in his mind until finally he kind of just blurted out the word, "Sorry!"

"Sorry who?" Katie said, not letting it go that easily.

"S-sorry ... Winter."

"Okay, now that's better," Katie said as she rose from her chair and made her way to the house with her dog in tow. Just before she went in, she turned to face them again. "Winter, I am looking forward to seeing you at my husband's birthday celebration coming up in just a few weeks."

"What?" Bart said. "I never said I was going to be there."

"Oh, believe me, buddy; you will be there, and Winter will be with you, unless ..." She hesitated for effect before continuing. "You want me to return your toys?" With that said, Katie turned and walked into the house with a very prominent smile on her lips.

No one could see it, but Bart was seething mad. He felt like a rat in a cage, and it was his mother who had placed him there, but the reality of the situation was that he himself had put himself there; what made it even worse was the fact that he knew it.

As he just stood there with Winter behind him, Bart thought back to the last time he had really had a conversation with his parents. The discussion was about Bart's allowance, what the amount would be and who would administer the funds on a month-by-month basis. Bart argued, of course, wanting control of the money himself, and it was at that point that his father just gave up and left the room. Then he was all alone with his mother, with him thinking he had won a victory and things would now go his way.

But if Bart thought that dealing with his father was a breeze, he totally underestimated his mother. He could remember that day as if it were just mere minutes ago. Katie had walked right up to her son with only a foot or so separating the two of them. Bart smiled slightly at the memory of what his mother had told him. Before she spoke, she stuck her index finger right up to his nose.

"Now listen here, buddy. This life of yours is not, nor will it ever be a free ride. Yes, your father has money, but don't you ever think for a second that it was easy money. He worked hard—that work ethic is something you lack greatly—for that money and the life we now live. It will be I who will be handling your allowance as your father has asked me to do. Yes, it is your money to do with as you please, but if you ever abuse it or refuse to do anything you are asked to do by myself or your father, well, then that money source can dry up real quick and the toys can be taken away!"

"Bart, are you okay?" Winter asked.

He heard her, but he did not acknowledge it. This was another thing that annoyed him, his mother telling him to treat her better and bring her to his father's birthday celebration coming up very soon.

She means nothing to me, Bart thought to himself. *She is just eye candy and another toy to be played with, but if it means keeping the toys, well, then I will allow her to hang with me for another few weeks, but as soon as the party is over, then she is over too!*

"Uh, sorry ... what did you say?" Bart said in a voice dripping with emotion.

"I was just concerned that you are okay. You looked like you were in so much pain when you were trying to get out of the pool," Winter said as she approached him now, lightly placing her hand on his right arm.

Get your hand off me! How dare you touch me without my permission, Bart thought to himself, but he held back the anger he felt towards her.

"I am okay. The pain just suddenly left when I tripped on the steps in the pool," he said instead.

"Okay, I'm glad," she said with genuine concern.

Bart suddenly realized that she was really concerned about him in that moment. He had always thought that she was just playing the game like he was, and he felt something deep inside. He wasn't sure of just what it was, but he knew he didn't want that feeling hanging around.

"Do you mind if I give you a ride home?" he said. "I think I am just going to relax for the rest of the day, but I will give you a call in a day or two."

"Yes, that will be okay," she answered with a faint smile.

With that said, the two of them headed for his car in the huge entrance oval at the front of the house. Bart drove her home to her condo apartment and gave her a light kiss as was his custom with her before she exited his car, being careful not to slam the door.

As he drove away, only two words were resounding in Bart's mind. *Eye candy, she's only eye candy!*

Earnest was not having a good day, but it was the day that he had cleared in order that his best friend and partner Thomas Hillman and he could play a round of golf at the country club. The tee-off time was scheduled for 1:15 p.m., but it was now only 10:30 a.m. and Earnest was distracted in his thoughts as he called his secretary.

"Marcy, would you please hold all my calls until I get back to you," he asked politely.

"Yes, Mr. Woodsworth. Just let me know when you are free again, sir."

Earnest hung up and reclined in his office desk chair. His mind wandered back to the last conversation he had had with Thomas and the mention of his family. *"Do you have any idea yet if your entire family will be there?"* Thomas had asked, referring to his upcoming birthday celebration. Those words had instantly, once again, brought his emotions to the surface as he thought of his family, especially Bart and Franklin.

Earnest knew that he had neglected them when they needed a father the most, and because of the lack of time he spent with them, Franklin had just up and left and had never returned home again. Bart, on the other hand, was getting back at him by spending his money while living a raunchy lifestyle.

He rose from his office chair and picked up something off his desk before he walked over to the vault in the center of the room. He produced a very special skeleton key and slid it into the heart-shaped lock built into the metal door. After unlocking the door, Earnest swung the solid wooden door open and entered into the room, closing the door behind him with a definite *thud*, heard only within the walls of his private office suite. As he slowly made his way into the room, the soft glow of special built-in lighting began to illuminate the room and the walls of framed photographs. Earnest turned right to the wall and pushed a button there. Softly, a panel slid from within another wall and covered the existing wall of photographs. This wall also had framed photographs, but it was only about half full. He then lifted his hands to the wall and placed yet another photo he had brought with him on the next blank spot on the panel.

Standing back now, he looked at the newly placed photograph of Franklin that showed him dressed in his construction work clothes, bent over a table as he studied a set of building plans. His children never knew it, but they were constantly being watched for their own protection by their father's hired photographers.

Earnest then sat back in the big leather easy-chair and closed his eyes as the soft sounds of voices began to flood his senses and the room. This room was the key to his heart and the key to his happiness. Over the years, not only had he taken countless photographs of his family and himself, but he had also made sure to record the sounds of them having fun. His reasoning was that one day, when he was older, not only would he be able to enjoy the pictures of them but also the sounds of laughter and better family times.

Soon the smiles were tears, and the man sat up in his chair with his head in his hands as he wept at the sound of Franklin and Bart play-wrestling with him on the living room carpet in their second home. As the tears flowed, thoughts also raced through his mind until they all culminated into one single thought: *I would give all of this up if it would just bring my children back to me!* Then all thoughts were drown out by Earnest Woodsworth's tears, there in his secret vault of memories gone by.

It was a gorgeous Wednesday morning with not a cloud in the sky. It wasn't overly warm, and the weather forecast was saying that it would be simply a pleasant day. As Earnest stepped up to the first tee, he was thinking to himself that a golfer couldn't ask for a better day. He could hear the birds chirping and see the butterflies fluttering their way across the luscious fairway in front of him. He couldn't quite put his finger on the reason why, but he felt good—really good for the first time in years.

"Hey, Bud, you gonna take the shot, or are you just gonna be one with nature?" Thomas chided as he waited for the man to make his shot.

"Yeah, yeah, yeah!" was all that Earnest had to say as he waved his hand as if to brush off the comment. "You in a hurry or something?" he said back to Thomas over his shoulder as he positioned himself just behind his golf ball.

The swing was perfect and that *ping* sound off the club told him it would be a great shot as his eyes followed the small white ball up into the sky and down onto the fairway about 150 yards out.

"Nice shot!" Thomas said as he walked up to the tee box after Earnest backed away from his shot.

"Well, thank you," Earnest said with a big smile.

"Somebody's in a good mood today, I see," Thomas said.

"Yep, you could say that."

"Is Katie in as good a mood as you?"

"Very funny!" Earnest said, rolling his eyes. "I could ask if Shelly is in a good mood this morning—hum?"

"Hey, she's in a good mood anytime I'm around," Thomas said with a grin as he readied himself for his first shot of the day.

As the two men rode in their golf cart out to their golf balls, they were bugging each other like two high school buddies having a chat about the women in their lives and how they were feeling this particular day.

Thomas loved the fact that even though they were business partners in the innovation sector, they were still best friends and they could bug each other and joke around about pretty much anything, including their marital relationships. But the one thing that he really wanted to talk about would have to come later in the game. For now, it was all about being happy and being friends.

"When did you first learn to golf?" Earnest asked Thomas as they rode along in the golf cart after teeing off the fourth hole.

"Actually I started golfing when I was 13 and was taught by my best friend at the time. In those days, the city course was sand greens and putting was a lot harder on those than the finely manicured grass greens here at the club."

"I have played a few sand greens myself over the years, and it's true; they are harder to putt on, but they still offer the same thrill, I find."

"Yes, I agree with that, and something else you might not know is that I still use some of my original golf clubs from that very first set. Over the years, I have added new drivers, but I still use my old putter and my number six and eight irons. They just feel really good in my hands, and I haven't found any since that feel that way."

"I think a lot of golfers still carry around some of their favorite clubs from over the years, and even in the Masters you find some top-ranking players pulling out a favorite club now and then depending on the situation at hand," Earnest said as the two men made their way to the number 6 tee box.

"Are we going to stop for a break after this hole?" Thomas asked.

"What's the matter, old man? You needing a nap too perhaps?" Earnest said with a chuckle.

Thomas was amazed by this happy tone in his friend's voice. It had been a very long time since he had seen him this happy, and it had nothing to do with work.

"Hey, remember that you are the senior here, not me, and I only asked, because I saw the beverage cart coming over the ridge on the next hole," Thomas said as he nodded his head in that direction.

"Yep, way ahead of you there, buddy."

The two men teed off and were headed out to their golf balls when they noticed the lovely beverage cart woman waiting for them to finish the hole just off to the left.

"Okay, seeing she is waiting there for us, it would be rude not to order something from her, so we'll take a break. Also, seeing we have an audience, you up for a loonie hole?" Earnest asked.

"Anytime, my friend, and just a loonie? Let's make it more lucrative. Let's say … 50 dollars—hummm? And the winner can use it to tip the beverage girl."

"You're on!"

The two men placed both of their second shots just short of the green, which would make the contest even that much more challenging, seeing it wouldn't be a putt that would determine the winner but rather a chip shot that would tell the tale.

"Okay, buddy, it's your lead," Earnest said to Thomas, whose ball was about two feet behind his own.

Thomas then pulled out his chipping wedge, and walking over to his ball, he sized up the situation. He squatted down to have a look at the lay of the green, its slopes and the distance. Then he stood up and positioned himself just to the side of the ball. He took a good look at the flag and mentally drew a line from the flag to his ball just before he took his swing. A small clump of grass was lifted with his ball as it arched high into the air and landed with a soft-sounding *thud* about one foot from the hole, where it stayed.

"Wow!" Earnest said. "That is quite the shot. Looks like you want to make quite the impression for the lovely lass."

"Well, yes, and the fact that I will be using your money to do it too," Thomas said with a grin as he looked over at the beverage girl, who was taking a keen interest in their competition.

"Okay, let's see if I can top that or not," Earnest said as he too walked over to his golf ball's position and squatted down to see the lay of the green, the slopes and the distance.

"Hey, Earnest?" Thomas said, causing Earnest to look his way and break his concentration. "Double or nothing?" Thomas said with a cocky look on his face.

"Yeah, whatever!" was all that Earnest had to say.

A couple of other players from a nearby hole had heard the friendly commotion and were now standing by the beverage girl as all of them took in the competitive wager between the two friends that gorgeous sunny morning.

Earnest was ready. He mentally blocked out all the sounds and people watching. He took a breath and stepped up to the ball. He wasn't sure why, but he felt as one with his club, like it was actually an extension of his arm. He felt perfect. The day was perfect, and now was the time. He swung his arms back as his custom-made golf shoes gripped the fairway solidly. Down came his arms with the chipping wedge, and the club made contact with the ball. As the ripples of vibration rolled up the club and through his arms, he knew in an instant that it was going to be a great shot. He then heard the gasp of the others looking on and the sound that made the game of golf all worthwhile. He saw his ball hit the flag shaft and actually walk its way down the shaft and into the cup with a soft *plop*.

Suddenly the air was filled with whoops and hollers from those watching the shot.

"What a shot!" said one.

"Way to go!" said another.

"Did you see that?" the beverage girl said.

"Okay, Earnest, I knew you were in a good mood, but not this great of a mood. Way to go, buddy!"

Earnest actually blushed at all the attention. He didn't understand it and would never be able to explain it to anyone, not even his best friend or his wife, but he knew this was only the start of something great about to happen in his life.

"You did say double or nothing?" Earnest said with a big grin on his face as he approached Thomas, who was sporting a fake pout on his face. Earnest was surprised to see that he already had the money in his hands as he stepped up and removed it from his friend's hand.

The beverage girl's eyes lit up like sparkling diamonds as Earnest handed her the 100 dollars.

"It's your tip," was all he said before he ordered a drink for both himself and Thomas. The woman insisted it was on the house, but both men would have nothing of that, paying instead for their own drinks and a snack too.

CHAPTER SEVEN

At around noon, Bart wasn't feeling all that well and decided to relax for a bit in his room before going to a downtown club in the city core to hang with a few of his friends. He really didn't feel like lying down, so he opted to recline in one of the large black leather recliners and play a video game. As he sank down into the chair, a really weird feeling came over him, almost as if he were going to have an anxiety attack. His mind began to swirl, and the room began to spin—at least that was what he thought was happening.

Bart was trying to get control of the situation, when suddenly the searing pain returned to his right arm just above the elbow in the exact spot that the racquetball had hit him and the stranger had placed his finger so many weeks ago. His mind began to spin, as did the room, and just when he felt he was going to throw up, Bart closed his eyes and bent forward in an attempt to stop it from happening. He was in that position for only a few seconds, but when he opened his eyes, he knew something was really wrong. He looked all around, but he knew he was no longer in his room.

Where am I? he thought, knowing full well that there was no one near him. As his eyes tried to focus in on something— *anything*—he knew that there was actually nothing there except for white. Bart couldn't even get his mind to accept what he was looking at, because really he was just looking at nothing. No matter where he turned his head, to the left, the right, up or down, all he could see was white! There were no walls, no corners, only white and nothing else.

It took him a few minutes, but eventually he knew that he was sitting down in what felt like the very comfortable armchair in his room. But as he looked downwards to where he knew the chair was, he was startled to still see nothing but whiteness. He stuck his arms and hands out in front of him, but still there was nothing to see but white. Suddenly fear began to creep into the situation as Bart was unsure if this was a dream or possibly some weird science fiction reality. So he just sat there wondering, listening and fearing.

Then he thought of the searing pain he had felt in his arm just moments before and realized that once again the pain was gone without a trace. Again he held up his arms and wiggled his fingers. He knew they were there and doing what they were supposed to do, but he could not see even a trace of them right up before his eyes. Bart felt as if he were in some sort of a milky-white room that was full of only the milky-white substance, besides himself and the chair he sat in. With nothing to look at but white all around, he closed his eyes and just sat there, waiting for something to happen. He felt as if he were waiting at least 20 or 30 minutes before he opened just one eye, peeking as if to see if anything had changed.

"What the ...?" he said out loud as both eyes immediately popped open. Bart realized he was back in his own room, and the instant that realization registered in his brain, the searing pain in his arm returned. "Ahhhhhh!" he screamed out in agony, as it felt like his arm was on fire. He tried to get up from his chair, but with the searing pain in his right arm, it was impossible to do. Bart moved his arm here and there, trying to see if he could find a position that offered him some relief, but nothing worked, and the searing, burning pain remained constant. Finally he found that if he laid his arm on the arm of the chair and held it completely still, the pain subsided just enough to be bearable, but if he even twitched his arm, the pain shot right back in.

Finally after about 30 minutes of intense pain, it just stopped as quickly as it started, but the one thing that Bart knew was that this pain had to be checked out; it was getting worse every time it showed up.

"Bart, are you okay?" Katie asked as her son staggered out of his room just as she was passing by.

"I am okay!" he almost yelled, but the instant the words left his lips, he regretted them, as he needed to tell someone about his arm and the pain. "No ... actually I am not okay. I need to go see a doctor."

At first, Katie was startled by her son's brashness towards her, but then when he mentioned the doctor, she settled down some as the caring mother came to the surface.

"What's the matter?" she asked quietly but with concern, and he knew it.

"I-I really don't know. I hurt my arm a few weeks ago playing racquetball with ... some guy," he said, hesitating with his words because he knew he would have to explain some things he didn't yet understand.

"Racquetball? I thought you had given up on the game because you couldn't find anyone to play with you anymore?"

"I ... uh ... you wouldn't believe me if I told you, so what's the point?"

Katie hesitated a moment before continuing, "Bart ... you are my son and whether you accept it or not, I still love you deeply and even more when you tell me something is wrong. I will always be like that because I am your mother. Please, never be afraid or upset to tell me when something is wrong with you, because I care deeply for you in any situation that you may find yourself in."

There it is again, Bart thought. *That same feeling I had when I think I was out of my body in my father's secret vault ... if that really happened.* "Y-yes, I know you do." Bart managed to get out around the anger that still burned within. It wasn't that he hated her, like he did his father; it was because of the association she had to the man.

"So tell me what happened in order that I can understand the problem you seem to be having."

Bart hesitated this time as he tried to think of just what it was he would tell her about that weird night on the racquetball court. But before he could answer his mother, she took his hand in hers.

"Let's go to the sitting room just down the hall, son," she said, amazed at the fact that he didn't rip his hand away from hers, like he had done countless times before. As Katie and Bart walked the short distance to the room, she was saying a silent prayer. *Oh, Lord, please don't let anything or anyone break this time together with Bart and me.*

The two of them entered the room. Bart sat on the love seat with Katie facing him from the opposing sofa. Neither said anything for a few moments as Katie waited on her son to start. Bart was running things through his mind, trying to figure out just what to say without sounding like he had lost a marble or two.

"I ... uh," Bart started, looking very uncomfortable.

"Take your time, honey, and just tell me what you can remember," Katie said with a big, reassuring smile.

"Okay, well, you know that no one was wanting to take me up on a game of racquetball because they are all wimps and sore ..." Bart said, but then stopped himself, knowing that complaining about such things was not going to change anything. "Anyway ... I was really mad that no one would take me on in a game, and then one ..." Bart stopped again. "No! I have to go back farther than that for any of this to make any sense."

"It's okay, Bart. Please continue."

"Awhile back, when I was having lunch one day in the corporate café, I was angry at the fact that no one would play me, and in my mind, I was telling a lot of people off. Suddenly I heard a voice that said, 'Bartholomew William Woodsworth, I hear you are looking to take anyone on in a game of racquetball ... and I am your man.' Of course I spun around to see who was speaking to me just as he spoke again. 'Yes, you heard me right. I will take you on in a game.'

"I was surprised to see a very good-looking man with a slightly darker skin tone, jet-black curly hair, and the most amazing eyes I had ever seen, standing there. Those eyes—I will never forget those eyes," he said as he remembered the sight of the stranger in his mind. "It was as if they were looking right through me or at least deep inside of me."

With that said, Katie sat straight up on the edge of the sofa. This all sounded very familiar to her, though she couldn't quite put her finger on it. All she knew was that the Holy Spirit inside of her was reacting strongly to her son's words.

"Bart, can you tell me more about this man? Can you give me more details?" Katie asked.

"Well ... okay, but I really don't know why that is important."

"I ... I just need to know. I can't really explain it to you right now, but I need to know more," she said, wondering if this tied in at all to the other night when she and Earnest were at Thomas and Shelly's home and talking about angels.

"Like I said, he was good-looking—for a man, that is. His skin was slightly darker than most white people I know, but it wasn't really dark."

"Maybe someone from the Middle East?" Katie cut in.

Bart thought about that for a few moments. "Yes, maybe. It is a possibility. He also had this curly jet-black hair, and there was something strange about it."

"About his hair?"

"Yes, Mother! I didn't really notice it when I saw him in the café, but when we were playing the game, I did get to see his hair up close and it kinda, like, shone or at least sparkled."

"Sparkled?" *Now this is getting really interesting*, Katie thought.

"Yeah ... anyway, that's about all I remember of the guy, at least until later."

"Was he a tall man? How was he built? And what about his stature?"

"What's with all the weird questions?"

"Please, indulge me, Bart. Call it being inquisitive at least."

"Okay," Bart said with a snide sigh, and for a moment, Katie worried that he was reverting back to the cruel son he had been just hours before.

"He was kinda tall, I guess."

"Taller than you?"

"Yes."

"By how much?"

"I dunno ... maybe like an inch or so."

"Okay, and was he in good shape?"

Bart stopped and thought about that for a moment; he pictured the man in his mind as he had seen him that day in the café and on the racquetball court as well.

"Actually, yes! Yes, he was in very good shape. Funny, I never thought of that before."

"Was there anything else at all?" Katie asked as she leaned way over towards her son, sitting on the love seat across from her.

"Nope ..." He hesitated. "Actually, there was one other thing."

"What?"

"He kinda looked outta place."

"Why do you think that?"

"Well, we were in a corporate business café with lots of people all around us, dressed in suits, ties and business outfits of all types, but not this guy—No, he was dressed in a plaid shirt with the sleeves rolled up and jeans."

"Really?"

"Oh yeah and he even had those wide orange suspenders holding up his jeans. Man, the guy looked like Paul Bunyan or someone like that."

Katie Woodsworth was just sitting there now. Her mind was racing at the feeling of the Holy Spirit inside of her.

This man was not just some stranger who had heard about her son Bart and wanted to take him on in a game of racquetball. No, this was someone special, possibly even an angel, she thought.

Katie had a special place inside her heart for angels, even from a very young age. She had heard stories from her father and others in his family, who had seen and even in one case interacted with angels. The story was told of a Sunday evening church service—in the days when churches had them—and of a stranger in the crowd, sitting in the very back row of the church. He was pleasant and joined in the service, singing and praying as the others did. But then near the end of the service, after the sermon had been preached, the pastor had invited the sick and anyone needing prayer to come up to the front, and he and the church deacons would pray with those people.

A number of people had come forward, and finally there was just one woman standing up there for prayer. She explained that she had recently become a Christian and wanted to be baptised in the Holy Spirit as she had read about in her Bible. The pastor had the deacons' wives lay their hands on this woman and then their husbands placed their hands on their wives, so that no man other than the pastor would be touching the woman.

The pastor then began to pray for the infilling of the Holy Spirit into this woman's spiritual life, and just when he said the words, he placed his hand on her forehead. The pastor felt the rush of the Holy Spirit in the room and then through his body but not into the woman. He stopped praying and stepped back, taking his hand off the woman. He talked to the woman, asking her if she knew of any hindrance that would be blocking the Holy Spirit. They talked for a few moments, and then he asked her about her salvation, when and where it took place. He found out that it was incomplete and then asked if he could lead her through the sinner's prayer to which she agreed.

For the next few minutes, the pastor led her through the sinner's prayer, explaining each part of it before moving on. Then he came to the last part where he told the woman that she needed to ask the Lord into her heart, and when she opened her mouth to do so, a chilling voice began to speak back to the pastor. Immediately he knew what it was, but the voice began to get louder and even scream until about half of the congregation began to panic.

Mothers began to hustle the children out of the sanctuary to the children's wing, and a number of deacons and their wives just up and left altogether. Still the voice coming from the woman continued until the pastor, now filled with the power of the Holy Spirit, began to speak to the voice. This continued for a few minutes with an intensity filling the room, and the pastor knew that if there wasn't a release soon from the demon controlling this woman that literally all types of panic and confusion could break loose within his church congregation.

It was then that the mysterious visitor at the back of the church rose from his seat and made his way forward to the scene taking place. He never said a word, never touched a single person there, but simply just walked up behind the pastor and stood there.

Suddenly the demonic voice began to cry and wail. "Get away from me!" it screamed. "Leave me alone, you servant of the Most High God. You will never make me leave this one; she is mine forever!" Then the stranger raised his hands above his head and glared directly through the head of the pastor in front of him to the woman standing there with her eyes closed. There was a terrible loud yell, followed by a trailing scream. Some people said that they actually felt the church building shake for an instant and most people there instantly shut their eyes in fear. Then all went silent, and finally when they all opened their eyes, they were surprised to see the woman now on her knees in front of the pastor and the stranger gone—vanished!

Even more astonishing than all of that was the fact that in that very instant, the woman was immediately filled with the baptism of the Holy Spirit.

"Mother?"

Katie thought she heard her name being called.

"Earth to Mother?"

Finally, Katie opened her eyes to see her perturbed son looking at her directly.

"Are you in there?" Bart asked as he realized he had her attention again. "Out for a visit in your head, were you?"

"W-what ... Oh, I-I am sorry, Bart. I was just thinking about something in my past that you kind of brought up, but please continue telling me about your encounter with this man."

As Bart began to speak again, Katie was thinking about the other things she hadn't mentioned about her past, like the fact that the mysterious stranger in the evening church service of long ago was quite tall and well-built with jet-black curly hair and piercing blue eyes and the fact that he was dressed like a lumberjack.

"Anyway I was at the court in the lower level of the corporate building in the city in the early hours of that morning. I was very angry and was killing the small rubber ball the best I could."

"What do you mean, dear?" Katie asked.

"I was playing a game against myself, Mother."

"Oh!"

"Anyway I was very angry and running around like a madman, trying to hit the ball. I was swearing and yelling at that man who wasn't there, wanting him to show himself, when all of a sudden, there was, like, this cool breeze that blew across the court. In all my years of playing the game, I had never felt anything like it. I just stopped right there in the middle of the court, trying to figure out just what was happening when I heard it."

"Heard what?" Katie asked.

"I heard a voice."

"A voice? I thought you were alone?"

"I was."

"What did it say—the voice, I mean?"

"I am ready."

"That's what it said, really?"

"Yes."

"Then what happened?"

"He was there."

"Who was there?"

"The stranger with the curly hair."

Katie said nothing, but she knew that whenever this stranger or angel—call it what you may—showed up, that something very special was about to happen.

"And then what happened?" she asked Bart.

"Well we had a game, a very intense game that lasted well over an hour until I got the first point, but ..." Bart's voice trailed off in thought.

"What is it, Bart?" Katie asked as she rose and came to sit beside him.

"It's weird, but I ... I think he let me get that point."

"Why do you say that, dear?"

"Because he was better than me—way better—and I knew it."

"Is that what you wanted to tell me?"

Bart did not answer right away, as he was thinking about what had really happened that night on the racquetball court.

"Wha? Uh ... no!"

"What was it then?"

"The game just went on as intense as before, but now I wanted to kill this guy with the ball. I mean, I really wanted him dead, as some sort of force was controlling me, it seemed."

Oh no, Lord, please don't let it be, Katie silently prayed.

"But then it happened. It shouldn't have, but it did and I have no idea how."

"How what happened, hon?"

"I got hit by the ball, and I got hit hard."

"Is that what you want to see a doctor about?"

"Yes, but there is nothing there to even indicate I was hit. It hurt when it first happened, but it got even worse when he touched it."

"Who touched what?"

"The stranger. He came over to me and touched the impact spot with his index finger."

"Then what happened?"

"I passed out, I guess."

"How long were you out?" Katie asked with a growing concern.

"I don't know, but when I came to, there were two security guards there."

"Were you in pain?"

"No, and they said that no one was there except for me, as they had let no one in all night."

"Are you having pain now?"

"Yes, but it comes and goes at will almost."

"Describe the pain to me."

"It comes on very fast and is very intense with a burning, searing feel to it."

"How long does it last?"

"Depends. Sometimes just seconds, but the last time, it was for at least 45 minutes."

"Well, then yes, you should go see the doctor," Katie said, but she knew in her spirit that there was a lot more to this incident than just the pain he was experiencing. She wanted desperately to tell him what she thought about it but knew that now wasn't the time.

"Yeah, I'm gonna go see him soon." With that said, Bart stood up and just looked at his mother for an instant before he turned and left the room.

Katie just sat there and prayed. She prayed for Bart and this experience he was going through, for Earnest and his upcoming birthday celebration, for Caroline and strength for the trials she was facing, and for Franklin, who would soon be in her life once again after all the years!

Earnest and Thomas were now playing the back nine at the country club, and Earnest was flying high after his terrific shot on the fourth hole. Not only had he made the shot of his golf life so far, but he had also done it in front of an audience and won a wager to boot, which his best friend had to pay out.

The two men had stopped at the clubhouse for a light lunch before heading out for the second round of golf, and the day was proving to be one of the best the two friends had ever experienced while playing golf.

This is a fantastic day, and I praise you, Lord, for it, Thomas prayed silently as he stepped up to the tee on the seventh hole. *Please, Lord, provide an opportunity for me to witness further to my friend Earnest.*

They were now playing their 14th hole of golf at the country club when Thomas took the chance to reach out to his friend.

"Earnest?" Thomas asked as they rode along in their golf cart.

"Yes?"

"I don't want to touch any nerves with you, so please bear with my question, but remember the other day when we were discussing the plans for the new cover-it project?"

"Okay ... Yes," Earnest said hesitantly.

"And remembering me asking if your whole family would be attending your upcoming birthday celebration?"

This time, Earnest didn't answer right away, so Thomas just kept on going.

"I have been thinking about your hesitation when it came to Bart and Franklin. As I prayed about it after our meeting, the Lord brought me to a passage in scripture that I think applies directly to your situation with your eldest son."

Still Earnest said nothing, just stared straight ahead as the two friends neared their golf balls out on the fairway.

"It is found in the book of Luke and tells the story of a son who had enough of working for his father, so he left home taking with him his portion of the inheritance. Now I know that some of this story does not line up with your situation, but please permit me to continue and you will see that a lot of it does apply, as it is a story of hope!"

The two friends then got out and played their next shots, but Earnest never said a word. As they climbed back into the motorized golf cart, Thomas just kept on going with his words. He was determined to share with his friend until either he came to the end of what it was that he wanted to say or until Earnest told him to stop.

"The story goes on to say that this young man left his home, his father and the life he knew to pursue his own ambitions and gain, but that he spent his inheritance foolishly on wine, women and earthly pleasures until one day the money ran out. Then he found himself in a foreign land with no money, no friends and no way to support himself. He began to look for a job so that he could at least feed himself, but the only job he could find was feeding pigs.

"The Bible says that he was so hungry that he started to eat the feed that was given to the pigs. Then one day he came to his senses and realized that this was stupid. He felt he should return to his father where he could at least work for the man and be fed just like all the other workers his father employed. So he began to make his way back home, unaware that every single day his father longed for him to return." With that said, Thomas turned to look at his friend and partner to see tears streaming down his face.

"I know, Earnest, the pain you have in your heart for Franklin, but I also feel that Franklin is making his way back home."

"H-how do y-you know that?" Earnest managed to say.

"It is nothing I know really, but I feel it in my heart that a day of great joy is coming your way, by the grace of God."

"W-what happened?"

"What do you mean?" Thomas said, unsure of what he was asking.

"What happened in the story? Did the son get home okay?"

"Yes, my friend, yes, and this is the best part for it shows hope, the hope of the father that his son would return and the hope of the son that his father would take him back.

"The Bible says that while the son was still a long distance off, the father got word that his son was indeed returning. The father quickly made his way out to meet his son before he even got home. The son was so ashamed and knew that he didn't even deserve to be forgiven, let alone accepted back, but the father swept his son up into his arms and proclaimed that his son was once lost, but now was found.

"The story goes on to say that the father accepted the son back into the family and threw a big party for him. It goes even further about problems with his other son, but for now this part of the story is all you need to know.

"The story is about a father who is expectantly waiting for his son to return home, just like you are waiting for Franklin to return home, but there is one more important thing about this story that is not written, but implied." Thomas paused to look over at Earnest.

Earnest just sat there, wiping the tears from his eyes with his golf towel, but Thomas was pleased to see that there was once again a smile on his friend's face.

"W-what's that?" Earnest asked very softly.

"It is implied that the Father in heaven is expectantly waiting for you to return as well."

Earnest said not a word, and Thomas was not expecting anything. He simply wanted his friend to see the biblical connection between the prodigal son and himself.

The two men approached their golf balls, but Earnest stopped the cart and then turned to face his friend and business partner beside him. He was all choked up with thoughts of Franklin and God rolling around in his mind, but he managed to say a few words.

"D-do you really think it will happen? Do you think my son will return?"

"Yes, my friend, I do. I don't know when it will happen, but yes I believe it will."

That was all it took, just someone to say those words of hope, and from that point on Earnest was like a changed man, a driven man, a man with hope. Up to this point in the game, Earnest had been having the game of his life, and on the 14th hole, he was shooting two under par.

This guy could play the Masters tournament based on this game, Thomas thought as the game progressed until they stood on the tee of the 18th hole. Earnest was now shooting a three under par, and his friend Thomas was only at par for 17 holes.

"So this is a par four, eh?" Earnest asked, turning towards Thomas. "Care to make a wager again?"

"Based on the game you are having, there is no way that is going to happen. How about if you make par on this long par four, you give the first course worker you see, after we reach the green, another generous tip, and I will even throw in a little myself," Thomas said as he wanted Earnest to make par and make his day on top of that.

"Okay, that will work," Earnest said as he stepped up to the tee box and placed his wooden tee into the soft grassy surface.

He then positioned his Ping golf ball on the tee and was amazed that it was the same ball he had started the game with earlier that morning.

He stepped up to the ball and positioned himself, his custom-made golf shoes gripping the grassy surface beneath him. It was all about concentration now. He cleared his mind of all the thoughts rolling around in there and set his mind to the swing he was about to make. He looked down the length of the fairway spread out before his eyes and drew a mental picture from the place he wanted the ball to land back to his small golf ball sitting on its tee.

He was set. The weather was perfect with not a breeze. The sun was not in his eyes, and the temperature was perfect; in fact, everything was perfect now as Earnest swung back away from the ball. He could feel the muscles in his arms and legs tense, and even those felt just right. Then just as suddenly as it began, Earnest took the swing and the *ping* sound off his metal driver told him that it was going to be another fantastic shot, if not the best one of the day. Sometimes a golfer just knows, and Earnest Woodsworth knew.

Both men watched the beauty of the ball arching high up into the cloudless sky before it fell back to the earth and landed with one bounce onto the well-manicured fairway out before them.

"Wow!" was all Thomas could say as he looked to where the ball sat, at least 250 yards out. "What club did you use for that shot?"

"Just my number-one driver with the enlarged head."

Then it was Thomas's turn to take his shot, and try as he might he still only went about 150 yards out. He was still in the middle of the fairway. He just didn't have the distance that Earnest had though.

As the two friends approached Earnest's shot, after Thomas took his second stroke, they were both amazed at what greeted them at the green. Lining both sides of the green were at least 80 people, all anxious to see the two men finish the hole.

"What is that all about?" Earnest asked as he turned towards Thomas.

Thomas looked down at the crowd and finally saw the answer standing off to the side nearer to the clubhouse. "Remember the beverage girl?" he said out loud while the two of them were still looking at the crowd.

"Yes. Why?"

"I believe she's the answer to your question. She is on the left side close to the clubhouse."

Earnest looked, and then he saw her talking to a couple of golfers who had just come out of the clubhouse. She was obviously talking to them and pointing towards the green, most likely telling them about the two men who had tipped her after the most amazing shot she had ever seen.

"I see her," was all he said as he walked up to his ball. "How far is it to the green now?"

"Just a sec," Thomas said as he pulled out his viewfinder and pointed it towards the flag on the 18th green. "It says 200 yards to the flag."

"If they weren't there, I think I could make the shot and at least get on the green, but now I don't know."

Thomas said not a word, as it was all his best friend's game now.

Earnest positioned himself just as he had at the tee box, and once again, everything felt just right. He had no idea where those thoughts were coming from, but man, did he feel good!

Again both men heard that telltale *ping* off the club, and this time, they were not surprised when the ball came down on the green about 10 feet from the flag and the cup. There was only a slight bounce straight up and straight down.

Then they both heard the loud cheer that went up from the crowd at the green, and that cheer brought even more people out of the clubhouse to see what all the commotion was about. Thomas's shot landed about 70 feet short of the green, and after he took his third shot onto the green, the men drove their cart to the stop box and exited the cart to the cheers and hollers of well over 100 people now lining the green on three sides.

Thomas walked over to his golf ball and simply picked it up before placing it in his pocket.

"Hey! Aren't you going to putt out?"

"The game is all yours now, buddy. They are all here to see you make this shot—not mine."

With that said, Earnest went back to his cart and placed his new putter in his golf bag, mounted on the back of the motorized golf cart. He searched for a moment before finding what he wanted. He then walked back to the green with a very well-used putter. The rubber grip on the handle was peeling, and the shine of the shaft was no longer there.

"What's that?" Thomas asked.

"This was my very first putter from my Arnold Palmer set of nine clubs, which I purchased when I first learned to golf. I think it is fitting to use it for this shot."

No words were said from that point on as Earnest made his way over to his golf ball. He stepped back from the ball, squatting to get a good look at the slope of the green as it pertained to the cup 10 feet away. Then he stood up and again walked over to his ball. He positioned himself before the ball and prepared himself for the putt of his life.

Before Earnest took the putt, he was thinking about the day so far, the perfect weather, the shot on 14, and Thomas's words to him.

God, if you are really the one behind this day and behind my game, then please show me something to let me know that everything Thomas has said will happen, Earnest thought. He wasn't testing God in any way; he just wanted some sort of hope—any hope at all that he and his son would one day be reunited.

This is it! Earnest thought as he was finally ready to make the putt. He mentally blocked out all the people, just as he did when he was in his secret vault. He took a breath and a swing back. It seemed as if everything was in slow motion. The club in his hand came forward and made contact with the golf ball. He could see the direction is was going to take in just the first few inches of movement, and every fibre of his being tensed, as he knew the ball was going to hit its mark.

Still in that feeling of slow motion, he saw the small ball fall over the lip of the cup and into the hole. He saw the crowd jump to their feet, saw the hands shoot up into the air, and felt the vibrations of a thunderous applause. It wasn't until he felt Thomas's arm on his shoulder that it all came up to speed and reality.

"Fantastic! Man, I don't know if I will ever play golf with you again. Maybe next year you should try out for the Masters!" Thomas said as he shook his friend's shoulders, and the crowd rushed the men to find out what Earnest's final score was. When it was announced that it was a four under par for the course, another shout went up from the crowd.

Finally all the cheers and praises died down as the two friends made their way to the country club's golf clubhouse. Inside were even more words of praise and amazement, with people wanting to buy Earnest a drink or even a meal, but he gracefully declined each offer until it was just him and Thomas at a table over in the corner near the viewing windows that overlooked the third hole.

"So when are you gonna pay up?"

"What?" Earnest asked with a surprised look.

"The wager—when were you planning on paying up?"

"Oh man! I totally forgot about that. I was supposed to pay a worker, right?"

"Yep."

"I forgot to even see who was there."

Earnest stopped for a moment, thinking, before he started talking again.

"Just a minute," he said, and he bounded up to the booking desk and talked to someone there. After a few minutes of talking, a manager showed up and handed Earnest an envelope.

"That should do it," he said as he sat back down at the table with Thomas.

"Uh ... do what?"

"Just give it a few minutes and you will see."

The two men sat and talked about all the great shots of the game they had just finished, and in about 10 minutes, a number of groundskeepers and workers began to enter the clubhouse along with the beverage girl.

Earnest finally stood and spoke to the crowd of workers now inside the clubhouse.

"Hello to you all. As many of you know by now, I am sure, I had a fantastic shot on the fourth hole earlier today."

Suddenly a cheer went up from the group, and now every eye in the building was on the commotion.

"Then on the last hole, I asked my buddy here if he wanted to wager again, to which he declined," Earnest said as a light laughter went up from the workers, who understood Thomas's reluctance. "But in return he suggested that if I made par on the last hole that I give a generous tip to the first worker I see and he would throw in as well. The problem is though that I forgot to look after I made my shot. So in thinking about it, and knowing the fantastic job you all do here at the club, I have decided to tip you all!"

Suddenly the whole crowd erupted once more with cheers and whistles until Earnest got them to settle down. Earnest then scanned the group and did a quick count, coming up with a total of about 20 workers.

"I will stand over there by the door, and as you exit, I will be handing you your tip, which you all deserve. Thank you!"

"I am sure that you will never be forgotten at the club now," Thomas said as the two men drove back into the city. "It is not every day that they get a 100-dollar tip, I bet."

"Yes, well, they all deserved it. They do a great job and need to be rewarded for it now and then, I think."

"Does that mean you will do that more often?"

"Yes! It was a great feeling to see the smiles on their face when I put that 100-dollar bill in each of their hands."

"Very true, but it is the look of the beverage girl that I will never forget."

"Yes that was precious for sure. How much was it you gave her again?" Earnest asked Thomas.

"Five hundred."

"I never thought she would break down and cry like that though."

"Brought tears to my eyes for sure."

"And mine too, my friend, mine too."

"What were you talking to her about just after that?" Thomas asked as he drove.

"I invited her to my birthday celebration!"

CHAPTER EIGHT

It was now the Monday before Earnest Woodsworth's 50th birthday celebration, which saw Earnest and Thomas on a flight to the nation's capital. Their trip was for business, as the two partners were meeting with government officials to finalize the patents for their latest invention.

"So how do you think these meetings will go?" Thomas asked Earnest about halfway through their flight.

"I don't expect any problems, seeing that we have all the necessary paperwork in place, along with all the detailed drawings. Thanks to you, my friend."

Thomas just smiled as he had a sip of his hot coffee. One of the perks he had always enjoyed in his partnership with Earnest was travelling in first class. It mattered not if it was a flight, a road trip, or occasionally by rail; they always went first class. Just one of the benefits of wealth, he surmised.

"Today we will just get settled in, and tomorrow the meetings begin," Earnest said, without looking up as he poured over the latest changes to the mechanical drawings and technical descriptions.

"Who will we be meeting with first?"

"Actually I thought that this time around, we would meet with the Canadian Intellectual Property Office, which is a branch of Industry Canada. We can check in on our National PCT application with them first, before we move on to our registration with Industry Canada."

"Okay, well, it sounds like you have it all together, as usual," Thomas said with a small chuckle.

"You know me, buddy. I find that things go smoother if every 'i' is dotted and every 't' crossed before we meet anyone connected with government."

"Oh yeah, I know that for a fact, my friend. So I take it you also have our PowerPoint presentation all ready to go as well?"

"Yes and I had our technical staff fine-tune it before we left, just to make sure that the government people see everything and even more than they are expecting from us. Better to make a strong presentation right off the bat rather than a poor one that requires further trips and explanations."

"Yes, true."

The two men then just sat in silence with Earnest looking over every detail of their presentation while Thomas just sat there lost in other thoughts.

Dinner had been served and the dishes removed by the flight attendant for first class before either of the men spoke to one another.

"So, Thomas, do you have any other ideas on your mind these days?"

"What exactly do you mean?"

"Any other inventions rolling around in that amazing brain of yours?"

"Well, I wouldn't exactly call it amazing, but, yes, I do have one. I am unsure if I have ever mentioned anything about it to you before, but I am beginning to get very excited about it—at least in my amazing brain," he said with a light laugh.

"What sector of life would it be for?"

"Trucking actually, and then maybe even the entire transportation sector."

"I am all ears, buddy," Earnest said as he rotated his seat so that the two men were now facing each other.

"Okay," Thomas started, "within the trucking industry today, great strides have been made to make the whole experience of the trucker a comfortable trip without too much physical labor required. A lot of trucking companies are switching to automatic transmissions, self-adjusting air suspensions, self-adjusting air pressures in the tires, and more pleasurable rides within the cabs themselves.

"We need to remember that a lot of truckers live on the road and their trucks are their homes, so with this in mind, I have come up with an idea that will make the whole experience more comfortable and affordable at the same time. Also, the security features are something unseen yet within the trucking industry."

"Now those are the words I like to hear," Earnest interjected. "Affordable and unseen!"

"Yes," Thomas agreed before continuing on, "What I am thinking about is a central command module within the cab of the truck that is voice-activated, using simple word and number commands. It is like the new home control panels where one simply says, 'Kitchen lights on to 30 percent,' and immediately the lights come on to that percentage.

"The difference with my idea, however, is that every single function that any driver does within a trip or even a lifetime of trips, for that matter, can all be controlled by voice commands from either the driver or his or her home base."

"Wow! I sure know how to pick 'em!"

Thomas didn't respond to that, but he knew exactly what his partner meant by it and he simply smiled back at the compliment.

"So tell me some of the unseen details," Earnest requested as he now gave Thomas his full, undivided attention.

"Okay, well, what I have pictured in my head is a central command panel on the dash of the truck along with a hand-held remote unit. With either of these units, the driver can issue whatever command he or she needs for any number of situations.

"A lot of trucks already have voice-activated louvers over the rad or manual controls to regulate the air pressures of any tires on the truck or the trailer or trailers. What I am envisioning goes farther than that."

"Of course it does, because that is what you do, my friend. You take a situation and make it better—much better in most cases," Earnest said, cutting in.

"Yes, I suppose I do, but getting on with what I was saying, there would be three main areas of this system. First would be safety. I am not sure if you know much about a tractor-trailer unit or what a lot of people commonly refer to as a *semi*, but there are a few problems that drivers encounter on a daily basis throughout the industry. One of those problems is when a driver leaves his unit to take a break at a truck stop, fuel up, or just park it for the night. Then some unsavory character comes along and thinks it would be funny if he just pulled on the release rod for the fifth wheel. The driver comes along eventually and, as a lot of them do, doesn't do a quick walk-around and just starts up to drive away. As they pull away from where they were parked, the unlocked fifth wheel allows the trailer to stay where it is, and as it uncouples, the trailer falls down to the dolly wheels, which makes it very hard to lift when it is fully loaded, let alone hook it back up to the fifth wheel.

"So with this control panel I am proposing, the driver would be able to give a voice command, such as 'pin lock' or maybe 'Five-PL' and the pin would immediately lock. No one would be able to release it without the control panel or the remote unit and the right command. This same idea could also be used for the trailer, and this is one feature that I am very excited about. It could literally eliminate highjacking of trucks and trailers," Thomas said before pausing a moment to have a drink of his coffee.

"I can see that excitement in you, my friend," Earnest said as the wheels of his brain were already at work, thinking about the potential investments in such a project.

"Right now, within the trucking industry, the only way to lock a trailer is with a padlock on the back unloading doors or any other additional doors, such as on refrigerated units or moving van trailers. What I am thinking about are voice-controlled commands that would activate pins located inside the trailers, which when activated would make it virtually impossible to open a trailer with the exception of a cutting torch or ripping it open in some way. The other, even more exciting aspect to the locking idea is to have the same system for all the wheels on the truck and/or the trailers."

"What exactly do you mean?" Earnest asked.

"The way it is now, it is very easy to highjack a truck and trailer, either by stealing a running unit or forcing the driver out with the threat of violence. In some cases, the thieves even have their own tractors and just hook up to parked trailers before taking off with them. With this unit I am talking about, the driver could issue a voice-command that would have pins slide into place that would lock each and every wheel on the unit. A further option would be that the home base could also issue the command at any time, so if they knew that one of their units was taken, they could just issue the command, and wherever that unit was, it would immediately lock down the very first time it came to a full stop!"

"One other thing I just thought of is that each unit could be programmed to only accept the driver's voice for commands and only the home base of the company would be able to override the system of each and every truck with a special command."

"My, my, my, Thomas, you have certainly outdone yourself on this one, and even I am very excited at the prospect of it. Maybe in our meetings coming up, we could ask some questions pertaining to this new idea, just to see what the feasibility of it would be from the government's point of view," Earnest said with raised eyebrows.

"Okay, sounds great!" Thomas said. "Then maybe in the future we can talk about a few other ideas I have too."

"You have more?"

"Yes."

"How many?"

Thomas thought for a moment as he mentally ran through the list.

"Seven."

"Seven ... Really? Does that mind of yours ever take a break?"

"Well, son," the doctor said to Bart and his mother, who had come along as well, "after all the initial tests, we don't see anything physically wrong with you. You, young man, are in very good physical health."

Bart just stared at the doctor across his desk, unsure just what to say now.

"But, Doctor, what about the pain he is occasionally experiencing in his right arm. It is real to him and very painful when it happens," Katie said.

"Yes, I have thought about that, and what I recommend is that the next time one of these episodes happens, he immediately gets to the ER in order that we can assess it while it is happening. It is very difficult, as I am sure you will agree, to give a proper assessment of the condition without seeing just what the pain does to him and exactly where it is located."

"You are correct in that, and I guess that is all we can do for now," Katie said as she and Bart rose to leave the doctor's office.

Once they were both outside of the clinic, Bart began to head off to his vehicle.

"Bart, I have some errands to run for your father's party this weekend, so I will see you at home later, okay?"

"If you are lucky," Bart muttered under his breath, never turning to even acknowledge his mother's question before he climbed into his car, fired it up, and roared off.

"Kids!" was all Katie had to say, rolling her eyes as she got into her own vehicle. Before driving off, she took the time to use her cell phone for a call to Caroline.

"Caroline? It's Mom ... What are you doing now? ... I am off to the florist's to see how the arrangements are coming. Would you like to join me for a light lunch in the city? ... Okay, meet me at The Salad Palace at 11:45, okay, honey? ... Great! I will see you there. Bye!"

The two women met as planned, and after picking their meals, they settled down at their table to admire the comfortable atmosphere and soft inspirational music playing in the background of the restaurant.

Katie always loved coming to this establishment, with its great choices of food items, music and greenery. The whole layout included a brook running throughout the entire eating section of the building, complete with gardens, walking bridges, waterfalls and seating benches. Spotted here and there, as well, were tables to eat at. The whole atmosphere was set up like going on a picnic, and after picking out a meal from the generous buffet section, guests would wander around until they found the spot they wanted to sit at to eat their meal and talk.

"So how are the floral arrangements looking?" Caroline asked her mother.

"They all look great, just the way we requested them."

"Are Dad's favorites included?"

"Yes, almost every arrangement has a few daisies included."

"Great! I'm sure he will be pleased."

"Yes, he will. And how are things going on your end of the planning?"

"Great! I have lined up a local string quartet that will be playing throughout most of the night, at least until Dad is presented with his cake and blows out all those candles," Caroline said with a slight laugh. "Then after that, I have more lively music arranged."

"You mean music for your generation, right, my dear?"

"Well, I'm trying to please everyone at the party, and I had thought about bringing in a group from Dad's past, but then changed my mind."

"What group?"

"Actually I had three groups in mind: BTO, Chilliwack and possibly even Crowbar. I heard Dad once talking about a Crowbar concert that he and his best friend attended and how much he loved the music."

"So why did you change your mind?"

"Basically because each of these groups would just be playing their brand of music and I wanted something that would cater to everyone."

"Okay, that makes sense, so what did you decide on?"

"A DJ."

"DJ?"

"Yes. A person who just plays CDs with a wide range of music."

"I do know what a DJ is, my dear. I'm not as old as you seem to think I am," Katie said with a smirk.

"Okay, but I just thought it would give us that wide range and we could even make it so that guests could go up and ask him to play their favorites and such."

"Yes, that would work and is a great idea, honey."

"You referred to the DJ as 'him,' so does that mean that you have hired a man?"

"Oh yes!" Caroline said with a very wide smile.

"Really now, you seem overly excited about this man. Is there something you need to tell me, dear?"

"Maybe!"

"So there is something going on. Come on, dear. Spill the beans."

"Well, his name is Mitch, and yes, he is a DJ and came highly recommended by some of my friends at church. He is a born-again Christian and is 24 years old."

"And?" Katie said. "I know there is more to this story."

"Okay. I first met him about six months ago when we got together to discuss the event and what I was looking for. When he found out that I was a Christian, everything seemed to change—for the better."

"Change?"

"Well ..." Caroline paused as Katie raised her eyebrows.

"Yessss?" Katie pressed her daughter.

"We have been seeing each other—only twice, but it has been nice and ..." She paused again, but this time, Katie just waited. "We are getting together in about another hour."

"How did this all come about?"

"I told you that he was highly recommended by some of my church friends."

"Yes."

"So I thought I would just contact him and see what he had to offer in the way of music. He has an extensive collection that will easily cover all of our needs, but there is one thing that really stood out when we talked, and it is what makes me like him so much," Caroline said with a big smile as she recalled that first meeting.

"What is that, dear?"

"He told me that when it comes to music, he will not play anything smutty or suggestive, no matter how much it is requested. He has even turned down job opportunities where they want that type of music. Mitch said that it goes against his personal stand for the Lord and he will not compromise that stand just for money."

I have got to meet this young man. Katie quickly thought to herself before responding. "That is nice to know, especially in this day and age when such moral stands are rarely heard of or seen by Christians."

"Yes, and I love him for it."

"It sounds to me, my dear that you and this young man are getting close. Is that true?"

"Oh, Mom! I am not a child anymore."

"I am not saying that at all, just that I want you to be careful and get your education before you start thinking about a future together with any man."

"Yes, Mom, I know all of that, and for now, we are just getting to know each other as friends—nothing more," Caroline said.

"Okay, dear, I can live with that," Katie said as she took her daughter's hands in her own, and with that said, the two women rose up and walked around to each other where Katie again cradled her one and only daughter in a hug.

As the women walked, enjoying the gardens, they continued to talk about the final details of the upcoming birthday celebration until it was time for Caroline to leave for her coffee date with her new best friend, Mitch. Katie was heading out to see the decorators and iron out a few other party details before she would head home for the day.

The instant Bart woke up, he knew something was wrong. He had been out the night before partying with his newest eye candy, whose name he still couldn't remember. He kept up appearances with Winter, just for his mother's sake, but once his father's birthday bash was over, he planned to dump her quick and hard.

Bart winced as he grabbed his right arm. The pain was back, and it was worse than it had ever been. Over the past few days, it had shown up occasionally, and in the beginning, he tried to get to the hospital as quickly as he could, but it seemed that just as he entered the ER unit, the pain would simply vanish. It had happened three times now, and finally Bart just stopped going to the hospital when it would show up, knowing that it would be gone before anyone could look at it.

This morning, it was even more painful than it had ever been up to this point and it had brought tears to the young man's eyes.

"Ahhhrrgg!" Bart cried out as the pain seemed to be in control and not himself, which was something Bart strived to maintain on a minute-by-minute basis. "What is this pain?" he cried out with gritted teeth, looking up at the ceiling as if it were God standing there above his bed. "Take it away. I command that it be taken away!"

Instantly everything changed, and Bart found himself in the big easy chair once more. He blinked to make sure it was real and knew instantly that he was in the white room again. All he could see was white and nothing but white. He raised his fingers to his face and touched his nose, even though all he could see was white. The one thing that Bart did know—and maybe this had happened the first time he was in this white state without him realizing it—was that the pain in his arm was completely gone.

He wasn't sure how long he just sat there, trying to see something different, no matter how small it might be, but all he could see anywhere was whiteness. Finally he began to reason some things out in his thoughts.

Okay, I know that I am really here—wherever here really is. I know that my body is all here, even though I can't see it, and I know that I am sitting in some kind of big and very comfortable chair, even though I can't see it either. With all of this taken into consideration, this place is kinda like a white room of darkness!

Bart just sat there for the longest time, unsure of what to do, until he finally got up the nerve to try to stand up. He reached for the side of the chair and found a handle that felt like any handle on most of these types of chairs. Slowly and apprehensively, he pulled on the lever until the footrest pulled back into the bottom of the chair and his back came up into a normal seated position.

Next, he gingerly slid forward until his foot hit something solid that felt like a floor of some sorts, and then in one quick, brave move, he stood up. It took him a few moments to catch his balance, and he was amazed that when he couldn't see anything but this white darkness, it was quite hard to stand up and stay up. He didn't know whether to try to move around, because there might be a drop-off point, so he carefully shuffled his feet forward and when he was confident that there was a full floor under him, Bart began to walk around.

He had moved forward about 15 to 20 feet when he bumped into something solid, and after feeling around in front of him, he realized it was a wall of sorts. Inching his way along the wall that he couldn't see, he finally came to a corner. In the course of an hour or so—at least he thought it might be—Bart found that he was in a square room of sorts and right in the middle of the room was the big easy chair. Finally he sat down and pushed back, which caused the footrest to come out, and then it was gone, and just like that, he was back in his bed.

"What the ...?" he said out loud, just before he screamed out as the pain instantly returned to his arm. Suddenly he heard banging on his bedroom door.

"Bart, are you okay?" He heard his mother's voice.

Bart cried out in pain once more as the searing pain began to radiate out from that very specific spot just above the elbow of his right arm.

"Bart, you hang on and I will get in as soon as I can!" she yelled as she tried and tried to open the locked door.

◼

It took the groundskeeper two tries before he managed to bust his way into Bart's bedroom, with shards of wood flying all across the room. The mess could be cleaned up and the door replaced, but everyone's immediate concern was Bart. All their attention was directed at him.

"Bart, honey, are you okay?" Katie asked as she rushed to her son's bed. "Is it hurting worse this time?"

Bart couldn't reply, and if he could have, his mother would not have appreciated what he wanted to say, but the pain was in control of him now. He rolled around on his bed, unable to get into any position that would lessen the pain in his arm.

"Call an ambulance!" Katie barked off to one of the maids who had just entered the room.

"No!" Bart managed to say.

"Hon, you need to get to the ER like the doctor said. I know that every other time you have gone there, the pain subsided and left before they could check it out, but I can see that it is much worse this time, and we will get it checked out even if it leaves. When the ambulance attendants get here, they will see the pain you are in and they can verify it to the ER staff."

Bart didn't argue this time. He needed relief, and he needed answers too, even if the pain left as soon as he got there. So he gave in to his mother's instructions, and the ambulance was called.

Katie pulled out her cell phone and made a call to Earnest, who would be on a flight back from the nation's capital, but she just wanted him to know what was happening with Bart.

"Hi, hon ... I just wanted you to know that we will be taking Bart by ambulance into ER as the pain in his arm is getting worse ... Yes, other than the pain he is okay ... Okay, well, just give me a call when you get back to the city and I will let you know where he is ... I love you too and will see you soon ... Bye."

Being that Bart was already in a lot of pain, Katie decided that she would help him get dressed for his trip to the hospital before the ambulance got there. It took quite a bit of endurance on her part, as her son cried out over and over again in agonizing pain, but finally she got him dressed enough to be presentable.

When the EMTs showed up in Bart's room, they were amazed at the pain he was in and the fact that he hadn't passed out by then, so they administered a shot of strong painkiller to lessen the pain. They suggested that he lie on the gurney, but there was no way that was going to happen, according to Bart. So they walked him out to the waiting ambulance, and he agreed lie down on the gurney once they had entered the vehicle. Katie rode along with her son as the siren wailed and they all made their way to King's University Hospital on the city's east side.

From the time that Bart had come back to reality from his latest white room experience until he got into the ER, the pain never subsided even for a moment, which the EMTs took note of. They were both amazed that there were no marks or any signs of broken bones or even trauma. The young man they were transporting was simply in inexplicable pain.

After about an hour of tests and being checked out by at least three ER doctors, his own personal doctor entered the room, closed the door, and sat down on the small rolling physician's seat. Bart was still in the same amount of pain as he had been when it first started earlier that morning, and nothing the doctors or ER staff had tried to do helped to lessen that pain.

"Bart. We have performed a number of tests that would have told us if you had muscular problems, broken bones, or severed nerves, and all of them have come back negative. I have conferred with some of my colleagues about your case, and it all comes down to one conclusion," the doctor said and then he paused as if he were unsure if he wanted to say what the conclusion was.

"What conclusion?" Katie asked.

"That it is a psychological problem."

"I-I am not n-nuts!" Bart spoke between clenched teeth, and the instant the words left his lips, the pain ceased completely. "Wha?" Bart said, obviously startled by it.

"What is it?" the doctor and his mother both asked at the same time.

"The ... pain is ... gone," Bart said hesitantly.

The doctor then took Bart's right arm and began pressing here and there, asking if it hurt at all when he did.

"No, not at all. It is completely gone, as if it never happened," Bart said, waving his arm around in the air after the doctor let go. "But you all saw that I was in pain?"

"Exactly my point," the doctor said, looking first at Bart and then at his mother.

"Okay, Doctor, what do you suggest?" Katie asked even as Bart started raising a fuss.

"I ain't going to see a shrink! This is not in my head. The pain is real, and it is in my arm, right where he touched me."

That statement caught the attention of the doctor.

"Who touched you?" he asked as he quickly turned to face Bart.

Bart did not want to answer that question, because if he did, then the doctor would really think he was nuts, and more than seeing a shrink, he might have him committed.

"Nothing. I don't want to talk about it," Bart said sharply, and with that said, he stormed out of the examination room and left the doctor and his mother standing there.

"Is everything okay?" Thomas asked after Earnest put away his cell phone.

"I'm not sure. It is Bart and this pain that he has been having in his arm. Katie said they were taking him to the hospital ER to have it checked out while it is actually happening."

"What do you mean by actually happening?"

"It seems that this occurrence, which is very painful, comes and goes as it pleases. Almost every time he gets to the ER or the doctor's office, it just disappears—no pain."

"Well, that sounds weird," Thomas said from his seat as the two men were returning home on a flight from the nation's capital.

"Yes, very true, but no one seems to know what it is. Hopefully the pain will still be there when he gets to the hospital."

"Hopefully."

The two men then sat in silence for a while, lost in their own personal thoughts.

"Earnest?" Thomas asked after some time had passed.

"Yes, my friend?"

"Remember earlier when we were talking about my latest idea for a remote control panel for the trucking industry?"

"Yes, vividly."

"I have been doing some more thinking on that idea and have come up with a possible solution when it comes to copycats."

"Copycats? Do you mean companies that will try to make cheaper versions of the product and also try to get around the patents?"

"Yes, exactly."

"Okay, talk away. I am all yours for the next couple of hours until we land; then I have to get over to the hospital."

So the two friends and business partners sat and discussed all the nitty-gritty details of Thomas's plan until Earnest understood it all.

"Yes! I can see it now, our own company with our own technicians and mechanics to install the system. Thomas, you are a genius, and I love the idea, because it means I can look for another failing company and redesign it to fit the system. It could employ salespeople all the way through to the final sale and uninstall of the fault you are talking about."

Then Earnest fell silent, and Thomas knew something was up other than what they were just discussing.

"What is it?" Thomas asked as he reached across the aisle and placed his hand on his best friend's shoulder.

"Ah! ... I don't know. It's ... just everything, I guess. My family is suffering in many ways, and for the first time in all these business years of mine ... I think I need a break. Can you understand that?" Earnest said as he looked directly at Thomas.

Thomas could see the hint of tears in the eyes of the successful businessman seated across from him on their flight.

"Believe me, Earnest, when I say that I really do understand that. But it seems as if something else is bothering you too. What's going on, my friend?"

"Please don't take this the wrong way, and I will explain later, but I am thinking about selling out," Earnest said as he turned in his seat and looked out the window, lost in other thoughts.

Thomas sat there for a moment before speaking again. He was not shocked in any way; in fact, he was pleased because he knew that this was what the man needed.

"Can you tell me what has led you to this line of thinking?" Thomas then asked.

Earnest kept looking out the window at nothing in particular as he thought. In the breaks of the cloud cover, he could see the farmland patchwork far below in the southwest corner of a prairie province, and it pleased him, bringing him a strange kind of peace.

"Remember the meeting I had in Texas?" he said suddenly.

"Yes, about the loading facility and your investment into the project."

"Exactly. They pushed me quite hard, but always in a professional manner, mind you. Still I tossed the idea around for the longest time before I came up with my decision."

"And what decision was that?" Thomas asked.

"I looked at the overall picture and realized that, yes, this investment would make me a lot of money, as oil is in high demand these days, especially from our vast fields of it in this part of the country."

"But?"

"There is always that 'but,' and with it, I realized that this project is all about making more money for those who already have money and does nothing to really improve the lives of the common workers. Sure, the workers out there building the structure or even the truckers hauling the crude oil to the facility are making 40, 50, and even 60 dollars an hour, but the investors are making millions on the backs of all the labourers out there," Earnest said as he paused again.

"And?"

"You know me, Thomas; I am not into that game. My philosophy is about helping the little guy, about bringing work and jobs back into small communities who feel lost when their only mill or manufacturing plant is shut down. I love ... no, I *long for* the looks on the common workers' faces when they come back to work the day their plant or facility is reopened. It is what I live for. The money made is only a side line for me." With that said, the man broke down.

Thomas said nothing for a few moments, leaving his friend to express his emotions until he composed himself again.

"I-I'm sorry about that," Earnest said finally.

"Sorry about what? The fact that you are a human man with human needs, wants, fears and trials? We all face these things at various times in our lives, and it seems that now is your time."

"Thanks, Thomas, you are a great friend."

"Anytime ... anytime."

Again, the two men fell silent for about 10 minutes, and Thomas figured the topic was over for the time being. In about 45 minutes, they would be landing and Earnest would be rushing off to the hospital to check on the condition of his son Bart. But such was not the case.

"Let me explain my thoughts to you," Earnest said to Thomas as the two friends and partners sat facing each other again. "Yes, I am going to sell out all my international holdings and get out of that line of work altogether, but I am not retiring. I want you and I to go into business together full-time with all your ideas and inventions. I can't really explain it, but I feel this is where I need to be right now in my life.

"All these ideas of yours help to enrich the lives of others, and that is what I really want to do deep down inside. It's not about the money at all. You and I have enough money and investments to keep us and our families going for a long, long time. I propose—if you are interested that is—that the money we make from these projects, we use in even more ways to enrich more people in the future. What do you say?"

Thomas had a big, wide grin on his face now as he answered, "Do you remember on our flight to the nation's capital just a few days ago when we were talking about new projects and you said to me 'Man, can I pick 'em'?"

"Yes, I do, and yes, it is true."

"Actually it's not."

Earnest's countenance suddenly changed, and he became very quiet in confusion at his friend's words.

"W-what do you mean?" he said. "These ideas are yours, right?"

"Yes, they are all my ideas, straight from my mind, but that is not what I mean. I am talking about you picking me. You didn't pick me, Earnest. It was God who led you to me. He has a plan for your life, and you just shared it with me."

Earnest said not a word, as he never liked getting into discussions about God and religion.

"God gave me all these ideas, because he knew they would benefit humankind in the long run, but he also knew that I would need a partner and a wealthy one at that. That is why he led you to me," Thomas said with compassion.

Still Earnest said not a word, but Thomas knew he was listening, taking in every word.

"In two days, you will celebrate a milestone in your life, as you become 50 years old. You have accomplished a lot in your life, my friend, but still you battle with demons. You long for a relationship with your eldest son and with Bart. You want to strengthen your marriage with Katie, and through all of this, you still are there for the underdog, the little man, those beaten down in despair and financially destitute.

"Do you think all of this is happening just because? You told me you had this feeling deep down inside. Well, that, my friend, is the leading of the Holy Spirit in your life, whether you accept it or not. I can see great things in your future, and I know it will all happen one day but not before you make the biggest and most important decision in your entire life. That decision, Earnest, is worth more than all the gold and wealth this life could ever give you."

It was now Friday evening, and the following would be a day filled with endless activities for the entire Woodsworth family. Everything was now in place with just the final touch-ups needed before the birthday celebration of Earnest Bartholomew Woodsworth to be held on site at their family estate just outside of the city limits in the forest to the east.

"So, Caroline, is everything in place on your end, my dear?" Katie asked her daughter, sitting across from her at the table on the stone patio.

"Yes, Mother, everything on my end is set to go just as planned."

"Even the DJ?" Katie asked with a suggestive smirk.

"Yes, Mother, even with Mitch."

"Mitch? Who is Mitch?" Bart suddenly cut in.

"Your sister's new ... uh ... friend," Katie said hesitantly, not sure of just where her daughter's friendship was headed with this new man in her life.

"Ha! I can't wait to meet him. I'll set him straight about a few things," Bart said with a sneer.

"Don't you dare," Caroline snapped at Bart, shooting visual daggers at him with her eyes.

"All right, you two, settle down. This is all about your father, and you remember that," Katie said. "Bart?" she continued.

"Yeah, what?" he snapped back at her.

Katie hated the way Bart treated her, but she knew that would all change one way or another and soon enough.

"When will you be bringing Winter around today?"

The words startled Bart, as he had hoped his mother would have forgotten about Winter with all of her planning and preparations for the birthday festivities.

"Winter? Who's Winter?" Caroline said this time.

"Winter is a very lovely girl that Bart has been seeing for a while now, and I had the pleasure of meeting her recently. Bart informed me that he would be bringing Winter to the celebrations tomorrow. Isn't that right, Bart?"

Bart felt like a trapped animal or like a bee caught in a sealed jar. He had no intention of bringing Winter to the birthday bash. He was gonna bring some bimbo, some eye candy who would serve his every whim and hopefully embarrass his father too.

"Bart?" Katie asked a little more sternly this time as both she and Caroline looked at him across the table.

"Yeah, she's coming," he blurted out in a disgusted tone.

"That's not what I asked you," Katie said.

"I don't know when ... sometime today."

"Does she even know when you are picking her up?" Katie said, knowing what Bart's real intentions were.

"You haven't told her yet?" Caroline asked, a big grin on her face as she rubbed it in all the more.

Bart just glared at her, but even though anger was fueling his thoughts now, he knew the consequences if he showed up without Winter on his arm.

"She will be here ... with me."

"Okay, great, then everything is about set. Please, both of you, remember to be at your best, as these are all your father's friends and business associates." Katie said as Bart and Caroline began to get up from the table. "Oh, Bart, one more thing son," Katie said as Bart was almost to the house.

"What?" he snapped.

"I plan on having breakfast with Winter on Monday, and I want you to be there too. I have something to discuss with you."

"Wha ...?" Bart said as he stopped dead in his tracks.

"Please make sure that you are here by 10:00 a.m., son," Katie said with the biggest smile she could muster.

Now Bart was frustrated, even more than he was angered. He knew what it meant when his mother wanted to talk to him in front of someone not family. It meant no arguing or back-talking on his part. His mother and father had installed in all the kids the rule that whenever someone other than family was present, they were to act civilly and with respect—something Bart fought against all the time.

He had intended on dropping Winter right after the party and just moving on to his newest conquest. The girls were plenty and willing to grace Bart's presence anytime he asked for their company. It was all just a game after all. They were there for the money, the cars and the parties, and Bart did his best to give them what they wanted in return for whatever he wanted from them.

"Yeah!" was all he said just before slamming the deck door hard behind him.

"Good," Katie said with a little chuckle. "Good!"

Bart exited the house as soon as he could. He had no desire to stick around for the evening with his do-good family. He wanted excitement, and he wanted speed. He climbed into his salsa-red Jaguar and burst out of the garage like a coyote hunting down a rabbit on the run. As he sped into the evening traffic, he punched a number into his cell phone and waited for the call to make its connection. The call rang and rang and rang with no answer until Bart ended the call in obvious frustration. He tried three more bimbos he knew, but for some reason, they weren't answering or weren't home. This lack of girlie action only fueled the raging anger inside, so he headed to the city core, sure he could find someone who wanted to hang on his every word tonight.

After over two hours of searching and a number of alcoholic beverages, Bart headed out alone into the night again. He drove aimlessly for some time until he found himself in the city's business section. Unsure of what to do, he headed for Woodsworth Industries International, intending on hitting the racquetball court, even if he was alone.

As he whipped the 100,000-dollar luxury sports car into the driveway of the underground parking lot, he almost hit a homeless man pushing his cart across the drive, forcing Bart to brake hard.

"What the ...?" Bart yelled as he quickly lowered his window. "Watch out where you are going with that cart, you useless bum. You could have scratched the paint, and then who's gonna pay for that?"

The homeless man kept pushing his cart, never looking back as Bart wheeled his car up to the security overhead door. He pushed a button on his dash, and the door began to open. Bart almost hit the door before it was fully up in his rush to get inside to his private world on the court.

"Why can't I find anyone tonight?" he said. He left his car, crossed the parkade and made his way into the building and then down to the lower floors of the massive high-rise corporate headquarters, made of glass and steel that his father owned.

For the next few hours, Bart played against himself, trying to release the anger and rage he felt inside. As he attacked the small rubber ball, Bart was wondering just where all the anger came from anyway. He was sure that it had nothing to do with himself, so it must be because of his father. Thinking this way had the opposite effect though, as the anger now rose to the surface and Bart began to throw things around. Anything he could find he would grab up and smash against the walls, the glass viewing section, or just the floor itself until he was spent and collapsed to the floor.

As he lay there, breathing hard, he felt a very small radiating pain, growing in intensity, just like his anger had earlier. Then in mere seconds his arm burst into the pain he had come to dread, and here he was, all alone on the lowest floor of the building. He now regretted telling the security guards to leave him alone until he was ready to leave.

He screamed out in pain as this bout seemed to be the worst so far, and no matter what he did with it, how he twisted it or rubbed it, the searing pain continued.

"Ahhhhhhhhhhh!" he cried out over and over again until he thought about running into the wall headfirst in order to knock himself out and temporarily end this pain. He mustered up what little strength he had, stood on wobbling legs, and ran as hard as he could towards the wall in front him. A few feet from the wall, he lowered his head and braced for the impact, hoping he wouldn't break his neck.

Suddenly everything just stopped, and Bart wondered if he were dead—until he opened his eyes and instantly he knew where he was. Once again, he was in the strange white room, unable to see anything but whiteness as he sat in the comfortable chair beneath him. He sat there for the longest time before he once again realized that the pain was gone. He twisted his arm around, even though he couldn't see it, and yes, the pain was indeed gone.

Suddenly the hairs on the back of his neck stood on end, as Bart felt uneasy. All he could see was this white darkness all about him, but he knew that someone or something was in this place with him. He couldn't see a thing, but somehow sensed that whatever was there was moving around almost as if it or he or she was walking.

"I-is someone there?" Bart said in a whisper.

Instantly the moving stopped, and Bart felt fear grip his innermost being until he was literally shaking in his seat. He knew that whatever or whomever was there with him could hear him as well, so that meant he or she or it was conscious of his presence in this strange place.

There was no answer and no movement that he could detect, and so it remained for the longest time until Bart finally got up the courage to talk once again.

"P-please tell m-me; is there someone here?"

Silence continued to fill the whiteness all around him for what seemed like hours until all of a sudden, on the wall he knew was directly in front of him, was the word "*YES*" in big, bold black letters, and Bart's fears were answered.

"Who are you?" Bart asked as his confidence began to build while the fear strangely subsided.

Again, all was silent and white as the bold word faded away moments after it appeared. Bart could still sense a presence with him, but the fear was now gone.

"Tell me who you are?" he said in a more demanding voice this time, as if he were the one in charge now.

Silence.

"Do you know who I am and just who you are dealing with?" Bart demanded now as anger began to replace all the other emotions he was feeling just moments ago.

Silence.

"I demand that you release me from this ... whatever ... this is right ... now."

Silence.

Then just as quickly as the anger rose, it was once again replaced with fear as he realized that this person or thing might actually be more powerful than he originally led himself to believe. So he just sat there in the silence and waited.

Then just as totally unexpected as the first word, a second word appeared in the same large black bold letters "*YAHWEH*."

"Huh?" Bart said sheepishly, confused by what he saw.

The letters faded away and after a few moments were replaced with the words "I AM THAT I AM!"

Bart was still totally confused but also relieved that the words were in English and now somewhat understandable. The words faded away like the others before had. Bart mellowed out a bit and tried to be nicer in his approach with whomever it was he was now communicating with.

"Please ... I still don't understand."

Silence again filled the white darkness around him as he just waited—again.

Then letters began to appear, one at a time, still black and large right in front of Bart's eyes now as if they had suddenly moved in much closer to his eyes.

"J-E-H-O-V-A-H."

Bart was startled to say the least. He knew that word, even though he wasn't sure what it meant or to whom it belonged.

Silence.

Then Bart felt the movement again, and even though he could still not see anything but whiteness, he knew that whatever it was was moving all around him as he sat in the comfortable chair in the middle of the room. But all fear was now gone, and he felt something he hadn't felt since ... He paused, trying to recall the last time he had felt it and suddenly remembered that he had had these same feelings when he had the out-of-body experience right after the stranger touched his arm there on the racquetball court.

Remembering being in his father's secret room with the chair and all the pictures, Bart recalled the feeling of love, and he was now feeling love once more. This time, it was different in that this love felt absolutely pure, as it permeated every fibre of his being.

Just when Bart thought he would be washed away in this intense feeling of love so pure and radiant, another word flashed on the whiteness before his eyes. The word was close, very close, so close that he thought it would slap him in the face. His body began to tremble at the sight of the word, and he also knew right then and there that the word was holy and deserved respect, no matter how he felt about it. Bart managed to speak, even though he had a big lump in his throat.

"God?"

Bart got no reply as he suddenly realized he was once again lying on the floor of the racquetball court, squirming in pain. He rolled this way and that amongst all the clutter of destroyed chairs, towels and railings that he had earlier thrown around.

It took about 10 minutes of screaming before the pain suddenly left, just as quickly as it came on until everything was normal once again. As he lay there looking up at the ceiling, Bart's mind began to wander, wondering just what all this pain and the white room were really all about.

"God, was that really you or a figment of my imagination playing a cruel trick on me?"

As the words left his lips, he felt a slight twinge of pain in his right arm once again, like that was the answer.

"Well, if you are really who you say you are, you know how I feel about you and what you have turned my mother into. I am in control of my own life now, and I don't need you or anyone else's help. So just back off and leave me alone!" Bart shouted out into the empty hollow of the court.

Instantly intense pain shot back into his arm, and no matter what he did, the pain would not leave or let up this time. Bart once again was screaming in burning, searing pain that radiated out from that spot just above the elbow of his right arm.

It was now about 4:30 a.m. when a security guard on the second lower level thought he heard screaming below and went to the lowest level of the building to check it out, radioing for help as he descended the stairs. As he entered the racquetball court area, the screaming was almost unbearable, and he immediately radioed central command to place a call to the Woodsworth residence.

Within 30 minutes, Earnest and Katie rushed into the lowest level of the Woodsworth Industries International building to find two security guards trying desperately to calm their son down as he thrashed wildly on the polished hardwood floor.

Katie knew what was going on with her son, even though she couldn't help him other than to be there for him, and Earnest was just bewildered by what he saw and heard.

"Let's get him an ambulance!" Earnest had to shout over the sound of his son's screaming and groaning all mixed in with a lot of profanity that seemed to be directed at God.

Then, just like that, Bart stopped screaming as the pain instantly left, just as it had in the past. Katie was amazed, and Earnest was confused.

How can a pain like that just turn itself on and off? Earnest thought as his son lifted himself off the floor and brushed past both of his parents like they were total strangers.

Katie was silently praying. *Oh, Lord, please show me what to do for Bart to help him through this time of trial, and please keep the pain away today so that all you have orchestrated will come to pass and the joy of love will return to this family.*

"Katie?" Earnest said. "Earth to Katie. Are you in there?"

"Uh … oh, sorry … I was just thinking," Katie said as she and Earnest began to leave the racquetball court area.

Earnest instructed the security guards to just leave the mess and he would see to it that someone would clean it up over the weekend.

Bart was out of the building long before his parents even got to the parking level. He quickly sped out of the building and noticed the homeless man's cart sitting alone just to the left of the building entrance.

Where is that guy? Bart wondered, which kind of amazed him, but he quickly shrugged it off as he accelerated down the street and out of sight into the early Saturday morning.

About two minutes later, Earnest drove his silver-grey Lincoln MKZ through the opened security door and out onto the entrance drive. Looking both ways and seeing nothing, he and Katie headed for home and—they hoped—another few hours of sleep before the day really got started.

CHAPTER NINE

As Earnest walked out onto the stone patio early that Saturday morning, he was amazed at the day, with the sun shining and the almost perfect temperature for that time of the day. As he took in the wonder of the day, a thought flashed in his mind. *I haven't seen a day like this since ... that day on the golf course with Thomas ... What are the odds that this day will turn out to be as great as that one was?*

Earnest hadn't slept all that well after the encounter with Bart at the racquetball court on the lower level of his office building, yet here he was, feeling like a million bucks, full of vigor and life.

He sat at the family table out on their gorgeous stone patio, which was now adorned with bushels of flowers and plants, all in preparation for the big birthday event later in the day. A maid appeared and asked what he would like for breakfast.

"Well, Maria, seeing that this is a special day for me, I would love to have ham and eggs with flax toast and orange juice. Thank you!"

"Would you like your usual coffee while you wait, Mr. Woodsworth?" she asked politely.

He didn't know if it was the morning with the perfect weather or the fact that he just felt physically great, but either way, he was feeling generous.

"Maria, please just use Earnest today and maybe even from this day on."

Maria didn't know what to say. For years, it had been so

formal, but now her employer was suggesting that formality could be tossed.

"Uh, yes, Mr. Woods … I mean Earnest … sir."

Earnest just laughed. "It's okay, Maria; you just call me whatever you feel comfortable with, and it will be all right with me."

As Maria turned to leave, Earnest spoke to her again.

"Actually, Maria, when breakfast is ready, could you please have the chef and the rest of the staff join me out here on the patio, as I have a few words to say."

Maria said she would, but all the way into the house, she was wondering if she had done something wrong and why it was that he wanted to see the entire staff so early in the day.

Earnest knew that the day would be full of prearranged events and that having any time alone with Katie was probably out of the question. Still, he had hoped that they could at least have breakfast together.

Katie hadn't slept all that well either, and the beautiful morning found her in her private office on her knees at her black leather sofa. Her heart had been heavy since the encounter with Bart earlier in the night on the racquetball court. She knew that today would be a very full day, but that no matter what—short of death or serious injury—she would take time to read her Bible, pray and spend time listening to the Lord.

"Oh, Lord," Katie was praying, "I pray that you will be with Bart in this trial of pain he seems to be going through at your hands." She knew that this was of the Lord and that it was a battle that Bart himself would have to face and fight. "Please give him the strength to go through the pain he is enduring, and please help him to not do something drastic. I pray as well for Winter. I sense something special in her, Lord, and ask that if she is in your will for Bart's future, that you will give me the insight I need to instruct her and guide her on the path you have laid out before her."

Katie was very emotional by this time, and she paused from her prayers to wipe her eyes and rise up from her knees to sit on the sofa.

"Lord Jesus, my God and my Saviour, you know full well that today is Earnest's 50th birthday, for you know every single thing about him. I pray for him today, with all the celebrations and the special surprises that are planned for him, that somehow he will see you through them all. I pray that his reunion with Franklin will be the best birthday gift that any man or father could ever want and that they can resume their father-son relationship in a positive way.

"I pray as well for Caroline and this man who has caught her attention, that this would be your will alone for her life. I realize that at her age, I really can't interfere, but I do, Lord, as her mother, want only the very best for her as long as it is your will too. I thank you that he knows you and has a very personal relationship with you, and I believe, Lord, that you have brought them together. Please watch over their every move and protect their lives and all of this family too.

"Please have all our efforts for this day of celebration be a success and the weather be perfect. All of these things I ask in your name. Amen!"

Katie stayed in her prayer position and just waited on the Lord, to see if he had anything to give her as was her practice in her daily times of prayer and Bible reading. Almost immediately after she had said "Amen," she felt a scripture verse come to mind, and she opened her Bible to look up Ephesians 3:20, which she read out loud. "God is able to do immeasurably more than all we ask or imagine, according to his power that is at work within us."

Katie smiled at the words she had just read and knew that it was a word of encouragement from the Lord for her today.

"Thank you, Lord God Almighty, for this word of encouragement found in the pages of your holy Word."

Katie was in a great mood when she walked out onto the stone patio at the rear of their large home out in the country and was surprised to see Earnest siting at the family patio table reading the weekend newspaper.

"Well, good morning, birthday boy," she said as she walked up behind him and wrapped her arms around his shoulders from behind.

Earnest put the paper down and hugged her arms, loving the feeling of her close to him. He realized how much he really did love her in that brief moment. With great wealth came great temptations, and it had been more than a few times that Earnest had been propositioned by women from all walks of life. But he was not a stupid man and knew that they were only looking at the wealth and not really at him as a man; the only one who had ever looked at him that way was his wife, just as she was doing now.

"Good morning to you too, gorgeous!" he said just before she broke away from him and leaned over to give him a peck on the lips, but he was having none of that on this day. He quickly stood up and swept her up into his arms for a long, tight, passionate kiss.

"Wow!" was all Katie had to say as they broke the kiss. "What's gotten into you, big boy?" she said with a slight laugh.

"Just feeling good today and wanting you to know it."

As she turned to walk to her side of the table, Earnest gave her a playful swat on her butt.

"Oh, Mr. Woodsworth!" She giggled. "I can see that you are in more than just a good mood, sir."

"Mmmmm, you got that right, Mrs. Woodsworth, and maybe later tonight I can show you just how good a mood I am really in."

"You sure know how to make a girl feel good with your words, kind sir, but make sure that you don't wear yourself out today, because I will be expecting you to make good on those words later."

As the two lovers sat at their family table, Maria came out once again to see what it was that Katie would like for breakfast.

"Oh, just the usual for me will be fine, Maria," Katie said.

With that said, Maria left and Katie returned her attention to Earnest.

"So what's on the agenda for today?" Earnest asked across the table just before taking a drink of his coffee.

"Thank you for asking," Katie said with a big smile. "After breakfast, we have a sitting with Pinetop Photography for this special occasion. Today it will be just you and I and Andre."

"Andre? Good! I love that man and his work. He truly has a gift when it comes to portraits," Earnest responded.

"I agree, love, and he made a big fuss about us coming in specifically today. I think it is just his way of saying happy birthday."

"Well, I would make time anytime for him."

"Yes, well, that is scheduled for 10:00 a.m."

"And after that?"

"At 11:30 a.m., we are to meet with Thomas and Shelly for lunch at the Evergreen Club. Caroline might be meeting us there as well and might be bringing a friend."

"A friend?" Earnest said, raising his eyebrows.

"Yes and his name is Mitch. He is a DJ who will be supplying the music for the second part of your birthday celebration tonight."

"A DJ, you say?"

"Yes, a disc jockey who supplies recorded music."

"I do know what a DJ is, my dear, but why not a live band?"

"It was your daughter's idea. She felt that live bands play too much of their own style of music and with a DJ, a whole range of songs can be covered. Also, guests can requests songs on their own."

"Okay ... that sounds good to me," Earnest said, just as breakfast was about to be served.

Katie was a little puzzled when not only Maria came out of the house but all the rest of the staff as well, lining up across in front of them.

"Uh ... what's going on?" Katie asked, puzzled to say the least.

"Don't fret, my dear; they are here at my suggestion," Earnest said with a grin.

"Oh ... okay."

Earnest rose from his chair and walked over to the row of staff. He then reached into his front pocket and pulled out 20 100-dollar bills, much to the delight of the staff.

"This is just a small token of my appreciation for each and every one of you, no matter what role you play in working for us. I know today is a very busy day for you all, but I personally wanted to give you a tip for your role in making this, my fiftieth birthday, a very successful and happy one."

With that said, Earnest started at one end of the row and first shook each staff member's hand before he handed them a crisp, brand-new 100-dollar bill.

"What was that all about?" Katie asked after all the staff had returned to their assigned duties for the day.

"Just a little something I picked up on the golf course."

"At the golf course?" Katie asked, totally confused now.

"I will explain it to you sometime when we both have more time, but for now, my dear, let's eat breakfast and get this day on the road."

Katie just nodded, and as was her custom, she bowed her head and asked the Lord to bless the food and this most special day.

"You said we were having lunch with Thomas and Shelly at 11:30, so what's happening after that?" Earnest asked about halfway through his birthday breakfast meal.

"Well," Katie said, "most of the afternoon is yours to do with as you wish ... as long you don't work." She pointed her finger in the direction of his nose. "I know you, Mr. Woodsworth, with your desire to be working all the time, but not today, please?"

"Okay ... well, I think I can find some things to occupy my time here at home."

"Uh, that will be a problem."

"Why is that?"

"Well, you know we are having the celebration here tonight, and I would appreciate it if you weren't around as we set up a few surprises."

"Surprises?" Earnest said with raised eyebrows and certain interest.

"Yes, dear, surprises, so please don't come home until you hear from me."

"Okay, but just what am I going to find to do all afternoon away from the house and the office?"

"Talk to Thomas about that; he says he has some new ideas to discuss with you."

"That's a great idea. Perhaps he will share his other seven ideas with me."

"Seven?"

"Yes, can I pick 'em or what?"

"I agree; he is a very talented man, hon."

"That he is indeed. That he is."

At precisely 11:25 a.m., Earnest and Katie Woodsworth pulled up to the Evergreen Country Club in Earnest's car. He had told his wife that that day of all days, he was going to do the driving for a change. This way, it gave him the freedom to go and do whatever he wished.

Katie had hoped that he would have used their driver; that way, she could keep tabs on just where he was and make sure that he wasn't sneaking off to work on something when he was supposed to be relaxing.

"Welcome to the club, Mr. Woodsworth," one of the club's

young valets said as he came and opened Earnest's door for him. Another valet was doing the same thing for Katie on her side of the vehicle.

"Here," Earnest said as he reached into the inner pocket of his blazer and plopped a 100-dollar bill into the young man's hand. "This is just a little thank-you for your diligence and good work here at the club." With that said, he went over to the other valet and repeated the same words as he gave him a 100-dollar tip as well.

Wow, Katie thought. *He has really gotten into the spirit of giving today. I shall have to ask Thomas some time just what this sudden gesture of personal generosity is all about.*

When the couple walked into the main dining area of the club, Earnest was instantly surprised to see it all decorated in celebration of his 50th birthday. In unison, as if on cue, everyone in the room shouted, "Happy birthday!"

Earnest was genuinely surprised and touched by the surprise, and he smiled while blushing at the same time. Then as the couple were led to their table, Earnest made a point of shaking as many hands as he could while he thanked them for being there and for thinking of him at this most special time in his life.

"Well there, Mr. Woodsworth, so good of you to join us on this most special day," Thomas said as he rose to give his best friend a huge bear hug and a pat on the back, while Katie and Shelly hugged as well.

"Glad you two are here as well," Earnest responded as the four sat down and settled in to their seats.

"You know, Earnest, there is this one question that I have always wanted to ask you, but I was saving it for such an occasion as this."

"What's that?" Earnest asked as he leaned forward towards his friend and business partner.

"I just wanted to know what it was like growing up with the dinosaurs."

The two women at the table burst into laughter, as did the waiter as he approached the table.

"Very funny," Earnest said, trying not to laugh himself.

"And then you got to witness the motor car, electricity, television and all those other wonderful inventions," Thomas continued, which only fueled the laughter.

Earnest just sat there with a smirk on his face as if to say, "Okay, let them have their fun."

Katie reached over and patted her husband's hand, as she and their best friends made light of his fiftieth birthday.

Then the waiter stepped in, handing them their menus and taking their drink orders. Finally he scooted away from the four friends.

"You know, Thomas, one of these days, it will be your turn, and I will be waiting patiently for that day," Earnest said with a big smirk as he sat back in his chair.

"Yes, I know that is true, but the one satisfaction I will always hold over you is the fact that you will always be older than me."

The women just laughed again, that is until Earnest spoke to them. "Okay, ladies, and what about you? Shall we go to the expense of making it big news of your 50th birthday when you get there, hmm?"

Suddenly the mood changed as both Shelly and Katie threatened both men within inches of their lives if they ever did that.

Thomas and Earnest just looked solemnly at each other before they broke out into sudden laughter.

"Hey, we're serious here boys!" Shelly said as she and Katie were shooting visual daggers at their husbands.

This time, the two men just sat still, not saying a word until Thomas chuckled softly and then both men broke out into laughter again, holding their stomachs and rocking back and forth in their chairs.

Finally they all settled down, each knowing that the others

were just kidding and it just made for a great time of visiting and celebration there at the Evergreen Country Club.

After a delicious, filling meal, the dishes were all cleared away and the men just sat back drinking their coffee while the women sipped on their tea.

"So what does Katie have you doing today, birthday boy?" Thomas asked.

"Actually not that much and she won't let me go to the office or do any work at home either."

"I did suggest to him that maybe the two of you could do something and discuss some of the many ideas I know you have rolling around in that brain of yours," Katie said.

"Yes, and I would like to hear about the other seven."

"What other seven?" Shelly asked this time.

"When we were on our flight to the capital the other day, genius here was talking about another idea he had and then mentioned that he also had another seven on the go," Earnest said.

"Oh those seven," Shelly said.

"You've talked to your wife about them?" Earnest said, surprised.

"Well, yes, we talk about everything in our day," Thomas said as he looked over at his wife and smiled. Then he gave her a wink.

"I have always tried to keep my work separate from my private life," Earnest said to which Katie simply nodded.

"I do understand that, my friend, but I have learned that Shelly is my best friend and confidante as we share this life together and I want her to know everything that goes on in my life just as much as I want to know everything that is going on in hers."

The four friends then fell silent as Thomas and Shelly held hands and just looked at each other. Katie admired them for their open love and dedication to each other. Yes, she and Earnest loved each other, but there had always been this sort of wall when it came to work versus family life, and maybe that had something to do with the way the boys thought about their father.

"So maybe we can sneak in a round of golf here today. What do you think, buddy?" Thomas finally said to Earnest.

"My thoughts exactly," Earnest said back to him. "But I guess I will have to go home first to change."

"No problem there, big boy," Katie said this time. "Everything you need is in your locker downstairs."

"Oh so you even had this planned out, eh?" Earnest said, turning towards Katie.

"It's what I am good at," she said back to him.

Earnest nodded and with a beaming smile, said, "Yep, ain't no denying that!"

The four friends had a great time at the Evergreen Country Club, laughing and reminiscing about the past, present and future of their lives. Eventually Shelly and Katie made their ways back to their homes while Thomas and Earnest set out to play 18 holes of golf on the club's prestigious 36-hole course. This course gave the golfer two choices of 18 holes of golf or four choices of nine holes. Each of the nine holes had a different level of rating that went from beginner to advanced.

Today Thomas and Earnest decided to play the advanced 18 holes in the back area of the 600-acre Evergreen Country Club layout. They were ready for the first tee off, complete with their personal golf cart, clubs and accessories.

Earnest won the tee toss to go first, and as he stepped up to the tee box and placed his wooden tee into the plush grass, he felt that this was once again all too familiar. There wasn't a cloud in the sky, just a slight cross breeze, and the temperature was perfect. Earnest lined up his shot, feet in position, and his grip on the club felt right as he took his swing and connected with his favorite Ping golf ball.

He watched the ball arc high into the clear blue sky and fall back to the earth, landing neatly in the center of the fairway at a distance of almost 200 yards.

"Way to go, buddy!" Thomas said from behind him as Earnest smiled briefly, making his way back behind Thomas as he readied himself for his first shot of the day.

Just like his best friend, Thomas readied himself and took the swing; then he stepped back slightly to watch his ball, which landed amazingly right alongside Earnest's ball.

"Well, imagine that," Thomas said.

"Bet we couldn't do that again even if we tried," Earnest responded.

The game progressed until they were both on the tee box of the fourth hole, which was a par three at 198 yards. Both men had almost identical shots on each of the previous three holes, which had both of them baffled, to say the least.

"Care to wager on this hole, my friend?" Earnest asked Thomas.

"Based on the way we have been playing so far, you bet I do!"

"Okay, name the cost?"

"How rich are you feeling today?"

"Okay, how about 100?" Earnest asked, eyeing his friend closely.

"Sure, and who does the money go to then?"

"Hum ..." Earnest thought. "How about the woman booking holes back in the pro shop?"

"Okay, that works for me."

With that out of the way, it was Thomas who was first to tee off this time, and once again, he went through the procedure he had so finely crafted after all his years of golfing—sizing up the lay of the fairway, positioning his feet, and then lining up the shot from the flag to his golf ball, sitting on his wooden tee. Using his favorite number 8 iron, he took his swing and watched the ball arc high into the air and then back down to earth. The bright-orange ball bounced once on the green's apron and then twice on the green before it simply rolled about three feet and into the cup.

"Yessssssss!" Thomas shouted, amazed at the fact that he had just shot his first hole-in-one in years. "Let's see you top that one, buddy!" he said as he brushed past Earnest, giving him a slap on the back.

For the first time this game, Earnest wondered if he could match that shot or even come close. He too followed through with his routine, positioning his golf ball on the tee, lining up and planting his feet, and then drawing a mental line from the flag far below up to the ball sitting on its tee just before he took the swing. As the metal golf club made contact with the golf ball, it sounded perfect with just the right tone of *ping*. Both men watched the ball arc high into the clear afternoon air just before gravity pulled it back down.

Earnest's ball landed right on the checker-patterned green and bounced once slightly before it plopped into the cup, sitting on top of the bright-orange ball that belonged to Thomas, his best friend.

"Wow!" Thomas said. "Is it gonna be like this every hole? And just how are we to pay out when we both make the shots?"

Earnest just stood there, almost unable to believe the game so far. *How could we both be playing our shots side by side like that?* he wondered as he retrieved his wooden tee and walked towards the golf cart.

Of course, Thomas was thinking the same sort of thoughts, but instead of being mystified by it all, he was grinning ear to ear as silently he said, "*Thank you, Lord,*" in his mind.

The rest of the first nine was the same, and when both men entered the clubhouse for a light snack, their scores were identical. They didn't know it, but word was getting around at the country club as to what was happening with their strange round of golf.

"So are you going to share any of the other seven inventive ideas you said you had?" Earnest asked.

"Yes, I suppose I should do that, seeing it is the reason we are out here today," Thomas said across the table. "But for now I am just going to give you a quick overview and we can get into the details at a later date."

"Sure, that sounds fine."

"Okay, then. Well, I have this idea of making use of one's personal cell phone in a way that would also allow one to measure the height, width and distance of any object. Then the app can calculate the volume of the object and model it in a 3-D image. Of course, this app is not just for anyone, but in specific fields of work, it would eliminate the need for measuring tapes, cameras and computers."

"Hum!" Earnest said, trying to wrap his brain around the idea.

"Then I have an idea for a golf club, specifically the driver that would greatly improve a golfer's game."

"Now you're talking my language. Please explain."

"Okay, the idea is to make the center of gravity within the head of the club adjustable vertically and horizontally. Then the golfer could tweak the ball's spin independently of the angle after the ball leaves the tee."

"Really? Has that ever been possible before?"

"No, not as far as I know."

"Wow! Now that's something I would like to see and test personally."

"Want to hear some of the other ideas?"

"You bet I do."

"What time is our tee time for the back half?"

Earnest checked his watch.

"We still have 20 minutes."

"Okay, that should give me enough time. So another idea I have, but have not thought it through too much, is that of thermal radar."

"What?"

"I know it sounds complicated, but really it's not. Basically how it would work is that the unit would mount a number of ways, but to make it easier to understand, just imagine a unit sitting on a tripod, just like a surveyor's equipment. The unit would warm objects, such as car engines, tires, people and such. The spinning camera unit on the tripod would take 10 to 16 or more thermal images per second, then software would piece the pictures together and then the heat signatures of these items are triangulated using GPS, giving their location as a dot or a blip on a radar-like screen, perhaps even the screen on one's cell phone."

"Now that is very interesting indeed, and I can already see the military and search and rescue agencies being interested in technology like that," Earnest said as he sat way back in his chair, checking out the genius seated across from him. He also finalized another thought in his mind and would make it known to everyone soon enough.

"Next?" he continued.

"This one may sound a bit funny, but I call it Heel and Toe Power, and it will be something totally new in the world of power."

"Mmmm, I love those words 'totally new'!"

"Again, basically it is a system built into one's shoe. The operating system would convert the energy of one's heel striking a plate that would create a rotational energy. This would be produced using magnets that would spin, like rotors. Then the spin of these rotors would create an electrical current that would be stored in coils of wire also embedded within the shoes. This current would then travel along wires or a circuit board, charging a lithium battery pack that would sit on top of the shoe just above the user's toes.

"The benefit of such a device would be to charge cell phones after a relatively short walk or run and would be great for hikers, long-distance runners and joggers alike."

"Where do you get these ideas?" Earnest asked, amazed at the man's ideas.

"I just like to think. I see situations that might require

additional technology or tweaking, and I just go with it until I come up with an answer; it is a God-given gift."

"Well, there is no doubt about the fact that it came from somewhere," was all Earnest could come up with at the moment.

"I know that sometimes it can all sound quite technical or detailed, so I hope I am not boring you."

"Boring me? Are you kidding? I think it is the most fascinating conversation I have had in quite some time, at least since we talked about the Green Heat system."

"Well then, just let me share one more idea before we head out," Thomas said as Earnest glanced at his watch.

"Okay, shoot."

"It is interesting that you brought up the Green Heat system because I have an idea that would further enhance the project as it now stands. This idea would be based on the Green Heat idea, but would be a generator, powered by the same items that create the heat for our existing units.

"These units would be small and great for home owners, campers, military situations and just about any situation that requires heat should the power go out, let's say. It would incorporate our Green Heat system along with solar power to charge a battery that could run a home refrigerator for up to 48 hours or light that same home for up to 24 hours. Anything electrical could be run off this unit. Thinking even farther ahead, it could be adapted to boost a vehicle battery or allow enough power for a 30-minute boost of a welder.

"The unit would be designed for a fast recharge and affordable enough for the average person to be able to own one or two units at a time. We could even look at changeable power pods with one main charging unit. What do you think?" Thomas asked his friend and business partner.

Earnest actually sat there with his mouth open and not a word to say about this fantastic idea, until Thomas suggested they hit the course.

No one had ever heard of two men matching their shots like Earnest and Thomas had so far, especially like on hole number 4. A crowd was beginning to form for the back nine, and one of those interested players was a news anchor for the city's local television station.

"Okay then," Thomas said. "Let's get back to finishing this extraordinary round of golf."

"Yep," was all Earnest had to say, at least until the two men drove up to the 10 hole tee box. "What the ...?" was all he had to say as both friends saw the crowds that were seemingly waiting to watch them play.

"Uh ... I take it that someone heard about our first nine?" Thomas said in a whisper as he leaned over in Earnest's direction.

"Looks that way."

"Sure glad it's you teeing off first," Thomas said with a grin.

"If ever there was a shot that one didn't want to flub, it would be this one."

"Yep. No pressure, buddy."

"Oh yeah, thanks."

Once again, Earnest prepared himself for the shot as the crowd quieted down. He took in the beautiful day and mentally blocked out the crowd, a talent he had acquired over many years of dealing with corporate crowds and board meetings.

The day was right, his positioning was right, and after he drew the mental line, he took his shot. Everyone there followed the ball this time as it arced high into the cloudless blue sky and landed softly with just a slight bounce 250 yards down the fairway.

The crowd erupted in a loud roar, which only helped to draw even more people towards the sounds at the 10 hole.

"Ha! Now the pressure is all yours," Earnest said with a grin as he slapped his buddy on the back.

"Thanks," Thomas grunted as he prepared to take his shot.

Once again, Thomas's shot landed just mere inches from his friend's ball, and the crowd erupted again as they witnessed the unbelievable shot. This type of play continued right up to the 16th hole, which was another par three, at 180 yards.

"What?" Thomas said this time as he stood at the raised tee box, high above the green below them. Lined all around the green were at least 80 people, including groundskeeping staff, the beverage girl and even a television crew, called in by the news anchor.

"What is with all these people?" Earnest said.

"I know we were having an awesome game, but didn't know that the whole world knew about it," Thomas said.

"Yeah!"

Both men knew that this was more than an extraordinary game of golf, as they had both matched each other's score to the stroke, including the two holes in one on the fourth green, but this wasn't what they wanted. They just wanted to finish the game alone and then go home feeling great about the game of their lives.

"So what now?" Thomas asked.

"We only have two choices. We quit and just leave, or we play it out to the end. This crowd isn't going to leave, so we have to decide."

"Let's toss a coin to decide."

"Works for me."

The crowd was now wondering just why the two men were preparing to toss a coin as Earnest flipped the dollar coin high into the air and watched it land at their feet.

"Guess that settles it then."

"Yep."

The two men just looked at each other and then out at the crowd down below, surrounding the green.

"Enjoy, Buddy," Earnest said with a slight laugh as Thomas prepared to hit his ball.

All went suddenly very quiet as Thomas swung his eight iron

back and then forward, contacting the ball with a resounding *crack* in the eerily quiet air. He watched as his ball rose into the air, not quite as high this time, and bounced about six feet from the green. The ball then bounced once on the green and rolled towards the cup. They all collectively held their breath until the ball stopped rolling just mere inches from the flag.

Again a cheer went up from the crowd at the great shot.

"Man, am I glad that didn't drop in." Thomas sighed as he picked up his tee and walked past Earnest.

"Why is that?" Earnest asked, unsure if he heard his friend right.

"Can you imagine what they would be like?" he said, pointing to the crowd below. "If they knew that I got two holes in one on the same day?"

"Yes, so then I hope it doesn't happen to me either."

Earnest played his ball perfectly, almost without trying, as if some unseen force was playing the game for the two of them. The pink-and-yellow ball bounced once on the green and rolled in the same direction as the bright-orange ball. Every single eye, including the eye of the camera lens, along with a few cell phone cameras, was trained on that ball as it rolled up the green towards the cup.

Then the crowd gasped in unbelief as Earnest's ball connected with Thomas's ball, which in turn forced both balls to drop into the cup. The crowd didn't know what to do or how to react.

Has that ever happened before? some were thinking.

What are the odds of that happening? others thought, but the vast majority simply went "Wow!" just before a huge thunderous roar arose from the crowd.

"No way!" Thomas blurted out.

Earnest remained silent, unsure just how to react. This day so far had been almost too perfect, he thought as he just stared at the crowd below. Just then he spotted someone walking away from the green as he took a double look.

It couldn't be, Earnest thought. Then he felt his friend's pat on the back, and when he looked back again, the person he thought he saw was gone. *Where did he go?* he wondered as he looked all around in that direction, but he saw no one, other than the crowd awaiting him and Thomas to come down to the green.

"Hey there," Earnest heard behind him. "Are you coming? Our fans await us."

Startled, Earnest turned and walked over to the golf cart, taking one last look back through the crowd, before both men descended the hill on the golf cart path to the steadily rising cheers below.

Later, both men sat in stunned silence at their table in the Evergreen Country Club golf lounge. They had answered more questions than they had cared to, including those of the news anchor and now just sat there trying to figure it all out.

"Has that ever happened before? I mean two men getting the exact same score, including two holes in one on the same course in the same game?" Earnest asked, even though his mind was on that young man he thought he saw walking away from the 16th green after their phenomenal shots.

"I don't know," was all Thomas had to say, and while both men sat there thinking, both of their cell phones chirped at the same exact time.

"Unreal," Earnest said.

CHAPTER TEN

It was 6:30 that evening when Bart pulled up to Winter's apartment on the north end of the city. It was a very warm evening near the end of August, so Bart decided to put the roof down on his convertible Jaguar. Even though he didn't really want to be seen with her any longer, he still played the part in order to please his mother, who controlled the purse strings of his allowance and his toys.

"Very lovely," he said, his words almost dripping as he commented on Winter's choice of attire for the evening's events about to unfold.

"Well, thank you, kind sir," Winter said as she took his arm. "My, my, Bart, sometimes you really do amaze me," she continued as he walked her out to his car, opened the door and closed it after she was seated. Then he bounded around to his side, hopping over the door rather than opening it.

"You must be in a really good mood," Winter said, surprised at his youthful moves.

"Well, we are going to a party, are we not? And a royal one it will be at that. Mother will surely have outdone herself for this one and Caroline too, as per usual. And as per usual they haven't asked for my input other than to order me to be there with you!" Bart said in a condescending tone before he sped away from the curb and roared down the street. As Bart came up to an amber light, he braked reluctantly for the coming red light. The last thing he wanted to do that night was get a ticket or be in an accident that might affect his mother's decision concerning any future money he might receive.

As they sat waiting for the light to change, Bart noticed a homeless person coming their direction from his right, pushing the typical shopping cart piled high with all his belongings. *Where do these people come from?* he thought in disgust. *C'mon, light, change, change.* Bart was trying to will the light within his mind, not wanting to have to wait for this person as he tried to make his way across the intersection. But the person made it onto the walkway just as the light changed to green, and Bart sat there gunning the engine in hopes of getting the person to move a little faster.

"Oh, look at that poor soul." Winter suddenly spoke up. "Maybe they need a hand with their cart?"

"What?" Bart said, startled at her words, as if they were directed to him. "I am not getting out to help that bum."

"Bart! That is no way to talk about anyone, especially one who is down and out, such as this person."

"He's made his own way in life. There are some who have the money and the rest who don't, and I will never be with the majority of those losers."

Just then, the homeless man stumbled and fell to his knees right in front of Bart's car, while the light was still green.

"What?" Bart shouted. "Get up, you bum! You're holding up traffic." But before he could say another word, Winter opened her door and rushed to the man's aid.

"Winter? Get back in this car, or so help me I will leave you here with him."

"Here, let me help you, sir," Winter said as she took the man's hand.

"Bless you, my child," the homeless man said, and with her help, he stood up once again, holding on to his precious shopping cart.

Winter suddenly stood transfixed as the man stared at her.

Never before had she seen such eyes. They seemed to be deep pools of emotion, and she was captivated by them, at least until Bart laid on the horn.

"Get in here, Winter, right now!" Bart shouted with obvious anger.

"I am sorry, but I have to go," Winter said as she turned and headed to her side of the car.

"Wha ...?" Bart began to say as the homeless man left his cart and made his way towards Bart's side of the expensive car. "Don't you dare touch the car!" Bart continued as the man came right up to his side and bent slightly to look into Bart's face.

Try as he might, Bart was unable to tear himself away from the dirty man's stare, and quickly he found himself staring into those same pools of mystery as Winter had just witnessed herself.

"W-what do you w-want?" Bart stumbled over his words, afraid that this might be a mugging in the making.

"The next time it comes, it won't stop," the homeless man said before he stood up and hobbled over to his cart. He began pushing it across the walkway and up onto the sidewalk.

Bart just sat there as the light changed from red to green once more and a vehicle behind honked for him to get going.

The next time what comes? Bart was mulling the words over in his mind, and he roared away from the intersection at a very high rate of speed, heading to his parents' mansion and his father's birthday celebrations.

Mrs. Katherine Sylvia Woodsworth had indeed outdone herself with the help of her daughter, Caroline. As she walked out onto the huge stone patio, she was pleased to hear the string quartet that Caroline had hired. The music was soft and soothing as Katie just stood there, swaying softly to the sweet strains wafting through the warm evening air.

Mmmmm perfect, Katie thought as she viewed the patio and backyard grounds. To her left, she saw the long rows of tables being filled with all kinds of fruit platters, a chocolate fountain at the end of each table, and trays filled with all types of elegant pastries, cakes and squares. Other tables were being filled with all types of cheese and crackers, complete with napkins, cutlery and toothpicks placed in each and every single piece of cheese.

Turning to her left, she saw a number of tables; each would seat six to eight people once all the guests began to arrive. Each table had a large floral arrangement and a greeting card welcoming people to Earnest's 50th birthday celebration. The card also listed the evening's events schedule, and she walked to a table and picked up one such card to have a look.

7:00	**Cocktails & Wine Bar Opens**
7:30	**Welcoming of Guests**
7:40	**Time of Fellowship & Food**
8:00	**Introduction of the Birthday Boy!**
8:15	**Meet & Greet**
9:00	**Gift Opening**
9:30	**Dance Begins**
11:30	**Late Lunch Served**

"Looks great!" Katie said softly as she walked over to the main staircase that took her to the lower patio level. There she could see close to 100 tables painstakingly placed at strategic locations, yet leaving a huge open area just at the bottom of the staircase. Here all the guests would stand as Earnest gave his little speech to thank them all for coming out to attend this momentous milestone in his life.

Looking even further beyond the tables, she could also see the huge tented area, complete with a built-in hardwood dance floor, and as she strolled in that direction, she could see another collection of similar tables all around the perimeter of the dance floor. Also, she could see all the strands of decorative lighting strung from support post to support post, flickering and sparkling in the warm night's air. As Katie passed the large corner post closest to her, she turned and walked into the tent. She was amazed at the sight she saw with speakers from the floor to the roofline on either side of a very colorful table system.

Busily working away with the finishing touches was Caroline's newest friend, Mitch. He was setting up some sort of table that had a laptop on each side of the square top. Katie was very impressed by the setup that she saw, with a table that was about six feet long. Above the table at about another six feet was some sort of digital readout box, and as she looked all around the tented area, she could also see a large screen mounted up in each corner of the tent.

"Mind if I ask just what you are doing?" Katie said, slightly startling the young man.

"Oh ... sorry, I didn't know you were there," he said with a huge warm smile on his face, and in that instant, Katie saw what her daughter saw in this man.

"Just thought I would walk over here and see what you were doing, and I must say, I am impressed."

"Well, thank you. I do try to provide the very best I can in any job I get."

"Yes, Caroline, told me about that, including your preference of music too."

"Are you Caroline's mother? You must be, as you look so much alike even in this low light."

"Well, aren't you the charmer, and yes, I am Caroline's mother. Very nice to meet you, Mitch," Katie said as she held out her hand.

He took it in a light handshake.

"The feeling is definitely mutual."

"About my music preference ... well, being a born-again Christian, I feel it is my path in life not to present a negative worldview, but rather an uplifting and happy one through Jesus, my Lord."

Katie just stood there smiling; then she just walked straight up to Mitch, who had now come around from his work to stand across from her. She gave him a long, loving hug and simply said, "Thank you," before she let him go and stepped back.

Mitch just stood there, unsure of what had just happened, but quickly, that warm, friendly smile returned to his face.

"So tell me, young man, what was it you were working on when I came in?"

"Uh … yeah … okay, well, this table you see here," he said as he moved back to the table with the four laptops behind him. "These laptops list all the songs I have in my catalogues, and people can come up here and scroll through the lists. When they find a song they would like me to play, they simply touch the number associated with that song, and it flashes up a message that tells them that the DJ has received their request. There is also a continuous message at the bottom of each screen that tells them to pick no more than two songs at a time in order that everyone gets a chance to hear the songs they like."

"Well, that is quite impressive, I must say, and just where did you get this system from?"

"Oh, it is something I came up with on my own."

"You made this yourself?" Katie asked.

"Yes, over some time, but yes, it was my idea. Would you care to see how it works?"

"Yes, that would be nice."

"Okay then … just give me a second to turn everything on. Please go to the table there and pick out a song," Mitch said as he pointed in the direction of the laptops table.

Katie moved to the table and began to scroll through the countless number of songs that he had, and finally she saw one that she liked. She pressed the screen, which lit up the number E26.

Instantly, Mitch received the request.

"I see you are a fan of the Electric Light Orchestra," he said to her.

"Yes, I have always liked their music, and this song is one of my favorites to listen to and dance to as well."

"Okay, great. Could you please move out into the middle of the dance floor where you will see the full effect of what I have to offer?"

Katie did as instructed, and as soon as she stopped walking, the music began to play in the very familiar style that only ELO could produce. More than that, Katie could see on the digital readout above the table, the words, "'Don't Get Me Down' by ELO ... Playing next ... 'Anniversary Waltz 1' by Status Quo ..."

"Wow!" she said and then noticed Mitch pointing at the four large screens in the corners of the tent. On one of the screens she was looking at, she could see the words of the song playing—much like a karaoke readout. "Wow!" she said again.

Then the music died down as Mitch shut down the system.

"So what do you think?" he asked, looking directly at Katie.

"That is fantastic, but why the words of the song?"

"That comes from a lot of time playing music at dances and such, where I noticed a lot of people who didn't dance and just sat there looking bored. So I added the screens and words so that those people and anyone who wanted to could at least sing along with the song while the others danced."

"Now that is a great idea, young man, and you invented all this yourself, you say?"

"Yep. Necessity is the mother of invention, so the saying goes."

Katie just stood there, her mind way ahead of her now, as she thought of the possibility of introducing Mitch to Thomas, wondering just what those two could do with their talents.

"Okay, well, I will make sure that I am one of those who try it out again later on this evening. Has Caroline mentioned Mr. Woodsworth's favorite songs?"

"Yes, she has, and I have a few of them loaded up and ready to go."

"Great! Thank you." With that said, Katie turned and walked

out of the tent back towards the stone patio at the back of the large house.

As she walked towards the house, she took in the vast grounds around her. Lights were everywhere. She could see strands of clear bulbs surrounding the stone walls of the patio strung from pillar to stone pillar. There were lights all across the back of the house and in almost every tree she could see, at least back to the tent she had just left, and it all looked oh so perfect.

"This is all just so beautiful," Winter said as she and Bart strolled out onto the backyard stone patio.

"Yeah, it's okay if you like this kinda stuff. Been going to parties like this ever since we got this house, so to me, it's just another boring party—at least it's not my kind of party," Bart said in a sarcastic tone of voice.

"Oh, Bart, I would love to host parties like this and do all the planning. I don't know if I told you or not, but I took several planning and decoration courses in college last summer, and I loved them."

"You went to college? Which one?" Bart asked, surprised at her words.

"Eastside Regional College back home," Winter said, still clinging to his arm.

"And ... where is home?"

"Toronto."

"You are from Toronto?"

"Yes, born and raised there."

"Now there is one exciting city, not like this boring place."

"Bart, how can you say that. This is a very exciting city, full of culture, history and religion."

"Religion?" Bart snapped as he pulled away from her, turning to face her now. "Why in the world would anyone be interested in religion when it comes to this or any other city, for that matter?"

Winter knew that she had said the wrong thing, and she just remained silent, not wanting to be the cause for his bad mood at his father's birthday celebration about to start very soon.

"Hello there, you two," they both heard as Katie walked up to them. She took Winter into her arms and gave her a loving hug, before she turned to give one to her son Bart, but he would have none of it and simply walked away.

"Bartholomew William Woodsworth!" Katie barked out, surprising Winter and stopping Bart in his tracks. "You turn around right now and get your sorry butt back here with a hug for your mother!"

Sheepishly Bart turned and did what his mother had told him, and again Winter got to see yet another side of Bart, but this one made her smile with a wide grin. She would have laughed if the situation were different, but instead, she just grinned, laughing hysterically on the inside.

At 7:00 p.m., the guests began to arrive—all 200 plus—and soon the celebrations were in full swing with guests milling around, greeting friends, and just talking to anyone who wanted to talk. The tables began to fill up as guests picked where they would like to sit before flipping over the schedule-of-events card, which read "This Seat Taken" on the reverse side. Others were filling their plates with many of the tasty delicacies that lay displayed on the various tables. Some were making use of the chocolate fountains while others were getting a drink from the many select beverage tables.

"Looks like things are going smoothly so far," Caroline said as she walked up beside her mother.

"Yes and everything is perfect in so many ways."

"I hear you had a chat with Mitch earlier?"

"Yes," was all Katie had to say.

"Just 'yes'? That's all you have to say?" Caroline said in mock surprise.

"You are already quite fond of him, aren't you?" Katie said, turning the conversation around.

"Well … I … uh … like him, yes."

"Come on, my dear; I know you better than anyone else, and I know there is more than that going on in that pretty head of yours."

Caroline didn't know how to respond. Yes, there was more going on, but she didn't want her mom thinking that they were rushing things. It was just one of those chance meetings where you know beyond a shadow of a doubt that this is the person for you. She wouldn't go as far as to say it was love at first sight, but it was pretty close to it.

Just then Thomas and Shelly walked in and over to them. Caroline greeted them politely and then told her mother that she was going to check on something and would talk to her later.

"Saved by the bell, eh?" Katie said to her daughter as she hurried away.

"Saved by the bell? Wasn't that a television show at one time?" Shelly said.

"Ha! Yes, it was, but I didn't realize you were into shows like that," Katie said with a chuckle to her best friend.

"Oh you!" Shelly said as she rolled her eyes. "At least it wasn't like you, all gaga over *Little House on the Prairie*."

"Hey, that was a great show that at least had some morals."

"Morals? That's not why you watched the show."

"Yes, it was."

"Come now, girls," Thomas cut in, thinking if this continued, he might witness a fight, right there on the stone patio of his best friend's home on his 50th birthday.

"And just why do you think I watched the show then?" Katie said, glaring at Shelly in a playful mood.

"Michael Landon!"

"Wha ...?" Katie said.

"Yeah, you loved him as Little Joe on *Bonanza*, and it just carried over to *Little House on the Prairie*."

Katie hesitated, thinking that through. "Yep, you are right!" Then the two women burst out laughing. "Hey, he was quite a hunk in his day." They laughed even more, and this time, it was Thomas who rolled his eyes.

"Oh brother!" was all he had to say, knowing that it was going to be one fun-filled, silly evening to say the least.

"Ladies and Gentlemen," Katie said into the microphone as she attempted to get the attention of everyone milling around the grounds. Quickly, the crowd settled down as she continued, "I just want to thank you all for coming out on the momentous occasion of Earnest's 50th birthday celebration."

A huge roar of approval, along with hands clapping and some whistles could then be heard through all the crowd.

"Now will be a time of fellowship and food. Help yourself to all the food tables, chocolate fountains and beverages located on the upper level of the patio," Katie said as she pointed in that direction. "In about 30 minutes, we will be introducing the birthday boy himself, so until then, just enjoy." Again, another roar of approval went up from the 200 or so people in attendance, and Katie made her way over to the table she was sharing with Shelly, Thomas, Caroline, Bart and Winter.

"There are a lot of people here," Winter said to Katie. "I have never been to a party with this many people before."

"Well, my dear, if it is the Lord's will, maybe you will be to more," Katie said as she placed an arm around Winter's shoulders and gave her a slight hug.

Bart was just staring at his mother in disbelief.

What is she talking about? he thought. *As soon as this party is over with and we meet with Mother on Monday, that will be the end of Winter as far as I am concerned, and then I can get on with my life again.*

Winter was also surprised at Bart's mother's words, but she was happy nonetheless, because the truth be told, she really liked Katie.

It's almost time, Katie was thinking, there at the table, while the others were chatting away. *I can hardly wait. Oh, Lord, help me to wait and help me not to blow it.*

After about 20 minutes, Katie made her way back into the house, up the huge, winding staircase, and into their bedroom, where she found Earnest fussing with his tie. She walked over to him and took over the task.

"What would you ever do without me?" she said teasingly.

Once the tie was set in place, Earnest drew Katie up close to himself. "I would be lost without you, my love," he said and then gave her a long, passionate kiss, which she returned eagerly. As they broke from the kiss, Katie stepped back and looked deeply into her husband's eyes.

"Remember, kind sir, to save your strength for later this evening, and I promise to make it worth your while."

"Just so you know, I have been thinking about it all day since you mentioned it earlier this morning, and I know it will be the highlight of my day!"

As the two of them hugged and teased each other there in their bedroom while 200 guests milled around just outside, Katie was lost in other thoughts. *It will be great, yes, but it will not be the highlight of your day, love … Indeed, it will not.*

Katie and Earnest walked through their home, thanking those who were serving food and doing various chores. Then they walked to the garden bay doors and made their way out to their many guests and family. People were coming up to them and greeting Earnest with birthday greetings or little jabs and jokes about his age as the two of them moved through the crowd. Finally they made their way up to a raised stage, and it was Thomas who met them there.

"Soooo, Birthday Boy, I have the privilege of introducing you, and I have taken a lot of time in thinking of just what it is I wanted to say about you." With that said, Thomas pulled out a piece of paper that looked like cards with notes on them. He flicked the paper notes, and they fell towards the stage floor with what looked like 20 or so cards all joined together, to give the impression that he had a lot to say.

"Thomas, my friend, I really do appreciate you introducing me, but I would like to speak before I reach my sixtieth birthday, you know," Earnest said as he laughed and slapped his friend on the back. "I'm just kidding, buddy. Get up there and do your thing."

"Ladies and gentlemen," Thomas began. "Most of you know the man as Mr. Woodsworth, but tonight we are all just his friends here to celebrate yet another milestone in this man's life, so without any further ado, I would like to introduce to you the birthday boy himself, Mr. Earnest Bartholomew Woodsworth."

Again, an even louder roar went up from the crowd of guests, family and workers, both outside and inside the large stately home. The cheering continued for a few minutes as Earnest stepped up to the microphone after giving his best friend a big bear hug. Finally the cheers, whistles and applause settled down as Earnest began to speak.

"I am humbled by such appreciation," he started, his eyes sweeping the huge crowd. "So here it is, my 50th birthday and yet I only feel like I am 30 or so. My, how the years fly by. First let me say a big thank you to my lovely wife, Katherine, and my daughter, Caroline, who have put this party together."

A huge roar went up from the crowd below him in their appreciation as well for all the work put into the event.

"I also would like to thank my son Bart for being here tonight. We haven't always seen eye to eye, but, Bart, I want you to know, son, that I really do thank you for showing up," he said in Bart's direction at the family table.

Katie was wondering what Earnest would say now, seeing that as far as he was concerned, Franklin hadn't showed up.

Earnest hesitated, unsure of just how to continue without bringing up Franklin's name and all the pain associated with it. "I ... uh ... my other son ... was unable ... to ... make it tonight sadly," he managed to get out. As he looked up, something caught his eye. While all the others just stood below him, Earnest saw someone dressed in a black tux moving through the crowd from his right to his left, but his head was turned and Earnest just couldn't see who it was. The person was like one you would see in movies where he was sort of there and then gone as he moved amongst people. *This looks all too familiar,* he thought before continuing with his talk.

"But you are all here and I am thankful, truly thankful. I am a man who has achieved more than I ever thought would be possible and a lot of it was with your help. I think of so many of you who have helped me along the way. I could name you all, but then I would leave someone out and I am not into that. Please just find me sometime this evening so I can at least shake your ..." Earnest hesitated as he saw the man in the crowd again. This time, he was standing still, but he had his back to him now. He was about five rows back from himself within the crowd of guests.

"Uh ... sorry ... yes, let me shake your hand in appreciation for all your help in making me the man ..." The man was turning now, Earnest noticed, and he just had to see who it was. *Yes, I remember this man; he was the one at the golf course who was walking away from the crowd at the green after that very weird shot that gave both me and Thomas a hole-in-one,* Earnest finally realized.

Earnest just stared, unaware that all his guests were staring back at him, wondering what was going on. Then the man turned around and finally faced Earnest.

"Oh my Lord," Earnest whispered as he almost collapsed to the floor of the stage, but he caught himself just as Thomas moved to his side.

Both of them heard an audible gasp from the guests, who were thinking that there was something wrong with Earnest.

"Are you okay?" Thomas asked, unsure just what had happened.

Earnest said not a word. He stepped down from the stage and rushed into the crowd below until he was standing in front of the young man. He was shaking now as tears flowed from his eyes.

"F-Franklin, is it y-you?" he managed to get out in strained and whispered words.

At first, the young man said nothing, as he too was swept up in the emotions of this meeting. Then he simply stepped forward and took his father into his arms in a long overdue hug.

"Yes, Dad, it is me," was all that Franklin could get out as the two of them clung to each other and wept tears of joy.

"What is going on over there?" Bart said, trying to get a better look by standing on his chair.

"I don't know. There are too many people in the way," Winter said.

Thomas turned to Katie. "You knew, didn't you?"

Katie couldn't say anything at first as tears washed down her cheeks, but finally she whispered out, "Yes, but he wouldn't let me say anything."

"Franklin, oh, Franklin ... I am so sorry, my son, for how I neglected you!" Earnest cried out, caring not who was standing around, for his son was lost to him but now he was back and he would do his very best to make sure that he never left again.

Earnest never did finish his speech to his guests, but as word got around as to who it was in the crowd, people were overjoyed at the reunion of father and son.

"Bart, they are coming this way," Winter said as she caught sight of his father walking towards them with some man she didn't know.

"Who?" Bart said from his chair where he now was seated.

"Your father and some younger man."

Then they were right there at the table, and as Bart looked up at his father and then the guy with him, his mouth fell open as he jumped up from his chair in surprise.

"Franklin!" Bart shouted.

"Yes, little brother, it is me."

Bart rushed around the table, and the two brothers, who had been so close growing up, hugged each other tightly.

"It really is you!" Bart said as they stepped back from each other. "Slightly older than I remember, but it is you."

Earnest was still in a state of shock and really couldn't say much as Katie joined them. She gave her eldest son a big, long hug as Caroline came rushing over to the table after she heard the news.

"Wow! Caroline, is that you?" Franklin said as he took her all in. "You certainly have grown up since I saw you last."

Caroline, like her father, could not speak a word as she rushed into her brother's arms, and they just stood there hugging.

Winter felt like the odd person in this situation.

"Uh ... maybe I should just go," Winter said as she started to move away from the table.

"No, Winter, stay here please," Katie said as she went to her and placed an arm around her. "Franklin, I would like you to meet Winter, Bart's girlfriend."

Bart turned towards his mother about to say something when Katie just shot him a look that said, "Don't you dare say a word," and he backed down.

From then on, it was time for the family reunion. Franklin introduced his fiancée Julie to them all as they sat at their table and reminisced about days gone by with laughter and joking all around.

I love this family and sure would love to be a part of it all if Bart would just let me into his life, Winter was thinking in the midst of it all. She wasn't born yesterday. She knew Bart was wanting to dump her, but she had been praying about it and knew it was all in the Lord's hands now. As Winter sat there taking everything in that was happening around her, her mind drifted back to earlier days and growing up at home.

Her parents were strong Christians and made sure that their children were well versed in the Bible, went to Sunday school and church, but even so, Winter had a hard time when she was in her teens and interested in boys. She was just like any other girl her age, wanting to get married and raise a family with her husband at her side. The more she dated though, the more she felt distant from the young men who wanted her by their side.

Winter would pray into the night as she lay in her bed, asking the Lord to please send her that special one who would make her complete. She became so sad, that she stopped dating for a time and her parents became concerned, thinking that maybe she had been hurt by one of her dates. One day while Winter was giving her father a hand in the garden, her father stopped her and asked that they sit on the porch for a few minutes. The day was hot and the sun was shining in all its glory when they sat on the porch swing together. After a few silent minutes, her father began a conversation.

"Winter, honey, your mother and I are concerned about your sudden departure from your dating life and want to make sure that everything is ok?" He asked softly as they two of them continued swaying back and forth on the swing.

Winter was quiet for a few moments as emotions began to well up within herself, so much so that she stumbled over her first few words.

"D...dad ...I don't know what to tell you."

"Did someone hurt you in some way?"

"No ... it's not them." Winter said as the tears came to the surface.

"Uh ... well is it your sisters or even ... us?"

"Nooo dad, everything is ok that way, it's just ... me I guess and ... maybe God."

Winter's father was a little shocked at his daughter's words, seeing that he and his wife had always tried to raise the girls in a good and happy Christian atmosphere.

"God?" Was all he could think to say, wondering just where this was headed?

"Yes dad ... but not in a bad way. It's just that ... I ... uh ...have been praying to him every night for quite some time, wanting him to help me meet that special guy ... you know ... the one, but still I am alone."

"Ok then." Her father thought to himself with a small smile as he knew this was something he and his wife could handle.

"Winter honey, what exactly are you looking for when it comes to that special man in your life?"

"Oh dad, you know, it's all the stuff like you and mom have and that's not even what I am upset about. It's just that I always thought I would know when I met him that he was the one for me and so far that hasn't happened at all. The guys who have taken me out, have all been nice and treated me well, but still ..." Winter said as her words just trailed off and the tears took over.

Winters father said not a word and just reached for her and pulled her to his side until at last the tears subsided.

"I know you know this already Winter, but God does have someone special for you, somewhere in your future life. You are just going to have to give it over to God and let him do the rest. This does not mean that you can't date anymore, it just means that you won't settle down and get married until you know he is the right one for you ... and when you meet him you will know for certain that he is the one God has for you, no matter his state in life or where he lives."

That was the best advice anyone had even given Winter on dating, so she made a point of going on with her life until the right man came along. She moved to the big city where she attended college. From there she had a couple of retail jobs and that is where she and Bart first met.

Bart had come into the clothing store she was working in and had become frustrated at the fact that he couldn't find what he wanted. She had gone over to see if she could help him find what he was looking for and the first time their eyes met, Winter felt a flutter in her heart, not only from being in the presence of the man, but also from the Holy Spirit.

After just a few minutes of talking, while Bart tried to impress her with his words and subtle hidden messages, Winter knew beyond a shadow of a doubt that Bart was the one! Now here she was, sitting with Bart and his beautiful family that she longed to be part of, especially now that she knew Bart was the one for her, even though he didn't know it yet.

After a good time at their table, Caroline excused herself and headed over to the tented dance floor. Earnest and Katie both watched her go.

"She sure seems to be in a hurry to get in there," Earnest said, still looking in that direction.

"Yes, she is at that," Katie said.

"Anything I should know about it?"

"I will explain it to you later, if you don't figure it out before then."

"Okay."

"Also, my dear?"

"Yes?"

"Remember not to wear yourself out tonight," Katie said as she winked at him.

"There is no chance of that, my dear. It has been on my mind all day long," Earnest said as he leaned over and gave her a kiss.

Mmmm, now that is love, Winter thought as she caught sight of the kiss on the other side of the table.

"Bart, look at your parents. Isn't that lovely?" Winter whispered in Bart's direction as she lightly elbowed him in his side.

Why are you touching me, woman? Bart thought. "Give me a break, you two. Why don't you get a room?" Bart said loud enough for everyone at the table to hear.

"Who says we won't do that?" Earnest said, surprising everyone there, but it only disgusted Bart all the more.

"Gross!" was all Bart had to say while the others just laughed at his reaction.

"Well, everyone," Katie said, "the dance is about to begin, so let's all make our way over to our table there."

Everyone rose from the table and started to head in the direction of the tent. People around their table realized where they were heading, and soon they were followed by all the guests attending Earnest's birthday celebration that evening.

As the huge group of people neared the tent and dance floor, they heard the music start up with the pulsing song "Get Ready for This" by Champs United blaring through the sound system. Soon people were grinding to the strong beat before they entered the tent and without even getting a table.

"Wow!" Franklin said as he entered the tent. "This is quite the setup. I have been to quite a few dances, and never have I seen anything like this."

"Look up in the corners, hon," Julie said as she noticed the flashing screens in tune with the strong beat of the song usually heard at NHL hockey games.

Soon they were all seated at their family table as all around them people began to sit down, while many still remained on the dance floor.

"You will have to watch the screens when the next song comes on," Katie said loudly.

Then the song ended, and instead of the next song coming on, everyone could hear a mic being turned on.

"Hello, ladies and gentlemen. My name is Mitch, and I will be your DJ for tonight."

A huge roar suddenly rose up from all the people in attendance. Then as the applause settled down, Mitch began to talk again.

"Before we get this party going, please allow me to explain the sound system you see here before you. First, this is my workstation, providing tunes for you to dance to. Please do not approach me at my station but over to my right here," he said as he pointed at the small round table. "You will see four laptop computers that hold all the songs in my catalogue. Please make your way there sometime through the dance and follow the instructions there to have your favorite songs played tonight. Also, please remember to only pick two songs at a time in order that everyone who wishes to will have an opportunity to pick their songs.

"Okay, so now if you look up into each corner, you will see a large screen mounted there. When a song comes on, the words will be displayed on these screens for you to follow and sing along with if you wish. Over my workstation here is also a digital screen that will announce the song being played and the one coming up after it. This is will help you decide if you wish to stay on the dance floor for the next song or not.

"That is enough said for now, other than to wish Mr. Woodsworth a very happy birthday, and we have something special for him a little later on in the evening. Remember that there is still plenty of food and beverages out there, but we will also be having a light lunch around 11:30 too."

With that said, Caroline took the mic from Mitch to make another announcement.

"Forgive me for interrupting, but I also want to mention that the gift opening will be at the time of the light lunch, seeing that it was missed while my family reunited with my long-lost older brother," Caroline said as she looked over at Franklin.

Once again, there was a huge applause from the guests and staff close by.

Suddenly the main lights were shut off, and all of Mitch's lights and the readout were flicked on, along with a large mirror ball in the middle of the dance floor.

"Are you ready to *partyyyyy*?" Mitch yelled into his mic, which was met with a resounding "Yes!" from the guests, and suddenly the song "Old Time Rock and Roll" blared out, which had many up to the dance floor in an instant.

"Hey there, old timer, you ready to dance your tush off with me?" Katie said to Earnest as she pulled him up onto the dance floor.

Just as Mitch had said, the overhead digital screen was showing: "'Old Time Rock and Roll' ... Coming Next ... 'How Long' Eagles ...!" On the screens, in the corners, the words for the song playing could be seen: "Just give me that rock and roll ... That kinda music is good for the soul ... We reminisce about the days of old ... with that good old rock and roll ..."

"Now that is what I call a sound system," Thomas said, still seated at the table.

"Yes, I agree. I wonder where he got it from, as I haven't seen anything like it before," Franklin said just before Julie pulled him up on the floor as well.

"So, big boy, you and I gonna make it out there at all?" Shelly said, surprising Thomas, who knew that she didn't like to dance much in public.

"Yes, ma'am!" he said as he bounded up onto the dance floor with his wife.

Sitting at the table now all alone were Bart and Winter, as Bart had no intention of dancing with her.

Don't want her getting any ideas, Bart thought as he stared down into his drink.

Winter, however, was tapping her toe and singing along to the words on the screens, all the while just dying to get up on the floor and dance as well.

The song ended, and "How Long" by the Eagles started up right after the last beat of the last song.

"Hey there, brother, aren't you going dance with Winter tonight?" Caroline asked as she bounded over to the table from Mitch's side.

"Nope!" was all Bart had to say.

"What? Are you crazy? Just look at this woman, Bart; she is gorgeous, and you are turning her down? What is wrong with you anyway?"

Bart said not a word, while Winter just stared at him.

"Well, I am gonna find someone to dance with you," Caroline said, looking directly at Winter.

"It's okay, really," Winter said, but Caroline was having none of that as she left the table in her search.

"A-are you upset with me?" Winter asked Bart.

Bart thought for a moment before answering. "No ... just don't wanna dance," was all he said, still not looking at her.

"Okay," Winter whispered in disappointment.

"Don't Stop" by Fleetwood Mac was the next song up, and as it played, Thomas, Shelly, Katie and Earnest came back to the table.

"Bart ... son, aren't you gonna dance tonight with this very lovely woman here with you?" Earnest asked, unaware of Bart's feelings about most anything, let alone Winter.

"Nope!"

Earnest looked at Bart and then at Katie, who just shrugged her shoulders, knowing she couldn't force Bart to dance with her.

Just then, Franklin returned to the table where he held the chair for Julie. He quickly grabbed Winter by the hand and pulled her out onto the dance floor before she could even refuse.

"Well, there you go. Looks like Franklin is going to cover for you, son," Earnest said to Bart.

Soon everyone at the table was talking about this or that while Bart just stared at his drink, not joining into the conversation.

Idiots! Bart thought.

After "Honky Tonk Blues" by The Kentucky Headhunters, "Hard Day's Night" by The Beatles, "Playin' in a Travellin' Band" by CCR, and "Boogie-Woogie Man," the music went silent and the mic was once more turned on.

"Okay, now this next song is only for the birthday boy and his wife. When we go to the song after it, you may join them on the dance floor for a more subdued time of dance and reflection," Mitch said.

There was a pause before the song "Color My World" by Chicago began to play. With the soft, slow piano strains in the song starting up, Earnest and Katie walked out onto the dance floor for a soft, slow waltz as the guests softly applauded them.

"This is my favorite song of all time, you know?" Earnest whispered into his wife's ear as they slowly made their way around the dance floor.

"How do you think he got the idea to play it, silly?" Katie said as she pulled in even closer to this man she deeply loved.

"Just how many songs did you tell him I liked?"

"A few."

As the song died down, the overhead digital readout was showing the next song: "Peaceful Easy Feeling" by the Eagles," and no sooner did it start than couple after couple began to join them on the dance floor.

"This truly is a peaceful, easy feeling, you know?" Earnest said to Katie as they continued dancing in each other's arms.

When the song was winding down, Earnest figured that the music would go to a faster song, but the screen showed next "Hey Jude" by The Beatles, and everyone just stayed on the dance floor, still dancing in the waltz mood.

"Don't they look so much in love?" Julie said to Franklin, as she hung on his arm at the table.

"Mmmm, yes," he answered her.

"Something on your mind?" she asked.

"Just wondering how they will react to our announcement is all."

"They will be okay, hon. Just leave it to the Lord; he knows what he is doing."

"Yes, you are right," Franklin said as he turned and gave her a light kiss.

The night continued, as did the songs. Earnest's favorite rock song "Get Back" by The Beatles came up next, followed by a swing tune by Don Messer and then "The Beer Barrel Polka" for all those who loved to dance the polka.

"This guy is very good in his selections of music. I am sure I have never heard any better at any dances I have ever been at," Franklin said. "But why the DJ? I would have thought you would have hired a live band for the dance?"

"Well, that was Caroline's decision, and I think there is more to it than just the music and setup we see here," Katie said as she looked at Caroline, sitting beside Mitch at his station.

"I have noticed that too," Shelly said as Thomas just nodded.

"What 'more' are you talking about?" Earnest asked his wife.

It was quiet for a few moments, other than the song "Mercury Blues" blasting away in the background.

"It's her new boyfriend!" Bart blurted out, tired of the conversation and the boring dances he was being forced to endure.

"Boyfriend?" Earnest asked with raised eyebrows.

"We will talk about it later, hon," Katie said, shooting looks at Bart across the table.

The rest of the evening flew by without a hitch, but because of the large number of cards and gifts that Earnest received for his 50th birthday, it was announced that the gift and card opening would be held in the dance tent the following day at 3:00 p.m. and that everyone was welcome to attend.

CHAPTER ELEVEN

"How are you doing, hon?" Katie asked Earnest as they were getting ready for bed in the wee hours of the morning.

"I am okay. How about you?"

"I will be there shortly," she replied from her dressing room.

"Okay, sweetie," Earnest said as he lay back in their bed, thinking about all that had happened earlier that day.

"What you thinking about so hard?" Katie asked as she slid into bed beside her husband.

"Oh ... just reflecting back on the day and all that happened."

"Were you pleased with it all?"

Earnest was suddenly at a loss for words, wondering just how he could ever put his true feelings into words for her, so instead, he put his arms around her and drew her to him.

"I love you," he finally managed to get out.

"Love you too," she said as she snuggled even closer.

They were silent for a few moments, just relaxing in each other's arms.

"Did you know?" Earnest finally asked.

Katie knew what he was asking but wanted to make sure before she answered. "Know what, hon?"

"That Franklin would be there?"

"Yes."

"Oh."

"He had phoned me awhile before your birthday and told me that you had phoned him."

"Oh … yeah, guess I should have told you about that."

"It's okay. I'm not upset about it."

"Okay, that's good, because it was never my intention to withhold it from you. He never said a word while I talked to him, so I had no idea whether he would show up or not," Earnest said softly.

"Well, when he called me, he asked me not to tell you, as he wanted it to be a surprise."

"Oh, it was a surprise all right. I almost had a heart attack when I realized it was really him standing there in the crowd," Earnest said with a silly grin on his face. "I know we talked a lot after that, but I still have one question I would like him to answer."

"What's that?"

"Why did he come? I mean, after all these years of not hearing a peep from him, he just decides to show up? That is not like him at all, and I guess I would just like to know why."

Katie was silent for the longest time, which told Earnest that she knew why, but he wasn't going to pressure her or Franklin, for that matter. They would have to tell him first.

"Do you know the story about his fiancée Julie? We were talking about her at the table, but I wasn't sure if you were there or up and about visiting with your guests."

"Actually no, I never heard it, but would love to know more about her. I was surprised when he introduced her to us. I mean, I never thought he would marry a sophisticated woman or anything like that, but she is so … uh … plain."

"Plain? What do you mean?" Katie asked as she sat back against the headboard of their bed and looked at him.

"Don't take me wrong here; I am not complaining at all. I think she is a very lovely woman, and I can see that they both love each other deeply, but I guess what I am trying to say is that she is kinda a woodsy girl or maybe the proverbial girl-next-door type."

"Well, hon, you have to remember that Franklin was a woodsy kind of man himself. That is why he got into the log-building business. I would think that he was attracted to the same type of woman—just like Julie."

"Yes, I guess that makes sense."

"Anyway Julie's parents were both killed by a drunk driver when she was very young. She apparently has no relatives that she knows of, because when her parents died, she was placed into the foster system. She was moved around a lot and really made no connection to any of her foster parents. Finally she was able to live on her own and got a job as a waitress in a roadside café.

"This was where the two of them met. She was working in the café, and Franklin was working on a large log home for some corporate CEO. Franklin would often drop into the café on his way to the job site, and that is how they met. After a few weeks of dropping in and just chatting with her as she served him, he finally asked her out for coffee, and the rest is history."

"Well, I think he has chosen wisely," Earnest said with a slight sigh.

"There is more to her story though, if you are up to hearing it," Katie said.

"Might as well hear it all."

"Okay then. Franklin told me that Julie had a wild side to her life before they met, probably due to being shuffled around within the foster system, but by the time they met, she had settled down some. He told me though that she was searching for something in her life and wasn't finding any answers."

"What was she looking for?"

"Peace! Peace with herself and the fact that she was all alone in the world. It must be hard to know that you have no living parents, siblings or even relatives."

"Yes, I would think so."

"Anyway, she finally made friends with one of the other waitresses in the café, and they became very good friends long before she met Franklin. The one thing though about her friend was that she was a Christian, and over time, her friend finally convinced her to go to church with her one Sunday morning."

"Oh ... okay," Earnest said quietly, not wanting to argue with his wife about religion after all she had done for him earlier with his birthday celebrations. "So did anything happen to her at church?" he asked, surprising Katie that he sounded interested.

"Well, yes. They had gone to a Pentecostal church that was very lively, with a great band and a very on fire praise and worship group leading, but it was the sermon that really touched Julie that day. The pastor was preaching about the prodigal son."

What? This is just getting way too weird, Earnest thought, as he had heard all about the Bible story from Thomas when they were out golfing.

"Oh really?" he said, looking directly at Katie now.

"Uh ... do you know the story?" Katie asked, very surprised now.

"Actually I do."

"Where did you hear it?"

"From Thomas when we were out golfing the second-to-last time."

"Wow, well, that is news to me," Katie said with a big smile at the fact that Thomas was making the effort to try to reach Earnest for the Lord. "I think that in the future we are going to have to work on our communications."

"Ha! Yep," Earnest said with a little laugh. "But please continue with Julie's story."

"Okay, the story goes that the sermon definitely spoke to Julie—not right away, but over the next few weeks, as she began attending church with her friend. Then one day when she was really down, feeling all alone, she cried out to God about it and instantly felt a peace, like God actually was giving her a real hug."

"Really? God would actually do that? I thought he was kinda ... you know ... out there, but not really here with us."

"Earnest, are you telling me that you believe in God?"

Earnest hesitated with that question, not wanting his wife to get the idea that he would be going to church with her and all.

"Well, yes ... yes, I do, but that is the extent of it. I am not into this Jesus stuff like you and Caroline are. I do think that there is a God out there, somewhere. I just can't believe that all of this just happened by chance and at the same time I do believe that God or whomever, took the time to create everything we see around us."

Thank you, Lord, Katie thought. *He might not know you, but at least he has a footing in you and something myself and Thomas can work towards.*

"That is very true, hon, about creation and the fact that God has made everything we see around us—including us too," Katie said with a big smile as she sat in their bed, facing Earnest on the other side.

"So what happened after the hug?" Earnest asked, still interested in hearing more obviously.

"To make the story short, Julie gave her life to the Lord and is now a Christian."

"She is?"

"Yes, sir."

"Okay, hon. That is a great story, and I am very happy for her, because I know that you are a happy person in your faith too. But I still need to know why Franklin is here, and please make it short, as it is quite late and I still want to take you up on your earlier comments," he said as he gave her a wink.

"Oh, you still think you are up for that, birthday boy?"

"Hey, it's been on my mind all day long as I have said before, and I am hoping you bought something special for the occasion too."

"Why do you think I am still wearing this silk robe, silly?"

"Mmmmm, you are just too good to me, you know."

"Only because I love you."

"And I love you right back, Mrs. Woodsworth."

"But in answer to your question, hon, yes, Julie is a Christian now and Franklin is too," Katie said. She leaned over and gave Earnest a kiss on his cheek; she could see the dots in his mind all connecting together.

"A Christian? ... Franklin is a Christian?" he said with surprise written all over his face. "Okay, then, yes, I guess that makes sense. It would have taken a major change in his life to get him to come home, and I could see God helping him with that," Earnest said as he plopped back down into his pillow.

Katie knew that the time for talking was over, and she slid out of bed and padded around to his side where she simply stood before him and let the silk gown slide down to the soft rug beneath her feet. She was pleased that he was pleased with what he saw just before she leaned over and playfully fell on top of him.

It was another glorious morning when both Katie and Earnest strolled out of the house arm in arm onto the now-clean stone patio. They were both amazed to see that everything was cleaned up and cleared away with the exception of the dance tent, which would be used later that day for the gift and card opening.

"I thought we told the staff to take the rest of the evening off after the party," Earnest said as he looked around.

"I think they were very happy with all the events that happened yesterday, including your tips that they just wanted to make you even happier today."

"Okay, I appreciate that, but I hope they don't think they are getting a tip like that again today," Earnest said with a silly grin.

"Oh you!" Katie said as she gave him a playful jab in his side.

"Mind you, after last night, I might just give everyone I see today a tip."

Katie just blushed a little and said nothing. She just welcomed the appreciation he was implying.

"You make this man very happy, Mrs. Woodsworth."

"Well, thank you, kind sir, and I had a fantastic time as well—just so you know."

They then walked over to the family table, which had been extended in order that eight people could be seated.

"Why eight? There will only be the family and Julie, which comes to six, I believe," Earnest said with raised eyebrows.

"I know that the family and Julie will be joining us, but I also invited two others to join us, I hope you don't mind?"

"Oh, no problem, as I do love Thomas and Shelly's company."

"It won't be Shelly and Thomas, love."

"Really? Well, who then?"

"Mitch and Winter."

"Ummm ... okay. Well, Mitch I understand, but why Winter? Are she and Bart an item that I haven't heard about, because if they are, then I am very disappointed in the way he treated her last night."

"No, they are not an item, but she and I have formed this special bond and I would like her to be part of the family even if it is without Bart's approval."

Earnest pondered that request for a few moments while Maria brought out their refreshments before returning to the house.

"Okay, my dear. I have always trusted your judgement, and besides that, I do like Winter as well."

With that said, both Earnest and Katie turned around to the words "Good morning, you two," from Franklin as he and Julie, hand in hand, walked out onto the patio to join them.

Earnest was up in a flash, followed closely by Katie, as they all hugged each other before sitting back down at the table, which was adorned with a very lovely flower-and-lace tablecloth.

"Franklin, I am so happy that you will still be with us today before you head back. Your visit has made me a very happy man indeed," Earnest said across the table.

"Just that?" Katie said with a sly smile.

Earnest chuckled softly. "No, not just that," he said as he leaned over and kissed Katie on the cheek.

"See, Julie, I told you that my parents are a picture of true love," Franklin said as Julie snuggled in close to his side.

"I knew that from the very first moment we met," she said with a beaming smile.

"Well, thank you, you two, those are very nice words," Katie said.

Suddenly there was a commotion in the house with someone shouting something, and then Bart came stumbling out onto the patio.

"Okay. Dunno what is so important that you want to see me this early ..." Bart was saying before he realized just who was at the table. "Uh ... oh ... hi there," was all he managed to get out.

"Bart, son, come sit with us at the table," Earnest said as he stood up to greet his son.

Bart said not a word but quickly sat at one end of the table, trying to avoid looking at anyone directly. His clothes were dishevelled, almost as if he had slept in them, which he had, but he wasn't about to let them know that.

"So is there a specific reason you wanted us all here today?" Franklin asked.

"There most definitely is," Earnest said with a large, beaming smile.

"May I ask what it is?" Franklin said.

"How about we wait until everyone is here first," Katie said this time.

"Yep, sure, no problem," said Franklin as he lounged back in his chair with his sweetie by his side.

Bart said nothing; he just sat there sulking.

Soon Caroline came bounding out of the house, smiling and happier than normal, it seemed.

"So what are you so happy about, Sis?" Franklin said, liking the sound of that on his lips after all this time.

"Oh, just things."

"Oh and do those things include a certain someone?" Katie asked.

"Maybe," Caroline said with a sly grin.

"Someone named Mitch perhaps?" Earnest asked this time,

which kind of threw his daughter off. She didn't realize that her father knew about her newest friend.

"Y-you know about him?" Caroline asked cautiously.

"Yes, I do."

"Uh ... okay."

"Your mom and I do talk, you know."

"Okay, I can see that now."

"Well, we are your parents after all," Katie interjected.

"Yes, I know that."

"And all we want is the best for you and the rest of you too," Earnest said as he looked each of his children in the eyes.

"Are we actually going to eat or not?" Bart finally said from his end of the table with a very sarcastic tone of voice.

"Hey, little brother, you got a bee up your pants or what?" Franklin asked, giving his brother the look.

"We will all be eating soon, but we are just waiting for two more to arrive first," Katie said.

"Who's that?" Bart asked, a bit calmer this time.

"You will see. I sent the car for them, and they should be here any moment."

"The car? You actually sent the driver and the car?" Bart said.

"Yes. Why not?" Katie said to her son.

"Ha! You never use the car unless it is someone really important, so why now?"

"Well, let's just say that some things have changed and will change even more around here," Earnest said with a little more fatherly authority in his voice, which made Bart quiet down.

The one thing that Earnest and Katie made sure to instill in their children was respect, especially for them as parents, for relatives, the elderly, and others in general, so when their father spoke in a certain voice, as he had just done, each one of them knew what that meant and how to react, even though Bart fought it with all he had. The only reason he did as he was told, even though reluctantly, was because of the money he received. He knew his parents didn't have to give him any money, so with that in mind he kind of towed the line - at least in his mind.

They all just sat in silence as they waited for the others to arrive, and finally after about 10 minutes, they heard voices in the house and all turned to see who was about to come out of the house onto the stone patio.

"What the ...?" Bart shouted as he jumped to his feet, pushing back on his chair so suddenly that it fell over backwards. "What is *she* doing here?"

"She is here because I invited her," Katie said as she rose from her chair to greet Winter. She gave her a big, warm hug.

"Oh!" Caroline said as a big, sudden smile washed over her face at the sight of Mitch. She jumped up to give him a tight hug as well and then Winter too.

Next, Earnest rose and greeted the two them with a hug before everyone finished the greetings and sat down at the table. Within mere minutes, the household staff began to bring out the pans of food that they had placed in the buffet-style warmers on a separate table just behind the table that everyone was seated at.

Before any of them got themselves some food, all eyes turned to Earnest as he began to speak.

"Franklin asked earlier if there was a reason we were all gathering today, and I just want to address that question now. The reason we are here is because this is the first time in over eight years that we have been able to sit down as a family for a meal."

"Not everyone here is family," Bart said, looking down at his drink.

"Your mother will be talking about that soon enough, so until then, Bart, I ask that you remain silent. Is that clear?"

Bart said nothing, but Earnest wasn't letting him get away with it this time. "Is that clear, Bart?" he said with a sharp voice while looking directly at his son.

"Yes," Bart whispered, still looking down.

"Yes, what?"

"Yes ... sir."

Wow! Winter thought to herself. *He does know how to respect others. Too bad he just isn't that way all the time.*

"Good. Now let me continue," Earnest said. "Your mother and I don't know how long it will be before we can all get together again, seeing that Franklin will be returning home, am I right?" he asked, looking at Franklin now.

"Uh ... yes, we will be returning within the next couple of days."

"So we wanted to have this alone time with you all today and then again this afternoon at the gift and card opening under the tent. So now I am going to let Katie say a few words before we eat breakfast," he said as he turned towards her, smiled and then sat down.

Katie never stood but rather talked to them from where she sat, with Caroline at her side and Mitch beside her.

"First let me say that through prayer and in talking with the Lord, I have felt him instruct me in what I am about to say.

"My heart is overjoyed that your father and I are sitting here with you today, our family together once more, but the Lord was the one who asked me to invite Winter and Mitch here today. I have felt in my heart from the first time that I met Winter that we share a common bond, of what I am unsure so far, but know that it will be revealed to me soon enough. So I invited you," she said as she looked at Winter across the table.

"I can't really explain it, but I want you to know that from this day forth, you will be considered as part of this family anytime we get together in part or as a whole, and the same goes for you, Mitch. This is the will of God, I believe, and he will reveal his will when his timing is right. Also, you two, this means you are free to come and go in this house and on these grounds anytime you wish and use any of the amenities we have at your disposal. That means the pool, tennis courts, hot tubs, vehicles and all the others that we will show you in the days ahead."

As Katie looked at Winter, she smiled at the tears rolling down her reddened cheeks and smiled as well at the look of blessed amazement on Mitch's face as Caroline clung to his arm. Bart, however, had a very sour, angry look on his face.

"Let us all hold hands to ask the Lord's blessing on this food," Katie continued.

Bart absolutely did not want to participate in any way, at least until he saw his father looking sternly at him, and quickly he complied.

"Lord God our Father in heaven, I come before you today on behalf of our newfound family. I ask, Lord, that you will bless this food that we are about to partake and that you would bless those who prepared it for us. Also, Lord, I ask that you will continue to draw us even closer together over the weeks, months and years ahead, and I ask it all in your name. Amen!"

The breakfast meal was excellent, and they ate with a little talking here and there. Then when the meal dishes were cleared away and their beverages were topped up, they began to get back into conversation. Bart was raring to get going, with no desire whatsoever to be a part of this any longer, but then he also knew he had to stay or risk losing some of his toys.

"You know, little brother," Franklin said in Bart's direction, "I was just telling Julie earlier this morning about some of the fun times were used to have in this family, in particular with you."

Bart just sort of grinned at his brother's words but still had no intention of participating, so Franklin just kept on talking.

"Yes, I can remember all that curly hair you used to have."

"Oh yeah and all the fun things you used to do to that hair too." Caroline piped up.

Franklin never said a word at her words though, knowing that she was right.

"Well, yes, and then your dad and I were the ones who had to deal with the fallout," Katie said with a rather stern look on her face.

Bart never said a word.

"Well, that hair was just so inviting," Franklin said.

"What kind of things did you do?" Winter asked this time, slowly getting used to the family.

"Ha!" Earnest piped up this time. "There were so many; where would we even start?"

Yeah, like you were a part of any of it, Bart thought, doubting that his father even had anything to do with any of them.

"I do remember the time when Bart was asleep and you put peanut butter in his hair and then just a little on his upper lip—just enough to have him itching there. Soon there was peanut butter everywhere, on his clothes, on the bed, all over his face and definitely in his hair," Earnest said, laughing out loud at the remembrance of it.

Franklin and Caroline were chuckling right along as well, but Katie had a not-so-happy look on her face at the recollection.

"Do you all know how long it took me to get that peanut butter out of his hair? In the end, I just had to cut most of it off," Katie said rather loudly, but that only served to have everyone at the table laughing away—with the exception of Bart.

"Yes, but remember, dear, that Bart wasn't always the perfect little angel either. How about the time he tried to set a fire in the window well at the back of the first house," Earnest said, looking at Bart first and then at Katie.

"Yes, hon, you are right; there were some trying times with that boy, then and now," Katie said, which at least had Bart look up at her.

"Well, at least I was the perfect little angel and nobody can deny that," Caroline said with a big smile.

"What? Are you kidding?" Franklin spoke up again, looking directly at his little sister. "How about that time when I was babysitting you and Bart? Mom and Dad had to do some shopping and just wanted some alone time, so I volunteered to watch the two of you guys."

"No, Franklin, please don't go there," Caroline said with a plea in her eyes.

"Go where?" Earnest asked.

"Yes, go where?" Katie added.

"Well, the little angel here invited some of her friends over that afternoon, as I recall, and they were all in her room, listening to music and just shooting the breeze. There was a phone call for her from some guy, and even though I called loudly, she never came to the phone, so I just went to get her. When I opened the door, this huge wave of cigarette smoke washed all over me. There on the bed lay Caroline on her back, cigarette in her mouth and a very shocked look on her face, along with all her girlfriends too."

"What?" Katie and Earnest said at the same time.

"How come we never heard of this before?" Katie demanded to know.

"Care to answer that, Sis?" Franklin asked, leaving the ball in her court now.

Caroline was in some sort of mild shock. She had always prided herself in the fact that her parents thought she could do no wrong, but now the truth was out and words would not come to her.

"Caroline?" Katie asked loudly.

"Well, obviously she can't say anything, and I think her halo is a little off-kilter now, so I will fill that part in as well.

Caroline looked at her brother now, shaking her head from side to side.

"Well, they want to know, and who am I to lie to them, Sis?"

Bart was now looking at Caroline too, wanting to hear what she had to say.

"Well … I … uh … I …" Caroline tried to say in her defense, but the words would not come.

"What she is trying to say," Franklin cut in, "is that she begged me not to say a word to you or Dad about it and she promised to do anything I asked of her if I would hold my mouth."

Caroline's head was down now. She was not looking at anyone, and she even withdrew her hand from Mitch's. Shame and worry consumed her now at what her parents and siblings would think of her.

"Hey, c'mon, Sis; this is all just in fun. A recollection of the fun times we once used to have as a family," Franklin said as he tried to get her to look at him across the table.

"Ha! Yeah, right!" Bart snorted out, much to the amazement of everyone there.

"All right, everyone, enough is enough," Earnest said. "We all have skeletons in our personal closets that we don't want anyone to know about. It is what makes us human, and it doesn't mean that we are bad in any way. Caroline, I am sure that everyone of us here has had a smoke or a drink at one time in our lives, but that doesn't make us bad."

"Your father is right. Even he and I have had things in our lives that we don't want to be reminded of, so let's get over it all right now," Katie said, softening her voice as she did.

They all talked a little more about everyday things.

"Bart, you are free to leave now if you wish," Katie said, and in one quick movement, Bart was up from the table and in the house before another word was spoken.

"Caroline, why don't you take Mitch and Winter on a tour of the house and grounds while your dad and I spend a little time with Franklin and Julie," Katie suggested of her daughter.

"Sure!" Caroline said as she rose from the table, followed by Mitch and Winter.

"Winter, I would love to talk with you when you are done with your tour," Katie said.

"Okay," Winter responded before she turned and caught up with the other two.

"Mom and Dad, Julie and I have something very important that we want to share with you right now, if you don't mind," Franklin said.

"Sure, son, anything," Earnest said. "How about we all move over to the sitting area first. That way, we can all get a little more comfortable."

Soon, all four of them were seated with Katie and Earnest on the outdoor wicker sofa and Franklin and Julie sat close together on the wicker love seat.

Earnest loved seeing his son obviously in love with Julie as the two of them sat very close together, almost hanging on to each other. However, the biggest joy in his life right then was the fact that his son was home, that all the anger Franklin used to hold against him was gone, replaced by this amazing love and joy he had found in Jesus. *Can Jesus really change a person like that?* he thought as Franklin began to speak.

"Well, we have this thing that we want to talk to you about. We have given it a lot of consideration and feel that now is the time to tell you."

"Tell us what, hon?" Katie said.

Franklin and Julie first looked at each other before continuing.

"We are planning on moving!"

Oh no! Earnest thought. *I have just gotten my son back, and now they are going to be moving even farther away?*

"Moving?" Katie asked, shocked as much as Earnest at the words. "Where?"

Franklin's face then broke out into a huge smile. "Here!"

"Wha ...?" Earnest asked, unsure of just what he meant.

"Back to the city."

"Oh, Franklin, that is wonderful!" Katie almost shouted for joy.

"Back here? You mean back to this city?" Earnest asked as he had to make sure he heard Franklin right.

"Yes, Dad."

Then Earnest could hold back no longer and broke down into tears with his wife at his side and his son and future daughter-in-law standing around him with their hands on his shoulders.

"It's okay, Dad. Everything is going to be okay!" Franklin said as he too cried tears of joy.

CHAPTER TWELVE

After the initial news of Franklin and Julie moving back to the city wore off, Franklin took a little time to talk to his mother alone, just before the gift and card opening started.

"Mom, we are going to be in need of something that I am sure you can help us out with," Franklin said to his mother just outside of the tented area.

"What's that?" Katie asked.

"Well, Julie and I will need a place to live after we are married. We are planning on having the marriage ceremony shortly after we move back here, so we will need a place to live once we get back from our honeymoon."

"Okay, and what would you like me to do for you then?"

"Do you think you would have time to look for a house for us?"

"Yes! I would love to do that. Would it be okay if Caroline helped me look?"

"Sure, no problem with that."

"So do you have any ideas on what you would like for a house?"

"Actually, yes, we do. We would like at least a three-bedroom home, preferably something with some character, not just a box-shaped home like a lot of them are. We would really like a country-style home with a high peaked roof, veranda all around the house, two-car garage with possible dormers and a stone fireplace."

"Well, that shouldn't be too hard to locate. Do you want it right in the city or out in the countryside, like ours?"

"Given the choice, we would prefer the countryside, as we have found that lifestyle most comfortable in the past couple of years that we have known each other."

"Okay, we will see what we can come up with. We can take pictures of what we find and e-mail them to you if you would like."

"Yes, that will work," Franklin said as he rose from his chair, but before he left to join the others inside the tent, he had one final word. "One other thing, Mom ... please don't buy the house for us."

Later that day at the gift and card opening for Earnest's 50th birthday, Franklin made a point of talking with his brother, Bart.

"So, little brother, I have heard that you are quite good at racquetball?" Franklin said as he pulled up a chair next to Bart.

"Who told you that?" Bart asked, surprised that his brother even knew.

"Dad."

Bart hesitated, surprised that his father would even take notice of his abilities, let alone racquetball.

"Dad told you that I was good?"

"Yep."

"Okay, so what's up then?" Bart asked, becoming interested in the conversation now.

"Just wondered if you would like to take me on in a game?"

"You?"

"Yes."

"You know how to play?"

"Yes, I do."

Bart thought that over for a few moments before responding. "Yeah, but are you any good?"

"League champion a couple of years ago."

"Really?" Bart asked, amazed. *Maybe now I can have a challenging, serious game with someone finally*, he thought.

"So you up for it?"

"You bet!" Bart said with a wide smile on his face that did not go unnoticed by Winter and Katie alike.

"Okay, well, let's set up a time to have a game or two before Julie and I leave later tomorrow evening."

"That soon?" Bart said with a twinge of disappointment in his voice.

"Yes, sadly. I have this house I am working on that has a deadline, and my crew are anxiously awaiting my return to the job."

"Okay."

"You figure out a time and place that we can play and let me know," Franklin said, and he gave Bart a pat on the back before rejoining the others.

Bart was anxious to have a game with his brother, so he wasted no time in setting it up at the Woodsworth Industries International offices the very next afternoon at 2:00 p.m. He let Franklin know of the time and said he would see him there.

Franklin, in turn, told his mother, who told Earnest, and when it was time for the game to begin, the viewing area was full to overflowing with family members, some of the corporate officers and workers who knew of Bart's reputation on and off the court.

"What the ...?" Bart said to himself when he walked out of the change rooms and into the racquetball court area.

"Uh ... what's with all the people?" Bart asked Franklin as the two of them met for the game.

"Well, I mentioned it to Mom and this is the result, I guess."

"Okay," was all Bart had to say. He just didn't really want a crowd around if things got a little wild in the game. He had no intention of hurting his brother, but he also knew that he had no intention of losing either.

The two brothers did a little warm-up, stretching their legs, arms and backs, as racquetball was a game that made use of almost every muscle and part of the body with an intensity that would wear down most healthy people in mere minutes.

Then the first game was on, and very shortly, Bart knew that he had finally met his match. It took a good 10 minutes before Bart finally scored, but his brother rebounded right back with two more points back-to-back, and he took the lead. From there, the game was fast-paced, back-and-forth action that had almost everyone holding his or her breath to see just who would win. In the end, Bart took the first game, followed by Franklin taking the second one.

So now it was down to the best of three games with both brothers each having a game win. This time around, it took almost 20 minutes before Franklin scored the first point, which caused Bart to become a bit more worked up at the thought of losing to his brother, something that he would not let happen at any cost, even if that meant playing dirty.

The problem was though that they were playing in front of family and, more important, in front of their mother. Bart knew that if he intentionally hurt Franklin with the ball, he could pretty much say good-bye to his cars and toys and so the conflict within him raged. Then Franklin scored another point, and Bart's anger began to seethe within him.

There is no way you are beating me! Bart was thinking. *I am the best of the best ... I am the king of racquetball, and soon everyone will be saying my name when it comes to this game.* But then Franklin almost scored again, and for the first time in his racquetball career, Bart realized that he could actually lose and that was when he snapped.

Bart then began to set his brother up, making sure that the little rubber ball was moving to the left side of the court with each play in order that he could play his "death stroke" as he called it and end the game once and for all. Finally the ball would be exactly where he needed it to be on the very next play. The ball made its way back to him off the wall in front of the two sweating

men, and Bart swung back his arm to finalize the game, when all
of a sudden, the paddle fell from Bart's hand and swung wildly,
still tethered to his arm.

"Ahhhhhh!" Bart screamed in pain as it radiated out of his
right arm just above his elbow. It had returned, and within
moments, Franklin was at his brother's side, trying to comfort
him as his screaming filled the entire court and lower level of the
building.

Earnest, Katie, Julie and Winter were at his side as well when
the EMTs arrived and tried to calm Bart down, but what they
didn't know was that the pain was at its full intensity and was not
leaving anytime soon.

Bart was rushed to the ER at the university hospital on the
west side where he was rolled into a secure room, due mostly to
his screaming. The EMTs had tried everything they could to get
the young man to calm down, but any painkillers they gave him
had absolutely no effect and they were at a loss as to how to help
control the pain.

"I am sorry to have to do this," one EMT in the ambulance said
as he placed a strip of bandage over Bart's mouth in order to cut
back on the loudness of his screams and moaning.

Bart was clutching his right arm, and even though he tried
to reach for the bandage over his mouth, as soon as he did so,
his hand shot straight back to his arm and the excruciating pain
there.

As the nurses and doctors came to his aid, the EMTs gave
them all of Bart's vital signs, along with their reasoning for the
tape over his mouth. The tape was removed, and Bart's screaming
continued. The doctors eventually had to replace it while they
tried to assess the problem with his right arm.

X-rays were taken along with a CT scan, blood work, and
vitals, but all to no avail and after about four hours, they were
stumped.

"I am sorry, but there is no logical reason for your son's

reaction to whatever it is that he thinks is hurting him," the ER doctor on call said to Bart's parents and siblings.

"Is there anything at all that you can do for him?" Earnest asked, obviously shaken by this bout of pain.

"We have given him the maximum amount of morphine that we can, and it has had absolutely no effect. We are now going to administer something to help him sleep and hopefully that will subdue the pain and help your son relax."

"Okay," Earnest said as Katie clung to his side.

"I am going to have you wait for a while yet until the sleep aid does its work, but when you see him again, hopefully he will be sleeping. This, unfortunately, will be the only way you will be able to see him for a while, at least until we can find a way to control the pain."

Katie and Earnest just nodded their heads in approval. Then the doctor turned and left the private waiting room adjacent to the ER area.

"What are we going to do now?" Earnest asked, obviously shaken by this turn of events. He had seen Bart in pain like this once before, but the pain quickly left him and he was good after that. This time, however, the pain didn't seem to be letting up and the doctors were basically saying that they were at a loss for an answer.

It took a while, but eventually the medication worked, and Bart fell asleep. Just as the doctors suspected, as soon as Bart fell asleep, the pain was gone and finally there was peace somewhat in that section of the ER unit. The tape was removed, and the nurses made sure that Bart's body was comfortable for the duration.

"We will be moving him to a bed in a private room soon that is used in cases like this," one of the nurses was telling Katie and Earnest, just after they had filled out the paperwork to have their son admitted to the hospital.

"What kind of a room is that?" Franklin asked as he stepped up towards the nurse and his parents.

"It is a soundproof room, as occasionally we get patients, such as your brother, who are in so much pain that it can get quite loud at times, so then they are moved to the room."

"Okay, that makes sense, I guess," Franklin said.

"Hopefully when he wakes up, the pain will be gone and then they can try to figure out just what it is all about. He has no physical reason to be in pain like that, so why is he?" Earnest asked, not really expecting an answer from anyone.

"Mr. and Mrs. Woodsworth, my colleagues and I would like to talk to you about your son's condition," the doctor said as the five of them sat in a finely furnished office up on the sixth wing of the university hospital.

It had now been five days with no solution in sight for Bart's continuing pain. When he was asleep, there was no pain at all, but as soon as he awoke, the pain immediately returned in its full force. The doctors had ordered that he be fed by tube and also that he be fitted for a catheter, to help with his bodily functions.

"We are sorry to report that all of our efforts to control your son's pain have failed. We have taken every test possible, with the exception of one, and can find no reasonable explanation for his condition. We do not feel that this condition is life-threatening but also realize that this pain will be ongoing with no relief in sight while he is conscious."

"What other test?" Katie asked.

The doctors looked at each other before answering the question.

"The test involves a psychological examination, but due to Bart's ongoing pain, we don't see how such a test would be possible."

"You mean you want him to talk to a shrink?" Earnest spat out. "He is not crazy."

"We are not suggesting that he is, Mr. Woodsworth, but we feel that the problems he is experiencing are from within and not from any physical condition."

"So if he can't have the test because of the pain he 'thinks' he is in, do you have any other suggestions?" Franklin asked.

"We have two suggestions, but please know that they are very aggressive in nature and will most certainly change his and your lives for sure."

The room became quiet at the doctor's words, and fear began to slowly creep into Earnest's heart, while Katie and Franklin were saying silent prayers.

The ER doctor finally spoke again.

"These possibilities are not life-threatening in any way, but they may alter Bart's life for a few years if not forever."

"O-okay," Katie whispered. "Tell us please."

One of the other doctors stood now and approached the family.

"The first suggestion will be the least traumatic in your son's case, and it involves putting him into an induced coma for an indefinite period of time until we can figure out what the problem is or until a technological advance comes along that can help him."

"A-and the second one?" Katie asked again.

This time, it was the third doctor's turn to approach the family.

"I know this will sound quite drastic, and we want you to take all the time you need to consider it, but the one way that we do know to remove the pain is to remove the source of that pain." The doctor then paused to let the implication sink in.

"You mean remove the arm, don't you?" Franklin asked as the reality of the doctor's words hit home.

"Yes."

"Oh no!" Katie cried out. "Dear Lord, no!" With that, she collapsed to the floor, and Franklin and Earnest quickly were at her side. They picked her up and placed her on the sofa in the room. As she continued sobbing, Earnest talked to the doctors.

"Those are the only two options?"

"Yes, I am sorry, Mr. Woodsworth," the first doctor said.

"Maybe there are some other specialists somewhere in the world who can help my son?"

"There is one other in this field of work, and I have conferred with him via the Internet. Based on our findings so far, he agrees that it is a psychological problem, but due to the constant pain your son is experiencing, it would be near impossible to try and resolve the problem through talking."

"Okay," Earnest said with defeat evident in his voice.

Franklin was silent too as the reality of the decision to be made sank into all their minds.

"Please take your time and make a wise decision. Then let us know, and we will proceed from there," the first doctor said again.

Later that morning, Bart awoke, and once again the pain immediately was with him. In his pain and anger, he swore at anyone who came into the room with the exception of his parents and siblings.

"Bart, I know it is difficult for you to listen to us, but please try, as we have a very important decision to make regarding the pain you are experiencing," Katie said, her face very close to Bart's, even with his screaming and anger. *Lord, please give him a moment of peace so he can hear us*, she said silently.

Instantly Bart was coherent and Katie could see it. The pain wasn't gone, but it was less intense as she proceeded to explain to him what the doctors had to say.

"So it is your life, Bart, you have to decide," she said as tears rolled down her cheeks, and in that moment, Bart actually felt his mother's pain alongside his own.

"T-take it o-off," Bart managed to get out, through gritted teeth. They were the first words he had spoken since he was admitted to the hospital.

Katie could not speak, but given the choice of being out of

touch with the world through a coma or having the pain removed totally, she understood his wishes.

"Are you sure, son?" Earnest asked as he leaned in too.

"Y-yes!" Bart whispered, and then instantly, the full force of the pain returned. It was so intense that he actually passed out.

"Bart? Bart, are you okay?" Katie shouted, thinking that he might have died. Quickly a nurse and a doctor entered the room, rushing to Bart's side. They checked him out and then backed away from the bed.

"It is okay. He has passed out, which is probably for the best right now," the doctor said before he left the room.

"Are we really going to let them remove his arm?" Franklin asked this time as he stood beside his mother with his arm around her.

"It was his wish," Earnest said quietly as he sat beside Bart's bed. "They can do wonders with prosthetics these days, and you can make sure we will get him the very best there is."

"Yes ... I suppose ... you are right," Katie said through her continuing tears.

It was three days later when the operation was scheduled for the amputation of Bart's right arm. Katie, Earnest, Caroline and Winter were at his bedside just before they were to take him down to surgery. Bart was still asleep, but the nurse had told them that they would soon have to wake him.

"Have you talked to Bart at all since he decided to have this done?" Winter asked sheepishly, still feeling like an outsider in this family situation.

"We haven't been able to do so, as the pain has only gotten worse. There have been many times since then that the pain actually caused Bart to pass out," Katie said as she moved to Winter's side and gave her a light hug.

"Too bad Franklin isn't here," Caroline said, her emotions right at the crest of flowing over.

"Yes. He wanted to stay, but he has a deadline for a log house he is building, and seeing that this isn't life-threatening, he just had to go, but he said his prayers will be with us all, especially Bart," Earnest said this time.

"W-who's there?" Bart managed to get out just before the pain hit him yet again.

Lord, please again, just a moment so we can talk to him? Katie prayed silently, and instantly the pain subsided enough for Bart to comprehend what was going on around him once more.

"W-what's happening?" Bart whispered, his mouth very dry.

"Son, we are all here for you as you go in for surgery."

"Oh," Bart said as he slowly turned his head to his left side, surprised to see Winter there too, but he said nothing.

"Are you sure this is what you want, Bart?" Katie asked again, hoping he would change his mind.

"Yessss! I want this pain to leave for good!"

Just then, the nurse came into the room to make sure Bart was awake, and as she looked at him, she saw something very strange.

"Mr. Woodsworth, is the pain gone?" she asked Bart curiously.

"No!" Bart screamed loudly.

"Why are you asking him that when he is obviously in pain?" Earnest demanded to know.

"Well, if it's not gone, then why is he holding his right leg?" the nurse asked as every eye snapped around in Bart's direction.

"What the ...?" Earnest asked as he saw his son clutching his right leg now about midthigh. "Why is he doing that?"

"Bart, son, what is happening?" Katie cried out, confused by this change in events.

Bart managed to look at her with very confused eyes himself.

"I am sorry, but you are all going to have to leave," the nurse said as she rushed out into the hall and called for help. Quickly one other nurse and a doctor rushed into the room. "Please just move to the waiting room, and someone will be with you shortly."

Shortly turned out to mean nearly two hours, but eventually the doctor overseeing Bart's condition walked into the waiting room and over to the family, who were seated by the windows. Earnest jumped up at the sight of the doctor approaching.

"Is everything okay?" Earnest asked with an anxious voice.

"For the moment yes. He has passed out again, but we must talk. The surgery is out of the question now with this new development, I am afraid. The pain seems to have a mind of its own, but probably it is more like Bart's mind is fighting off the suggestion of removing the pain through surgery."

"W-what do we do now?" Katie asked.

"We are going to have to go with the first option."

"A coma?"

"Yes."

CHAPTER THIRTEEN

This time it only took Bart a few moments to know where he was. The pain was gone, and whiteness enveloped him just as before. He felt the big easy chair beneath him as he just sat there, waiting. He waited for what seemed a long time before he felt the urge to speak.

"Is anyone here?"

Instantly on the screen or wall or whatever it was came the word "Yes."

Bart remained silent again, hoping that whoever was there would strike up the conversation, but after a while, he knew it would be up to him.

"God?" he finally said in the form of a question.

"Yes?" came up on the wall again.

"How do I know this really is God?"

"You don't."

Bart fell silent again, trying to figure out how to get this conversation going in a direction that would get him some answers.

"Just ask me," flashed on the wall.

"Ask you what?" Bart said, confused now more than anything.

"Anything you want—in order to get this conversation going."

"Y-you can read my mind?"

"Yes."

"How?"

"I am God ... Am I not?"

Bart felt himself getting smaller and smaller with the possibility that this really was God.

"Just ask me, Bartholomew."

I hate that name! Bart thought angrily.

"Why?"

"Huh?"

"Why do you hate that name?"

Again Bart was silent as he tried to come up with a good, reasonable answer.

"It was the name given to your parents through me."

"Th-through you?" Bart stammered out.

"Yes ... because it is a respectful name and will suit you well later in life."

"Uh ... okay."

Silence filled the room once again, and after a while, Bart felt as if God had left the room to attend to something else perhaps.

"Are y-you still h-here?" he whispered hesitantly.

"Yes."

"Okay."

"You have my undivided attention for however long you like."

"Okay, but don't you, like, have other things you have to do?"

"They are being taken care of."

"But how can that be if you are here?"

"Obviously you weren't listening to anything you were taught in Sunday school."

"You know all that too?"

"Bart, let me explain some things to you, and then we can move on to the main reason you are really here."

"Okay," Bart squeaked out.

"I want you to know that I knew you even before I started creation, even before I created the angels and everything before that. You have always been on my mind, and I even knew that one day you and I would have this conversation.

"You are fearfully and wonderfully made in every single detail, right down to the atoms that make you who you are. I knew what color your eyes would be, what color your hair would be, how you would talk and think and reason. I also knew all the hardships you would face in life, who you would marry, and how many kids you would have.

"But, my child, you are now at a crossroads in your life. You are here to make a decision, even though I know the answer already, but that is the way it works with men. They first need to make the decision themselves before we can move on."

"Decision?" Bart said. "What decision?"

*Why are you so angry, Bart?"

So now you are using the name I prefer, Bart thought before he said anything, forgetting what he already knew.

"I am using it for your benefit, so that you will feel more comfortable as we talk."

Uh-oh, I forgot that he can read my mind, Bart thought and mentally scolded himself.

"It is okay, as you are still operating in your earthly self."

"O-okay, sorry."

"No apologies needed, my son."

Silence again filled the room as this time Bart thought in earnest of an answer to God's earlier question.

"B-because my father ignores me for his money," Bart said, his head down and eyes closed in the milky whiteness that surrounded him and everything in this place.

"Yes, you are right," Bart read when he finally opened his eyes.

"Yessss!" He shouted on the inside.

"But you are also wrong," came the next message on the wall.

"What the ...?" Bart said out loud this time without even realizing it, and then he felt ashamed that he almost swore in front of God.

"Feel free to say anything that comes to mind, my son, except to take my name in vain. I have heard everything imaginable from humankind in their complaints to me."

Bart said nothing; he just continued sitting in his chair.

"You can get up and walk around anytime if you like."

This is amazing, Bart thought. *We could actually have a conversation without speaking.*

"Yes, we could, as I designed it that way. This helps out greatly when someone is wanting to communicate with me, but can't do it out loud."

Silence again filled the room, but only for a moment as Bart began to feel something strange happening to him.

"Whaaaaa ...?" Bart managed to get out just before he felt himself sucked right through the chair beneath him and then through the floor, but all in one piece and with no pain. Instantly he was in another room, one that he recognized as his father's office in the Woodsworth Industries International corporate building.

As he stood on the floor, he was amazed that although he could see everything around him, he still could not see himself. He could hold his hand right up to his face, but he could not see it.

"You can't see yourself, nor can anyone see you," Bart heard inside his head this time. "Walk inside the secret room."

Bart moved in the direction, assuming that he was actually walking even though it did not feel like it. He reached out his hand to use the door handle, but his hand passed right through it, and he realized that he could pass through things with ease. So he moved forward again and felt himself pass through the wall to the inside room he had seen once before.

"Just stand still and do not be alarmed, as no one can see you," the voice said in his head again.

After a few moments, Bart heard a key being inserted into the lock and was surprised to see his father enter the room with a picture frame in his hand.

His father then sat on the single chair in the room while looking down at the picture frame he held tightly in his hands.

Bart was startled to see tears begin to fall from his father's cheeks onto the picture below.

What is it he is looking at? Bart wondered as he strained to look without moving.

"You may move in for a closer look," he heard in his head.

Bart gingerly inched forward until he was looking over his father's right shoulder and down at the picture in his hands.

"What?" Bart said out loud, and even though no one heard him, he still covered his mouth with his hand.

"It is okay; no one can hear you either."

As Bart continued looking down, he was surprised to see a picture of himself, taken while he was playing a game of racquetball at a city competition that he had easily won.

Okay, it is a picture of me, but why is he crying? Bart asked silently.

"Oh, Bart, I am so sorry, my son, that I haven't been able to support you in this game that you love so much." Bart could hear the words in his head, but this time the voice itself was different and he realized it was his father's own thoughts as he sat there in tears. *"But I do love you so very much, even though you are so angry with me. I would do anything for you, Bartholomew, even give up everything I have achieved to make sure that you will always be happy and fulfilled in life."*

Bart stood up straight, unable to take in what he had just heard, but the voice continued on in his head anyways.

"God, I don't know if you are really out there or not, and I must be honest that I do not believe in your son, but please, please, please somehow bring my family back together. I will give up everything I have just to have them back with Katie and me, as a family once more."

Once more? Bart thought to himself. *We never were a family to start with!*

Instantly Bart was in another setting, in a home that he didn't remember, but he somehow knew that this was home at one time. He was in the kitchen but could hear laughter coming from another room, so he wandered that way, knowing that probably no one could see or hear him here either.

As he entered what appeared to be the living room, Bart was startled to see his parents at a very much younger age. They were both sitting on the floor, apparently playing with two boys. The one boy, who he somehow recognized as Franklin, was seated on his mother's lap, while he himself was sitting upright between his father's spread legs. His mother and father were tickling each of the boys as the laughter of all of them filled the room.

"Yeah, well, this must have just been a one-time thing," Bart spat out the words as anger arose at the fact that they were all having a good time.

Again the scene changed. His mother and father, Franklin, himself and a baby were in a trailer of some sorts. Bart finally figured out that it was a camping trailer and that the baby was Caroline, his younger sister. They were all sitting at the table and were playing a game of Sorry!, which was quite popular in its day. Every time one of them would pop the dice in the middle of the game board and then move their playing piece until it landed on someone else's, they would laugh or groan at being sent back home.

This time, Bart was quiet, as obviously his father and mother did spend time with them when they were younger and it looked like they all loved and enjoyed each other too.

But what happened then? Why did he stop spending time with us? Bart asked in his head, and instantly he was back in the white room.

"Bart, what do you think this place is that you are now in?" Bart saw come up on the white wall in front of him as he was seated in the comfortable white easy chair once again.

Bart had thought about this every time he came to this place, and he had a ready answer for God's question.

"I call this place the white room of darkness."

"Okay, yes, it is truly a white room, but why the darkness?"

"I think it is like being in a totally black room with the lights out. I know things are in the room, but I can't see them, I can only touch them as I feel them or bump into them."

There was only silence after he said the words, but Bart knew that God was not finished with this conversation yet. Time seemed to drag on and on with no response, and when Bart was finally going to say something, he saw words forming on the wall again.

"Yes, the whiteness could be like that, but that is not the darkness."

"Huh?" Bart said. "Then what is the darkness?"

Again there was a long time of silence as Bart just waited for an answer, but he grew tired of waiting and eventually shouted out the question again. "What is the darkness God?" Bart felt he had stumped God until a single word came up on the wall.

"You!"

Bart said not a word, knowing that to do so might implicate him in something he had no knowledge of. Once again, silence dominated the room and time ticked by, while Bart just sat there and waited as long as he possibly could, before he finally had to ask the question.

"Why am I the darkness?"

This time, the answer was almost instantaneous.

"What did you learn about in church concerning man ever seeing me?"

Bart thought for a moment as Bible stories and scripture ran through his mind. He was even more surprized that he could actually remember them, after all these years. Finally though, the answer came to him.

"The Bible says that a man cannot look at God or he would die."

"Yes."

"But doesn't the Bible say that Moses saw you at the burning bush?"

"No."

"I am sure that he hid behind a rock or something and he saw you."

"He saw my shadow pass by, but not me."

"Okay so what does all of this have to do with me anyway?"

"Why can't I look at humankind?"

"Uh ... because ... we are sinners?" Bart stammered out, wondering just where these answers were coming from.

"What else do you know about sin?"

This time, he knew the answer from something he had heard in Sunday school, several years ago.

"It is ..." Bart hesitated as it suddenly all made sense. "Darkness ... and that dark and light can't live together."

"So, my son, you really were listening, I see."

"Okay, I get it now, but why am I the darkness?"

"You are sin in my eyes."

"If that is true, then how can I really be having a conversation with God?" Bart said kind of smugly, like he had one up on God.

"Because you are covered in white and I can see no darkness from you."

The answer startled Bart, but at the same time, it all made sense and he knew now why he was in the room he was.

"Okay, God," Bart continued. "If you really are God, then I have some questions for you."

"They all do."

"What?" Bart said.

"Anytime man tries to confront me, it is all about a list of questions they have."

"Uh ... okay."

"But go ahead, my son, ask the questions; I have nothing but time on my hands."

Bart wasn't sure if God was serious or playing with him, but he went ahead anyway, wanting to see if this was really God. He also had some burning questions, and he was dying to know the answers.

"I hear people say all the time that they could never love a God who would let there be so much suffering and death on the earth. Why is that?"

Again there was a period of silence in the room, and once more Bart felt that he had the upper hand.

"This is an age-old question, and many people all through the ages have asked this question of me, but there is only one answer."

With that said, there was only silence once again.

Why is he waiting? Bart thought. He rose from his seat and slowly made his way around the room as he waited. Finally after a long period of time, at least in Bart's view, words began to show up on the wall.

"There is no easy answer to the question, but I will explain it in terms that you can understand with your limited mind."

Limited mind? Bart thought. *Who are we kidding here?*

"I never intended for the world to go the way it has, because in the beginning there was no sin, but man always has to test the waters and do it his own way. It matters not that it was the woman first and then the man, but sin is sin and I cannot be a part of it.

"I hear humans praying, asking or yelling at me all the time for me to end cancer, AIDS, poverty, war and a myriad of other earthly problems, but they simply do not understand the meaning of free will.

"Adam and Eve decided that they could do it their own way at the deception of the serpent and so I had to give them their desire to choose their own path, otherwise known as free will. But this free will has consequences and this is where man's reasoning falls short."

Bart had now returned to his chair, taking in all the words flowing onto the wall and across the wall and then simply disappearing off the other end as God continued with his answer.

"If I were to end cancer once and for all, then humans would be happy and rejoice and they might even give me credit for it, but it wouldn't be very long before they would want me to end AIDS and so I would do that, but then it would be a steady flow of end this and end that, until ultimately I would be in control of every aspect of the human life and they would simply be acting like robots to follow my every command ... but that was not my plan. I wanted humankind to be able to make their own choices and that would include choosing me or not and in that way they would make their choice to fellowship with me for eternity.

"Sadly though, those who choose not to follow me are basically saying they want it their way, and that way does not have a happy ending."

"You mean hell, right?" Bart asked.

"Yes, but many even have a misconception of that. They all say they will have a great party there, but they are so far from the truth of that place that it saddens me to have to leave them there."

"Why can't we all just go to heaven?"

"We have already talked about the answer to that."

Bart stopped talking and thought for a few moments before speaking. "Because we are sin?"

"Yes and I cannot even be in the presence of sin, so that would never work."

"W-what about m-me?" Bart finally had to ask.

"Bart, I am about to show you exactly where you stand with me so far. I want you to look at your arm where the pain was."

What? Bart thought but did as he was told.

"What do you see?" the words read on the wall.

"Uh ... nothing except whiteness."

"Look closer."

As Bart concentrated on his right arm just above the elbow,

which he could not see, he started to notice that the color was softly changing from the pure white to a soft yellow and then to a soft warm orange. The warmth he felt began to get hotter and hotter as he witnessed an opening of sorts within the area of the pain he had experienced before.

"What?" he said out loud as he felt his gaze being drawn in deeper and deeper until it looked as if he were staring down into a bright-orange sinkhole, there within his arm, which he still could not see. The burning sensation was getting worse, and suddenly he remembered the pain, he had experienced outside of this white room.

Next thing he knew, Bart was standing on the edge of this hole of heat. He could see himself wearing the very best of clothes with fine white linen slacks, which were billowing around his legs. He had on a pair of expensive patent-leather shoes, a very expensive and fine-quality leather belt around the waist of his slacks, complete with a buckle of solid gold. His shirt was pure silk, and on his wrist, he wore a very expensive gold Rolex watch. His hands were on his hips, and with his head thrown back, he was laughing at the world.

He looked down into the hole once more and could now see people, millions upon millions of people all flailing around, their hands reaching up to him, begging him to help them get out of that place. Looking even closer, he could see that the bright-orange colors were like molten lava that was burning everything and everyone it touched. Then he could hear screams, moaning and groaning amongst the anger towards God.

Bart suddenly saw someone he knew. It had been the first grown woman that he had spent time with. He grinned at the recollection that she had been his first of many women who had thrown themselves at him for his money, toys and sex. She was crying out, begging Bart to get her out of this place, but he only responded with even more laughter.

Suddenly her hand shot up out of the top of the hole and

grabbed hold of Bart's left ankle, causing his fine linen slacks to instantly burn away where she had grabbed him.

"Ahhhhh!" Bart screamed out at the hot burning fire in his left ankle. He fell to the ground as the woman tried to pull herself up out of the hole, all the while dragging Bart closer and closer to the edge.

"Let go of me!" Bart was shouting and screaming as he felt himself being drawn closer and closer to the edge. He was desperately trying to find something to grab hold of that would stop him from sliding towards the fiery hole.

As he was dragged closer and closer to the edge of the hole, Bart could not only hear the screams, moans and groans of millions if not billions of people all struggling within their torment, but he could also feel the tremendous heat coming up from within the hole as well.

Frantically he was clawing at the ground, but then realizing that there was absolutely nothing to grab hold of that would stop him, Bart rolled over on his back and began to kick the woman's head as it began to come up out of the hole beneath her.

"Nooooo!" she screamed. "Don't make me go back. Save me, Bart, for the love of God save me."

Her cries and screams were so loud now that they were ringing in Bart's ears, but he still kept on kicking and kicking until he felt his legs clear the edge of the hole and he began to tilt downward. Just as he began to slide into the hole, he kicked one last time and the woman let go.

As she fell back into the hole, she was screaming all the way down.

"Save me, Bart ... Please save me from this place ... Bart, save meeeeeeeee!" he heard until her voice was drowned out in the billions of other cries, screams and pleadings.

Suddenly Bart was in the white room of darkness again. Instantly after he realized where he was, he looked at his right arm and caught the last glimpse of the soft yellow glow fading back into the whiteness that filled and covered everything in the room.

CHAPTER FOURTEEN

Earnest was in his at-home office, just finishing up some correspondence that had to do with the latest invention that he and Thomas were working on when his cell phone rang. Looking at the number, he realized that it was from the office of the doctor who was treating Bart's case at the university hospital. Instantly he answered the call.

"Hello?"

"Mr. Woodsworth?" came the doctor's voice on the other end of the call.

"Yes. What is it? Is everything okay with my son?"

"Sir, I can't discuss this you right now, but you and your wife need to get to the hospital as soon as possible."

"W-what is it? Is he okay?" Earnest shot back.

"Please, sir, just get here as soon as you can."

"Okay, we will be there soon."

"Thank you, sir. Good-bye."

Earnest quickly clicked off and frantically called another number on his cell phone.

"In-City Flights. How may I help you?" came the greeting on the other end of the call.

"Mr. Earnest Woodsworth here, requesting a flight from our home to University Hospital, ASAP. This is a family emergency. Have the flight land on our front lawn. We will be waiting."

"Yes, sir, Mr. Woodsworth. Just a moment, sir," the woman

said, and the line was silent for a few moments before she came back on the line. "How many will be taking the trip, sir?"

"There will be three of us."

"Yes, sir, just one more moment please." Again the line was silent as the receptionist relayed the information to the pilot of an aircraft that was already returning from another trip. "Estimated time of arrival will be 10 minutes," she finally said.

"Thank you," Earnest said.

"You are welcome, sir, and, sir?"

"Yes?" Earnest asked.

"Good luck."

Good luck, Earnest thought as he clicked off the call and quickly made his way out of his office in search of Katie and Caroline. *I think Bart is going to be needing more than luck this time.*

"Katie? ... Katie?" Earnest was shouting as he ran down the long hallway of their stately home. "Oh, Lord, Katie, where are you?" he was shouting now, almost frantically.

Suddenly Katie and Caroline burst out of the sitting room about 20 feet ahead of Earnest. At first, they looked the other way in search of Earnest but then turned back to see him quickly hurrying up the hallway.

"What is it? What's wrong?" Katie shouted back as they met and halted their pursuit of each other.

"I ... just ... got ... a call ... from the ... hospital," Earnest said as he tried to regain his breath. "They want us ... there as soon ... as possible."

"Why?" Caroline asked this time.

"The doctor wouldn't say but ... said for us to get there soon. I made a call, and a helicopter ... will be here shortly to take us there."

"Let's go!" Katie shouted as the three of them hurriedly headed for the front entrance of the house and the front lawn outside.

As they exited the house, they could already hear the helicopter approaching in the distance.

All three of them stopped at the edge of the cobblestone driveway. Maria had hurried out of the house as well just behind them, and Katie quickly told her what was going on and gave her some instructions before the helicopter landed out on the lawn about 50 feet from where they all stood.

Within mere moments, they were all onboard and belted in as the sleek corporate helicopter lifted away from the expansive lawn of the Woodsworth estate. Once in the air, Katie quickly called Franklin's cell phone and told him what was going on, asking him to pray right then for his brother.

Within 10 minutes, Earnest could see the big red H on the helicopter landing pad at the university hospital, and in another three minutes, they had touched down. Before departing, Earnest told the pilot that if he needed them again, he would call their number and for now he could return to his home base. The three family members never saw the helicopter lift off, but they heard it just before they all rushed through the automatic doors into the ER.

As they approached the ER desk, they could see the doctor there waiting for them and he quickly made his way to them.

"Mr. and Mrs. Woodworth, I just want you to know that Bart is still with us, but at the same time something drastic has happened that must be addressed, and that is why I have called you here," the doctor said as he directed them in the direction of a surgical room.

"Is Bart not in his room?" Katie asked as they walked briskly.

"No, I am sorry, but due to the nature of this development, we needed to move him into the burn ward."

"Burn ward!" Earnest said loudly.

Caroline and Katie just looked at each other and then grabbed each other's hand as they made their way to the burn ward of the hospital.

Earnest never said a word, knowing that he wouldn't get any answers until they got where they were going.

Then they were there, and the doctor stopped walking and turned to face them all.

"I think that at this point in time it would be best if just the parents entered the room with me, and then if you think it is all right, your daughter could come in later."

"Caroline, please, honey, just wait out here and I will come and get you after we see what is wrong," Katie said as she quickly hugged her daughter before going through the large swinging door of the burn unit.

As they entered the room, they could see their son Bart attached to all types of hoses and wires, just as he had been when they placed him into a coma, but this time, there were more of these devices attached to his left leg and ankle.

"W-what is wrong with his leg?" Katie asked in a whisper.

"That is why I have called you here. First, I will show you what is wrong and then we will discuss it," the doctor said as he motioned for a nurse in the room to leave, which she did.

The doctor took hold of a white linen sheet that covered Bart's left leg and slowly pulled it back until the effected skin came into view.

"Oh!" Katie gasped, quickly turning her head from the sight.

"What is that?" Earnest asked sharply at the sight of Bart's badly burned ankle.

"Bart's leg has been severely burned, as you can see. We are treating him as we would any burn patient, but there is one difference in your son's case."

"What's that?" Earnest asked as Katie collapsed into a nearby chair.

"It's the nature of the burn. Most cases that we see here are due to house fires, forest fires or vehicle fires and such, but this one is very different and actually the first case I have ever seen in all of my career as a medical doctor. The only time I have seen a case such as this has been in a textbook."

"Okay, so what is this case then?" Earnest asked again, almost in a whisper, as he was afraid to hear the answer.

"This is the type of burn that can only be caused by something as hot as lava."

"Lava?" Katie and Earnest both said at the same time, stunned at what they had just heard.

"Yes, incredible as that may sound, it is what it is."

"B-but why? He is in a hospital, and there is nothing like a volcano around here for thousands of miles," Earnest said in a bewildered voice as he slowly shook his head from side to side.

"It is very puzzling for sure, and we have no answers, I am sorry. He was in his room and being monitored by our staff when all of a sudden his core temperature began to dramatically rise and his vitals began to go off the charts. Our staff were powerless to help him as he was and still is in the coma."

Katie had come back to the bedside now and was looking at the size and shape of the burn.

"Doctor?" she asked.

"Yes, Mrs. Woodsworth?"

"That burn pattern looks familiar. Do you know what it is?" she asked, not taking her eyes off the burn as she spoke.

"Yes, that is yet another piece to this very mysterious puzzle. What you are looking at is the pattern of a human hand that is gripping your son's leg."

"What?" Earnest said. "How is that even possible?"

"We have no explanation, sir. I am sorry, but nothing recorded in any medical book that I have read is like this. If I had to give you anything, I would say this is somewhat like spontaneous combustion, but even that theory is questionable in the medical world."

"But a handprint?" Earnest said, obviously flustered at even the possibility of what the doctor had just said.

"Doctor?" Katie asked.

"Yes, Mrs. Woodsworth?"

"Have you had a really close look at this pattern?" Katie asked as she had her face just inches from the burned hand pattern on Bart's ankle, despite the smell coming off it.

"Uh, not that close. Why do you ask?"

"Well, I have been taking a closer look and have noticed a couple of interesting things."

The doctor moved over close to Bart's ankle now as curiosity crept into his thoughts.

"What do you see?" he asked.

"I am not absolutely sure, but I think I can see a scar on this handprint, and if you look really close at the finger marks, I think you will even be able to see actual fingerprints."

"Wha ...?" Earnest said. "Are you telling me that this is an actual handprint of another human?"

The doctor was looking very closely at the handprint now and suddenly stood up. He turned to face Earnest before he spoke. "Yes, I believe it is, and I think we better contact the authorities."

"The police? Why?" Katie asked this time.

"To have that handprint fingerprinted of course," the doctor said before he turned and hurriedly left the room.

Katie and Earnest just stared at each other and then left the room as well, to go and talk to Caroline out in the waiting area. They stayed in that area of the hospital for another 30 minutes or so until the doctor returned with a couple of possible plainclothes police officers. One of them was carrying a metal briefcase of sorts.

"These officers are going to fingerprint the palm print on Bart's ankle to see if they can identify just whose hand they belong to, and then we will proceed from there, but I don't think we will get any answers until Bart comes out of the coma and then only if he can remember anything about it at all," the doctor said to the three of them. Then he turned and directed the officers into Bart's room.

"Fingerprinting?" Caroline asked with a very confused look on her face.

"It will be okay, hon," Katie said as she hugged her daughter. "When they are done in there, we will take you in to see what all the fuss is about, but know this, that what you will see is very hard to believe."

"Okay," Caroline whispered into her mom's shoulder, almost scared now to see anything.

"W-what was that all about?" Bart asked after a few moments.

"Your future."

"Are you saying that is where I will end up?"

"If you keep going the way you are ... yes!"

Bart said not a word as the full weight of what he had just witnessed and read came to bear on his mind and soul. Thoughts raced through his mind of childhood days gone by, moving onto his teenage years and finally up to the recent days just before that racquetball game with the stranger, that seemed to have started all this in the first place.

"D-did you cause me to get hurt in that racquetball game?" Bart asked quietly.

"No, Bart, I don't work like that. Yes, I allowed you to move into that situation and I even used a few of my servants to get you there, but the cause of this pain did not come from me!"

"Where did it come from then?"

"*You!*"

"From me?" Bart said loudly. "What do you mean from me? How could I hurt myself like that?"

"The pain that you have been experiencing was not a result of the injury you received from the racquetball game, my son."

"But what about the pain I felt right after that guy touched me there?"

"That was only done to allow you to concentrate on that exact spot, but again, I tell you that the pain that you have been experiencing was not a result of the injury you received from the racquetball game."

"What? That doesn't make sense, as I know that I am really in a lot of pain."

"As you are, my son, as you are."

Bart stopped talking for a few moments, trying to make sense of what God was telling him, until finally he changed the direction of his questions.

"Okay, so what is the cause of the pain then? Are you saying that it is all in my head?"

"No, it is all in your heart."

Bart was thoroughly confused, but by this time, he knew better than to argue with God.

"I understand the words that I see—at least in my mind I do—but I still need you to explain it to me," he whispered.

Again silence filled the room, and again Bart had to wait for the answer that he knew would be coming for sure. So he just sat back in the chair beneath him that he still could not see and waited.

Slowly the words began to form on the white wall directly in front of him.

"Bart, have you ever seen a child's toy that has a lot of certain-shaped holes? The intention of the toy is for the child to place the same-shaped items into the same holes."

"Yes, I think I know which toy you are talking about."

"Well then, my son, your heart and every human's heart is like that child's toy. Every one of them has certain holes in it that are the exact shape of things, such as love, knowledge, talents and such, but there is one hole that is shaped the same as myself and all humans have to do is to place me in that hole to have peace, happiness, joy and hope. The problem with humans though, ever since the fall, is that they all feel this hole, this loneliness that only I can fill, but they try to fill it with everything but me. They try alcohol, drugs, sex, money, thrills and anything they can find to give them true happiness. Even people with wealth have a real problem finding the answer, because they think that wealth itself is the answer.

"We did not create humans to be this way. You were created to have fellowship with us, to be at peace with us and to place your hope in us—not in the world, as so many unfortunately do.

"So, based on everything I have shared with you, Bart, again I ask you, why are you so angry? It is not because of your father or parents. I have shown you that they truly do love you, so tell me, my son, just why do you have so much anger inside?"

Bart knew the answer to the question. He had known it for a very long time but had not breathed a word of it to any living soul. It was hidden deep inside of his being, surrounded by walls he himself had erected over the many years as the anger began to rise up. Even now he was resisting the urge to speak it out.

"Don't fight it, Bart. Let it out and let my light shine in."

Tears began to form in Bart's eyes as an overwhelming desire to let it all out began to build within him. So many years he had hidden behind those very high stone walls that guarded his heart, but now he could actually feel those stone walls beginning to crumble.

Then Bart felt something that he was sure would have startled him in any other situation, but here in this white room of darkness, he felt an arm going around his shoulders and drawing him into the presence of pure love. It was enough. He felt the walls crumbling all around his heart, and the words began to form on his lips.

"I ... I am ... lonely," he barely whispered, and any other human probably would not have heard, but God heard and drew Bart in even closer to his presence.

"I know, my son," Bart heard softly in his ears as he closed his eyes and just allowed himself to fall deeply into this feeling he dearly loved and needed.

"The time is coming when all your fears and hurts will be gone forever and I will give you the peace and love you have longed for all these years."

"Can you do that now?" Bart asked, his eyes still closed.

"No, my son, but my servant will lead you into the truth that will set you free. After that, you will meet your best friend who will guide you into the mission I have for you and your future wife."

Bart did not say the word, but he heard himself say it in his mind. "Winter?"

"Yes. She is mine, and I called her to pray for you and to be there for you in this time of trials you are facing."

Bart was silent as he drifted into this dream world of white, lost in the strongest feelings of love he had ever experienced in his life. Time had no meaning and seemed to stand still as he felt the love of God wrap him up in a cocoon-like blanket. It was a feeling he never wanted to come out of and wondered if this was what heaven felt like.

Suddenly something registered in Bart's dreamlike state.

"Best friend? Did I hear you say something about my best friend?"

Then Bart heard a voice out loud this time, which startled him, even though the sound of that voice was like billions of bubbles of pure love bursting all around him, just before everything went dark.

"Yes, Bart, you have already met him, and when you talk to him again, you will be surprised to know that the two of you share the same name."

Bart was surprised to see Winter sitting beside his bed, holding his hand when he finally opened his eyes. Her hand was very warm and felt good in his. Her eyes were closed, and he thought maybe she was sleeping, but then her eyelids fluttered and somehow he knew that she had been praying.

Her eyes opened, and they just stared into each other's eyes for a few moments, but to Bart, it was like an eternity of wasted time had just come to a very pleasant end.

"Bart? Are you okay?" Winter whispered as she squeezed his hand.

Bart felt the squeeze and squeezed back just before he nodded his head in affirmation.

Winter's heart leaped as she felt his squeezing fingers, and she knew right then and there that her prayers had been heard and answered.

"Are you in any pain?" she asked.

Bart had to think about that one for a few moments, and then his eyes sparkled when he realized that the pain was all gone from his body, although he had a tingling sensation in his left ankle.

"N-no," he managed to whisper, his throat very dry from the tubes still there.

"Okay, don't talk. Let me go get your mother. I'll be right back," Winter said excitedly, but Bart wouldn't let go of her hand.

He rocked his head back and forth slightly as if to say no, so Winter stayed put for a few moments.

Bart looked up at her and for the first time in his life, as far as he could remember, realized that he truly loved someone more than himself and it brought tears to his dry eyes.

"Bart, it is okay," Winter whispered to him as she bent low to his face. She could see that he was trying to say something through the tears so she just waited for him to get it out.

"W ... Winter ... I am ... so sorry ... for ... hurting you."

Winter was at a loss for words, but she knew that something profound had happened to this man and only the Lord himself could change a man like Bart. Her heart was pounding in her chest from the excitement she now felt at his words to her. She knew he loved her, and she too loved him. She knew that God had answered all her prayers except one so far. He had even gone so far as to make her a part of the family before she was an actual part of the family.

Tears flowed from her eyes at Bart's words, and she couldn't say a thing. She just looked down at this man she loved and leaning over placed her wet cheek on his. She didn't see it, but her tears mixed with his as he too cried in joy.

It was then that Katie entered Bart's hospital room, and she stopped dead in her tracks at the sight before her. A huge smile came to her face as she took in the sight of her son and his girlfriend connecting in the way it was meant to be.

Thank you, Lord. Oh thank you, my Saviour, for your goodness to my family, Katie silently prayed, before she made her presence known.

"Bart? Are you with us again?" Katie said as she made it look like she had just entered the room. She rushed over to his bedside as Winter quickly sat up and moved over to the chair she had earlier pulled up to the bedside.

"M-mom!" Bart managed to get out, and Katie's heart melted at the sound of that word, because to her it was as if her true prodigal son had returned.

"Don't talk, Bart. You are still hooked up to all this equipment. We will get the doctor in here to check you out."

Katie then turned to Winter. "Winter, hon, would you please go get a nurse or the doctor and let them know that Bart has returned to us?"

Winter smiled and then nodded the affirmative. She quickly stood and did as she had requested, almost leaving the room in a run—a quick walk to be sure.

Within mere minutes, Bart's room had three nurses and two doctors in it, checking him out and amazed that he had simply just woken up. Most patients who were in an induced coma had to be brought slowly out of it when the time was right. Even more than all of this was the fact that he was the picture of perfect health, with no pain and no complications either.

By the time that the doctors and nurses had all left Bart's room, the rest of his family had arrived at the hospital, including Caroline and Mitch and Franklin and Julie, who had flown in on a helicopter requested by Earnest earlier in the day. It took another 30 minutes or so for the hospital staff to unhook Bart from all the equipment that was supposedly keeping him alive and fed while in the coma, but eventually his hospital bed was wheeled from the soundproof room into a family gathering area.

"Bart! Buddy!" Franklin shouted at the sight of his brother being wheeled into the room where they had all gathered.

"Great to see you, son," Earnest said as he pulled Katie tightly to his side, happy that he had his youngest son back with them safe and alive.

"Hey there, brother! You gave us quite a scare back there in that room, you know," Caroline said as she stepped up to his bed and gave him a light punch on his left arm.

Winter said not a word, as she knew that she and Bart would catch up on things later. She was uncertain if she would ever share the words exchanged between her and Bart when he first came out of the coma. Time would tell if it was real or not, but she was willing to wait and see what would happen.

"Hi," Bart said, and everyone smiled at his first word. More amazing than that first word was the fact that Bart really had nothing more to say, at least not in anger anyway. In three days, he was released from the hospital as a picture of perfect health that still had the doctors scratching their heads in wonder.

Bart was startled to learn that he had been in a coma for well over 10 months but even more than that was the handprint on his ankle.

"Branded by the hand of God!" he would be heard to say later on in his life. He learned from the police that the fingerprints on his ankle burn were indeed from a woman he had dated who had died in a car accident, but Bart knew even more than the police where the woman was now and it saddened him greatly every time he saw the hand-shaped burn pattern on his ankle.

In the time he had been in the coma, his brother Franklin and his fiancée Julie had moved back to the city and were now living in the spacious country home his mother and sister had found for them. Also, his father had sold his business empire and had gone into business strictly with Thomas in the invention and innovation sector of the business world. His sister, Caroline, was now engaged to Mitch, and both of them, along with Franklin and Julie, were waiting for Bart to come out of the coma before they got married.

Bart was surprised to learn from his mother that Winter had sat by his bed almost every day since he had gone into the coma. She had prayed for him in those times, as she was a born-again Christian, which Katie had found out one day when the two of them were doing lunch in the city. Katie talked to Bart about Winter and how special she was. She told him that she had been praying that one day, Winter would be an *official* part of the family. Bart had nothing to say about that, but the one thing that greatly got Katie's attention was the fact that Bart was no longer arguing with her; in fact, he hardly said anything anymore.

He didn't need to be told anything about Winter, because Bart knew in his heart that he loved the woman, and one day, he knew that she would be his wife, but right now was the time to get to know her in the proper manner, free of his sexual advances and insinuations.

CHAPTER FIFTEEN

I t had now been one month since Bart had come out of his coma. It was a gorgeous warm morning that found Earnest, Franklin, Bart and Thomas out on the Evergreen Country Club golf course. As Earnest stepped up to the first tee box, he was struck by the fact that this all seemed so familiar once more, referring to the weather and the day. As he stretched and prepared to hit his ball, he took a quick moment to look at his two sons goofing off over by their golf cart, and he smiled, knowing that it could have been oh so different, but here they all were, a father and his sons along with his very best friend, about to enjoy a round of golf.

The game progressed at a normal rate with Bart and Franklin making fun of the "old guys'" shots, but everything stopped when on the fourth hole, their father got another amazing hole-in-one.

"How do you do that?" Thomas asked in shock at the fact that this day seemed to be a repeat of another golf day not so long ago.

"Don't say anything about it until you take your shot, my friend, and if you do what I just did, then I might think that there is really something to your faith."

Earnest and his boys were at a total loss for words as Thomas's golf ball hit the apron, bounced once onto the green and smartly rolled up to the hole, hit the flag pole and simply plopped into the cup.

As Thomas walked back up to the other three, he was grinning from ear to ear.

"Uh ... about that faith thing," he said with a goofy grin, looking at Earnest.

"Okay ... okay, you certainly do have my attention now. There is no way in the world that our two shots are just a fluke; there has to be something more ... something supernatural at least," Earnest said as they climbed aboard their golf cart and headed down the hill towards the green.

"What did you think of that shot, Bart?" Franklin asked as they followed the old guys in their own motorized golf cart.

"When I heard about the first time it happened, I was certain it was a fluke or even made up for that matter, but to be here now and actually see it with my own two eyes, I must say that it definitely has me thinking," Bart said.

"Thinking about what?"

"About if God could actually make something like that happen, but then I know better than that."

"You doubt that God would do something like that?"

"No, not at all."

"Well then, little brother, I think you lost me," Franklin said with a strange expression. Ever since Bart had returned home from the hospital, he had been very quiet, spending lots of alone time in his room. He hardly ever drove his cars anymore or played with any of his other toys, and his parents were becoming concerned that maybe he was slipping backwards into some type of self-pity. So his words now were concerning and at the same time confusing to Franklin.

"I know for a fact that it was God himself that allowed those shots to happen both times," Bart said as they approached the green and stopped on the motorized cart path.

Wha ...? Franklin thought to himself. *Lord, did I just hear him right?*

At that point in the game, Franklin really didn't care about his game, as the old guys were obviously shooting way better than he or Bart was. Franklin's mind and silent prayers were about Bart and his profound words.

After two more holes, they switched seating positions on the golf carts with Thomas and Franklin sitting together, while Earnest and Bart shared the other cart.

"So what do you think about the old guys' golf game so far?" Thomas said with a chuckle.

"Yeah, it's okay, I guess," was Franklin's response.

His response bothered Thomas somewhat, seeing that Franklin had always been so positive and upbeat in the time he had known the younger man.

"Is something bothering you?" Thomas asked.

"It's not that it is bothering me, but just what Bart has told me so far this morning and also it is the Holy Spirit."

"Well, young man, you certainly have my attention. I am all ears, so lay it on me."

Franklin then took the time to explain to Thomas the conversation he had had with his brother, Bart, and how he was feeling somewhat confused and at the same time, he could feel the moving of the Holy Spirit and that something profound and wonderful was about to happen.

Thomas was not at all surprised, but he was thankful to the Lord Jesus Christ about what was going to transpire very soon, right there on the golf course.

"You know, your father and I had a very interesting conversation as well," Thomas said.

"Oh really? And what was it all about?"

"Well, we were riding along in the cart, and I could see a change in your father's face, so I asked him about it. He then told me about all that had happened in the past two years or so, including your forgiveness and coming back into his life. Then he talked about Bart and what he went through recently and how he is acting now. Earnest paused for a bit then, before he brought up a subject that I shall never forget or ever tire of hearing."

"What subject was that?"

"He went on to tell me that he should be the happiest man

alive with his eldest son home and his youngest son changed from being a royal pain to something better, even though he couldn't quite put a name to it. Then he said to me, 'I have everything a man could ever want out of life now, but I still feel like something is missing and I need it badly to make me whole.'"

"Wow! He really said that?"

"Yep."

"Okay, so you and I both know where this is heading, so what is the next step?" Franklin asked, even though he knew the answer before the words were totally out of his mouth.

"I have been praying about that for a while now, and the only thing that I get from the Lord is that it is totally your show now."

"Mine?"

"That's what I felt in my spirit—yes."

"Ummm okay."

"Do you have a problem with that?"

"Actually, no, I don't. It's just the where and when I am concerned about."

"That's a no-brainer."

"Huh?"

"The time is right now, and the location is right here."

"Here? ... You mean like right here on the golf course?"

"Yes."

Franklin took a few moments to process that information, looking a time or two back at Thomas and then at his father and Bart in the cart just in front of them.

"Okay, let's go for the next hole, somewhere on the fairway."

"That works for me."

Katie, Caroline, Julie and Winter, were all back at the house, sitting out on the stone patio, talking and having a good time in each other's presence. As she looked at the three other women before her, Katie smiled and silently thanked God. This was what she had wanted ever since her kids were born, that one day they would all be this very happy family that included their daughter's husband and the boys' wives. Soon it would all be a reality with maybe the exception of Bart and Winter, who were still getting to know each other, but every time she saw them together, Katie knew that they were in love.

The girls were all talking about the upcoming wedding plans for Franklin and Julie, to be followed shortly thereafter by Caroline and Mitch's wedding. Both of these women had accepted Winter as just part of the family and loved her just as much as they did each other.

After about 30 minutes of laughter, teasing and wedding plans talk, Katie was lounging back in her chair by the pool when she suddenly felt the moving of the Holy Spirit. So she simply closed her eyes and listened for the sound of the Lord talking to her.

Winter saw Katie with her eyes closed and knew that she was in prayer about something, so she too closed her eyes to support her in prayer. Within mere moments, all four of the women were in prayer, upholding each other in prayer.

"Quick, girls, we must all pray for Earnest and Bart," Katie suddenly said, but when she opened her eyes and saw the others praying, she knew that her request was answered before she even voiced it, so she simply closed her eyes again and returned to her time of prayer.

On the very next hole, each man played his golf ball and to the amazement of each one of them, all of their golf balls landed within a few feet of each other on the far left side about halfway up the fairway.

"Wow, talk about a game of surprises," Earnest said as the four of them walked back to their golf carts.

"You ain't seen nothing yet," Franklin said softly.

"What did you say, son?" Earnest asked, but Franklin remained silent.

The two golf carts then left the tee box and made their way out to the individual golf balls where they lay in the soft green grass of the fairway. As it turned out, due to the position of the golf balls, they had to park the golf carts one behind the other just on the edge of the fairway about 20 feet out from the trees. Being where they were now, golfers in front of them and any coming up behind them would be able to see them clearly before any other shots were made.

"I think that maybe a storm is brewing," Earnest said as suddenly dark clouds seemed to roll in and the rumblings of thunder could be heard in the distance. "Maybe we should think about taking cover somewhere?"

"It will be okay," Thomas said with a silly grin on his face that made Earnest wonder what his friend knew that he didn't.

Before the men made their way out to their golf balls, they all just sat in the carts talking, Bart with Franklin again and Thomas with Earnest as well. Within a few moments, the four men left the carts but did not grab a golf club or head out to their balls; instead they just stood on the side of the carts that faced the trees.

As Thomas looked back behind them to see if any other golfers were approaching, he was amazed that there were none. On a perfect day like today, with the exception of the approaching storm, this course would be packed with golfers on all 36 holes, but as far as he looked, Thomas could not see a single other golfer in sight. He could hear thunder all around them now, with flashes of lightning punctuating the darkened sky here and there, but nothing in their general area, and Thomas knew that this was the work of the Lord.

Thank you, Lord, for what you are about to accomplish, Thomas silently prayed as he turned back to the other three men.

"I-I am not sure what to do?" Bart stuttered.

"Maybe we should just wait until we get home," Earnest said then.

"No!" Thomas said. "Now is the appointed time."

Franklin had his father and brother get on their knees, facing the golf cart while he stood before them, leaning up against the cart. Thomas then moved in behind the two men on their knees and placed a hand on each man's shoulder.

"Okay," Franklin started. "The Bible tells us of four spiritual laws that are instructional in leading men to Christ. I am going to tell you each of these laws and then have you answer some questions that you can both answer at the same time. When we are done, we will all pray the same prayer together. I will say the words, and you can repeat them after me. Thomas will pray with you as well. Are you ready?"

"Yes," Bart said with his head bowed.

"Yes," Earnest said as well in a whisper as his emotions quickly rose to the surface.

"The Bible says ... for God so loved the world that he gave his one and only Son, that whoever believes in him shall not perish but have eternal life.

"It is God's plan for you and me to experience peace in our lives here on earth and in eternity as well. That is why he came up with the plan to send his Son to us. But there was a problem in that we were separated from God because of sin. He did not want us to be robots and just do whatever he wanted, so he gave man the freedom of choice. As mere men and women, we have chosen to go the way of the world. This started with Adam and still continues to this very day, and because of this, we are separated from God. Do you understand this?"

"Yes," Bart said, his eyes still closed.

"Yes, I do," Earnest said.

"Then the Bible says ... For all have sinned and fall short of the glory of God. It also says ... 'For the wages of sin is death, but the gift of God is eternal life in Christ Jesus our Lord.'

"God has a plan for anyone willing to accept it," Franklin continued. "He sent his Son Jesus who died on the cross for our sins. He paid the penalty for those sins and basically provided a bridge between us and God. After Jesus died on the cross and was buried, he came back to life, and he is alive today. The Bible says ... 'But God demonstrates his own love for us in this: While we were still sinners, Christ died for us.' Do you believe that you are a sinner?"

"Yes," Bart said as tears streamed down his face and he realized that he was in fact a sinner.

"Yes," Earnest was barely able to say as the guilt of all his sins began to wash over his soul.

"So in doing all of this for us, we must trust Jesus as our Lord and Savior and ask him to forgive us of our sins and be a part of our lives.

"The Bible says ... 'Here I am! I stand at the door and knock. If anyone hears my voice and opens the door, I will come in and eat with that person and they with me.' ... It also says ... 'If you declare with your mouth, "Jesus is Lord," and believe in your heart that God raised him from the dead, you will be saved.' Do you wish to ask Jesus to forgive you of your sins?"

"Yes, oh God, yes," Bart blurted out as he felt those heavy sins begin to depart from him.

"Yes, I do," Earnest said as well through a torrent of tears and sorrow.

"Okay, so this is the plan of salvation. First, you must admit that you are a sinner. Second, you must be willing to turn away from your sins and repent before God. Third, you must believe that Jesus Christ died for you on the cross and rose from the grave. Then fourth, through prayer, you need to invite Jesus to come in and control your life through the Holy Spirit as you receive Him as Lord and Savior. So I am going to give you just a few moments to silently talk to Jesus. Admit you are a sinner. Ask Jesus to forgive your sins. Believe that Jesus gave up his life for your sins, and then we will pray the prayer."

The two men on their knees were sobbing and praying at the same time until after a few moments they were silent.

Right then the storm seemed to really intensify with wild rumblings and lightning evident all around them, so much so that the ground actually shook with each crack of thunder. Thomas felt that this was a reflection of the battle that was now raging within the life of Earnest and his son Bart as they neared salvation.

"Okay, let us pray, and I will say the words and you repeat them out loud after I have said them," Franklin instructed them. This time, he did not wait for an answer but went straight into the sinner's prayer.

"Dear Lord Jesus ... I know that I am a sinner, and I ask your forgiveness ... I believe that you died for my sins and rose from the dead ... I turn from my sins and invite you to come into my heart and life ... I want to trust and follow you as my Lord and Saviour ... In your name, amen!"

Bart instantly jumped up from a kneeling position. "Wow!" he shouted. "I praise your holy name, my Lord and Saviour," he continued, much to the surprise of both Thomas and Franklin, but when they looked back at Earnest, he was still on his knees, his head still bowed and the tears still flowing.

It took another few minutes before Earnest finally raised his head and struggled to stand up, but with the help of the other three, he was soon sitting on the seat of his golf cart.

"Dad, are you okay?" Franklin asked as he knelt down on one knee to make sure that Earnest was okay.

"Y-yes," Earnest whispered and then remained silent for a few moments before continuing, "I-I have wasted so much of my life. I could have done so much good with what the Lord has given me." The tears continued, and his body was racked with sobs.

"Dad, look at me!" Franklin shouted, getting everyone's

immediate attention until Earnest looked up at his son. "Dad, did the Lord tell you this?" he then asked.

Earnest just shook his head no before he spoke. "No, not really."

"Then why are you beating yourself up?"

"Because I know I could have done so much more. I could have been a better father to you boys. I could have helped so many lost people, but I ..." His voice trailed off.

"Earnest," Thomas said, "we have all felt like this just after we got saved, but God ultimately is in charge of your life. I don't believe for a second that he is disappointed in you, and in fact, the Bible says that all of the angels rejoice when a sinner comes home. So right now, there is much celebration going on in heaven over the salvation of you and your son. Now is the time to celebrate, my friend."

Slowly, Earnest seemed to come around. The tears stopped, and finally he smiled and the peace of God that so easily confuses all the unsaved washed over the man right there on the golf course. He then rose to his feet and hugged both of his sons until Thomas joined in on the group hug.

As they all broke the hug, Thomas looked around and was stunned to see that it was once again a bright, sunny warm morning with not a single cloud in the sky, and after a few moments, he could see other golfers beginning to emerge here and there on the golf course.

"Well, boys, I think we better finish this game," Thomas said as he pulled an iron from his bag and headed over to his golf ball.

"I wonder if we will see any more amazing shots today," Bart said.

"I think we have already witnessed the most amazing thing that could ever happen today," Franklin said as he placed his arm around his brother's shoulders and pulled him close.

After the golf game, the four men made their way back into the country club dining room for a light lunch before heading back to the city, but Bart declined.

"I have got to get home. I have something very important to do, that is, if Winter is still there," he said as he literally was bouncing on the tips of his toes. With that said, Bart was out of there in a flash before Earnest had a chance to ask him not to mention anything to Katie.

"Okay, well, I guess it is just the three of us then," Earnest said as he turned back to his son Franklin and his best friend and business partner, Thomas.

"No problem, my friend, no problem," Thomas said as the three of them found a table and seated themselves.

"Actually, this is good, as I wanted to talk to you, Thomas, about our latest project and to you, Franklin, about a business proposal."

"Oh really?" Franklin said.

"Yes, well, you know a bit about Thomas here and the work he has been doing for me and with me, but now it is time to add another person to the picture."

"Why is that, Dad?"

"In case you haven't noticed, I am not getting any younger, and it is time to pass certain things on."

"Are you okay?" Franklin asked with concern.

"Yes, yes, but I want some alone time with my sweetie, time to travel and see the world in a pleasure sense instead of the business one."

"Well, okay, I can relate to that as long as you are okay?" Franklin said again.

Earnest just turned to Thomas then. "So maybe you could bring Franklin up to speed on the current projects."

"Okay then. Our current project may sound complicated, but really it's not. It is a thermal radar unit, and basically how it works is that the unit would mount a number of ways, but to make it easier to understand, just imagine a unit sitting on a tripod, much like a surveyor's equipment. The unit would warm objects, such as car engines, tires, people and such. The spinning camera unit on the tripod would take 10 to 16 or so thermal images per second; then software would piece the pictures together, and after that, the heat signatures of these items would be triangulated, using GPS, giving their location as a dot or a blip on a radar-like screen, perhaps even the screen on one's cell phone. We have looked at the feasible uses of such a unit and feel it could be used in the areas of the military or even search and rescue."

"Wow!" Franklin said, his face showing obvious excitement.

"My exact reaction the first time I heard of it too," Earnest said.

"Just how many projects have you two worked on so far?" Franklin asked, becoming very interested in these two men's line of work.

"Umm, three, I believe," Earnest said.

"No, it is actually four if you count the Heel and Toe Power Unit," Thomas said.

"Oh, yes, I had forgotten that one."

"Heel and Toe ... what?" Franklin piped up.

"Again, basically it is a system built into one's shoe. The operating system would convert the energy of one's heel striking a plate that would create a rotational energy. This would be produced using magnets that would spin, like rotors. Then the spin of these rotors would create an electrical current that would be stored in coils of wire also embedded within the shoes. This current would then travel along wires or a circuit board, charging a lithium battery pack that would sit on top of the shoe just above the user's toes or at the top of the back of the shoe above the heel, and the benefit of such a device would be to charge cell phones after a relatively short walk or run and would be great for hikers, long distance runners and joggers alike."

"Unbelievable!" Franklin said.

"Yes, he is a man full of surprises, and at first, I thought I was just lucky to have met him, but now I know that it was the Lord who brought us together, to make a difference in the world together," Earnest said, looking across the table at his best friend. "Thank you, my friend; you were right."

"It was all the Lord's idea, not mine," Thomas said with a smile.

"Yes, true, true," Earnest answered.

"Okay, so could you please tell me the other three ideas you brought to the world?" Franklin asked as the excitement continued to rise within him.

"Well, it all started with the Green Heat project, which is a radical new idea in home and building heating. After that, we worked on the Cover-It project, which is in wide use in the construction industry today. After those two, came the Commando-Com Unit, which is a centralized unit in tractor-trailer units that controls every aspect of a driver's job inside and outside the unit. Then there is the Heel and Toe unit we just talked about, and now we are delving into a new project that is named Green Heat II."

"Does this have something to do with the Green Heat project you already mentioned?" Franklin asked as he drank his coffee.

"Yes, it does. I have been working on an idea that would further enhance the original project as it now stands. This idea would be based on the Green Heat units, but would be more like a generator, powered by the same items that create the heat for our existing units.

"These units would be small and great for home owners, campers, the military and just about any situation that requires heat should the power go out. It would incorporate our Green Heat system along with solar power to charge a battery that could run a home refrigerator for up to 48 hours or light that same home for up to 24 hours. Anything electrical could be run off this unit. Thinking even farther ahead than that, it could be adapted to boost a vehicle battery or allow enough power for a 30-minute boost of a welder.

"These units would be designed for a fast recharge and affordable enough for the average person to be able to own one or two units at a time. We could even look at changeable power pods with one main charging unit instead of having to purchase multiple main units."

This time, when Thomas looked at the two men, they looked almost dumbfounded as their brains processed the information they had just heard. Earnest was thinking about the financial gains and how he could use that money to further fund even more projects, besides helping out the many charities he worked with. Franklin, on the other hand, was thinking of how such units could greatly improve the lives of many humans in some of the most remote locations on earth.

"Amazing ... simply amazing!" Franklin finally said. He found himself to be overwhelmed by this man, his vision into things and the fact that he was a born-again Christian.

"So, son," Earnest said as he turned to face his son, who was seated beside him. "do you think you would be interested in working with Thomas and myself?"

"Are you kidding me? You bet I am. When do I start?"

The four women were just milling around now on the stone patio when all of a sudden they heard a commotion coming from within the house, and before any of them could go to see what it was, Bart burst forth from the garden bay doors out onto the patio, looking in their direction until he spotted what he was looking for.

He started moving towards Winter until he was running. He came right up to her, swept her into his arms and kissed her passionately, while she had a look of shock that turned into pleasure on her face. The other women just stared in surprise, to say the least.

"I-I love you!" he said breathlessly as he broke the kiss and held her to himself tightly. "Thank you oh so much for never giving up on me," he whispered in her ear as tears rolled down both of their cheeks. Then the two of them just stood there, clinging to each other as they slowly swayed back and forth.

"What?" Katie finally said loudly. "What did you just say to her, Bart?"

Bart and Winter broke the hug as Bart turned to face his mother along with Caroline and Julie. "You heard right, Mother. I love this woman with all my heart and right here, right now ..." he said as he then turned to face Winter. "... and now I am asking you if you would be my wife."

Katie almost passed out, swaying slightly. Caroline and Julie rushed to her side and helped her sit in one of the patio chairs.

Winter was in shock. Yes, she had prayed to the Lord for such a day as this, but this was all so quick, all so sudden. She already knew the answer. "Yes!" she shouted. "Yes! Yes! Yes!"

Then Bart did something that shook even his mother's resolve. He pulled away from Winter and began to dance around the patio, his hands raised in the air as he shouted loudly. "Thank you, oh, God, my father, for exposing the darkness in the room of white. I praise your holy name now and forever more."

"H-he's saved?" Katie said. "My boy has found the Lord!" she said even louder as the tears flowed over her face. "He was lost, but now he is found. Oh, thank you, Lord! Thank you, Lord! Praise your most holy name!"

Caroline and Julie joined in on the praise celebration as well, and soon, all of them were on their feet, hands raised in the air, praising their Lord and Saviour.

Finally all of them settled down and were seated around the huge family patio table. Katie stood to talk to them all. Tears were still trickling down her cheeks as words came to her mouth.

"With so much excitement happening here today, the thought just occurred to me ... that perhaps you should all ... get married on the same day?"

CHAPTER SIXTEEN

Bart couldn't believe how good he felt every single day when he woke up. He was alive and flying high with the Lord, but one thing did puzzle him though and that was what to do with his life now. The experiences in the white room led him to believe that God had a purpose and a mission for his life with Winter, even though he still had no idea what that might be.

That day, Bart had a special thing in mind though. He had gotten permission, via his father, to go back to the racquetball court in his father's former building downtown. He just had a burning desire to go back to the location where his life-changing trip began, and that day would be the day. He had from 10:00 a.m. until 10:30 a.m. before he would have to leave, but he knew that would be more than enough time.

Bart bounded out of bed at 6:00 a.m., had a shower and shave before breakfast and was on his way downtown way earlier than his appointment. He just wanted to get out for a drive. As he drove along the avenue that would eventually get him to his destination, he was daydreaming about his experiences in the white room of darkness, his fiancée Winter, and their wedding, which would be shared by Caroline and Franklin as well.

His mind really wasn't where it should have been as he drove, and when he suddenly came to his senses, he realized he was about to run down a homeless man pushing his cart across a well-marked intersection. Bart immediately applied his brakes and came to a loud, screeching stop, but not before bumping the

---

man and his cart to the ground. Bart was out of his car in a flash as he rushed to the homeless man's aid, making sure that he was all right with no injuries. It wasn't that he was worried about any implications, such as being sued or anything like that, but he sincerely wanted to make sure the man was okay.

"A-are you okay?" Bart asked as he helped the man to his feet and then righted his cart back up. "I am so sorry. My mind wasn't where it should have been, I guess." Then Bart stepped back and had a good look at the man before him. Suddenly he recognized the man as the one who had walked up to his car the night of his father's 50th birthday.

"I think we have met before," Bart said.

"Yes, we have, my friend. Yes, we have," the homeless man replied.

"Please let me say how sorry I am for treating you the way I did, but I was a different man back then than I am today."

"Yes, I know."

"Uh ... you know what?" Bart asked, confused by this man's words.

"I know that you are now a different man," the homeless man said with a big smile on his face.

Bart didn't know what to say, so the man kept on talking.

"I know that you are now a born-again Christian along with your father."

"Wha ...? How in the world would you know that?"

"My Lord told me."

Now Bart was really confused. This homeless man was telling him that he too was a born-again Christian, and he wondered how that could even be.

"I ... uh ... h-how can that be?" Bart finally managed to get out. "Y-you are a ... uh ... a ..." But he couldn't finish the sentence.

"A what? A dirty, ragged homeless man?"

Bart was silent as he realized that the words the man had said were exactly what was on his mind, and now it all sounded so wrong, so un-God-like. He hung his head in shame in even thinking this way of another of God's marvelous creations.

"It is okay, son," the man said as he walked up to Bart and placed a gloved hand on his shoulder.

Bart raised his head and looked into the man's eyes. He saw love, pure and simple. The man then stretched out his arm for a handshake.

"Hello, my name is John," he said.

Bart took the man's hand in his own before he spoke.

"Bart is mine."

"That is an uncommon name for sure, with the exception of Bart Simpson," the man said with a chuckle. "What is your full name?" he asked.

"Bartholomew William Woodsworth."

"Hummmmm!" the man responded.

"W-what is it?"

"Your name, well, it's a coincidence, I am sure, because my full name is Johnathan Bartholomew Wiggins."

Bart froze right then and there as he recalled the words of God when he was in the white room of darkness.

"No, my son, but my servant will lead you into the truth that will set you free. After that, you will meet your best friend who will guide you into the mission I have for you and your future wife. ... Yes, Bart, you have already met him, and when you talk to him again, you will be surprised to know that the two of you share the same name."

"Y-your name ... is the same ... as mine," Bart said in a hesitant voice.

"Yes, it is, and now isn't that quite the coincidence?" the man said.

There was silence between the two men now, standing out in the middle of an intersection in the early morning light, before the city came to life.

"I ... I would like to take you to coffee?" Bart said.

"Right now?"

Bart searched his mind, trying to remember why it was that he was down there in the first place until finally the trip to the racquetball court popped into his mind. He looked at his watch before answering.

"Yes, sure, now would be a great time, as my morning appointment is still three hours away. Are there any coffee locations close by?" Bart asked.

"Yeah, but the only close one wouldn't want my kind in there."

"Your kind?"

"The homeless, dirty kind."

"What?" Bart asked, astonished.

"My life is miles apart from yours, Bart. People such as myself simply can't walk into a fine dining establishment, you know."

"Well, why not, as long as you have money?"

"That is not the way the real world operates, I am afraid."

Bart thought about it for a few moments.

"Do you have a place close by where you could leave your cart?" Bart finally asked.

"Uh, yeah, but it is a block or two away."

Bart looked at the cart and then his car and realized that it would not fit in easily.

"How about I just push it there and you can follow me?" John said, as if he were reading Bart's mind.

"Uh ... okay ... that will work, I guess. You're sure you are okay to walk?" Bart asked again just to be sure.

"I am fine, Bart. Don't worry," John said as he began pushing his cart down the avenue to the next corner where he turned left and went another two blocks. Finally he stopped at a padlocked door, produced a key, opened the door and disappeared inside with his shopping cart full of all his worldly possessions. After a few minutes, he appeared again, locked the door and made his way over to Bart's car.

Finally after about 10 minutes of driving, Bart swung his car into the parking lot of an out-of-the-way diner that looked more like a railway car that had been converted into a rusting old coffee shop, but the interior looked well-lit and comfortable, with even a jukebox in the corner by the door. After ordering what the two of them wanted, Bart paid for the food and drinks before they settled into a red-leather upholstered booth.

The two men chatted for about 20 minutes or so about life in general before Bart asked a question that had been burning a hole in his brain.

"So, John, why is it that you are living on the streets? I mean, what did you do before life on the streets?"

"Well," John said with a laugh, "I know you are going to find this hard to believe, but I was a world-renowned chef in my earlier days."

"A chef? You?"

"Yes, it is amazing how far the proud have fallen," John said.

"What do you mean by that?"

"Bart, you grew up with money and have lived a life of luxury, even though it was not your money to play with."

How does he know these things? Bart wondered, still listening to John's words.

"You and I both understand how money can warp a person's perception of the real world, right?"

"Yes," Bart said ashamedly.

"Don't feel ashamed, my friend. God knew what walk you would have in life to bring you to this point. Take those feelings and use them positively from here on in though. As for myself, it was more than money; it was the fame and being a somebody in the world. I was a wanted man by the rich and famous. I have been to more special high-society occasions and parties than I can count. Then I got into television and eventually had a chain of restaurants here in the city and the Midwest."

"So what happened then? ... I mean, look at you now."

"Have you heard the saying that for every action there is a reaction?"

"Yes."

"Well, I was the man of the hour for about 10 years until one day I was introduced to the wife of a very influential and powerful political figure. She was about 20 years younger than her husband and very lonely too. I started off as her personal chef in her quest to shed a few pounds, but over the course of a few weeks, it became evident to me that she wanted more than just my cooking. One morning after I had cooked her routine breakfast and was cleaning up, she came into the kitchen where I was washing a few things up in the sink. When I heard her voice and turned around, you could have picked my mouth up off the floor at the sight of her in a very revealing sheer gown that showed off the little lingerie she wore underneath. She walked right up to me and told me what she wanted and expected of me."

As John paused, Bart asked a question.

"You didn't?"

"Actually, no, I didn't."

"Then what happened that put you into the state you are today?"

"She was so offended that I would reject her offer that she swore I would never see another kitchen again, and she was true to her word. She let it get around that I came on to her, and when her husband heard the rumors, he saw to it that I was stripped of everything I had worked for, including my dignity, even though in the end, he arrived home early one day to find her with the pool boy in their bed."

"You've never worked since?" Bart asked as he drank his coffee.

"No."

"So then tell me, where did the Lord come into all this?"

With that question, John's eyes lit up followed by a broad, wide smile.

"One sure way that a man will turn to the Lord is to take

away all that he has, especially the ability to use his gifts to make money. I was destitute, depressed, losing my own family and considering suicide when I was watching television one night in my hotel room. I was mindlessly flipping through channels when it came to a man sharing a story of where he had lost everything in life, kind of like me. He went on to say that he finally cried out to the Lord, and just like that, the Lord heard his cries."

"What television show was that on?"

"The Billy Graham Evangelistic Crusade. I don't know where it was, but I was down on my knees in mere moments, crying out to the Lord to forgive me, accept me and restore me too. Then I called the phone number at the bottom of the screen and the rest is history."

"You became a Christian?"

"Yes."

"Okay ... but ... why?"

"Why am I like this?"

"Yes."

"I really don't have an answer to that, except for one thing maybe."

"What's that?"

"That evening, after I got saved, I had a dream that showed me like I am today. My family all left me, and I was living off the streets, ministering here and there when people would listen. In that dream though, I was having a conversation with God and he said something to me that was intriguing, to say the least. He told me that I would meet a man with the same name as mine that we would be the best of friends and that we would share a ministry mission together!"

"So seeing I am kind of naïve to your whole world, may I ask you some questions to bring me up to speed?" Bart asked John across the table as the two men shared a meal.

"Sure, what would you like to know?" John said as he licked his fingers clean of the sandwich he had just consumed.

"Well, first, how long have you been living the life?"

"You mean as a homeless person?"

"Yes."

"Next month will be five years for me."

"Five years! You have been living this way for five whole years?"

"Yes."

"Why? I find that a man with your qualifications might have been down on his luck for a year maybe, but five?"

"The answer is simple, my friend."

"Simple?"

"Yes, because that is where the Lord wanted me to be."

Bart had no comeback for that answer, but he was still new to the whole Christian walk thing, and with time, he would understand more, at least that was the hope.

"Let me ask you something?" John said to Bart as he stared intently at him.

"O-okay, what?"

"How much would you be willing to give up if the Lord really wanted you to go to the mission field or another country? Would you be willing to give up everything you have and know, to do his will?"

Now that question threw Bart for a loop. He knew that he would be giving up all his toys and such, and that was not a bother to him these days, but give up everything? That was a whole other ball game.

"If you never had the call to do so, then it is very hard to give it all up. One needs to be sure that it is the Lord's calling they are hearing; otherwise, they may be into a whole world of hurt down the road," John said.

"What do you mean when you say calling?"

"Ah, you are a good listener, I see. Well a calling or the will of the Lord for your life is the path that the Lord has for each of his children to walk through their lives here on this planet. The problem though, is that many have felt they have 'heard' from the Lord, when in fact it has been their own personal desires that led them here or there."

"Is that wrong, to do that, I mean?"

"Getting out of step with the Lord may not be a wise decision, but the Bible does say that the Lord works everything to his good for those who believe. What this means is that God will use a willing person, no matter where they are or how they got there, for that matter. However, it would be far better for a person to be doing God's will and have it all work out the way he planned it to be."

"Okay, I can see the logic in that."

"Great! You and I are going to get along quite well," John said with a wide smile on his face. "What else do you have for me?" he asked Bart.

"What?"

"You said you had some questions for me, but that was only one question."

"Oh yeah," Bart said with a chuckle as he remembered his earlier words. "I would venture to say that you have a ministry of sorts with your type of people, right?"

"Yes ... yes, I do at that."

"Okay, remember that I am still new to all of this, but how many people would you estimate are homeless in this city?"

"About 5,000, as far as I know."

"Five thousand people!" Bart said in disbelief. "There are that many people living like you do?"

"Yes."

"Well, I find that hard to believe."

"Bart, do you even know what the population of this city is?"

"Hummm, I think I heard it was around 300,000."

"Maybe 10 years ago, but presently, after the last census, the population of this city was pegged at 500,000-plus people."

"Wow!"

"So take only 5,000 people out of that number, and it really doesn't affect the overall number, does it?"

"No, I guess not."

"Okay then, let me ask you this. Out of the 5,000, how many people do you impact with your ministry?"

"Sadly only about 300," John said with a sadness in his eyes. "Why do you ask?"

"How would you like to increase those numbers?"

"Now you are talking my language, friend. What do you have in mind?"

"I am not sure where this idea came from, but while we have been talking, I kinda got this picture in my head of an old hospital converted into a homeless shelter."

"Praise the Lord!" John shouted out, which caught the immediate attention of the other patrons within the diner.

"Huh?" Bart asked, not sure why John was so happy.

"What you just saw in your head was what we call a vision. The Lord let you see something that will happen in the future."

"I saw into the future?"

"Yes, well, sort of, but I will explain that to you another time. So please tell me what you saw in this place?"

"Uh ... okay. Well, there were a lot of people all over the place, making use of the various departments. I saw a fully staffed kitchen with state-of-the-art equipment and ..." Bart hesitated, and John could hear emotion welling to the surface of his new friend.

"Take your time, my friend; I have all the time in the world."

"Uh ... oh ... sorry about that. I don't know where that came from?"

"That is the Holy Spirit interacting with you, and there is absolutely nothing wrong with being emotional or even crying— no matter what the world will tell you. So please continue with what you saw in your vision."

Bart wiped his eyes and cleared his throat before continuing, "I saw a chef with those tall white hats, you know?"

"Oh, believe me, that I do know."

"Okay, but when the chef turned around, I saw that it was you!"

This time and for the first time in the entire conversation, it was John who had nothing to say as tears formed in his eyes.

"After that, I saw a huge crowd of people seated in a huge dining area, having a great meal, while outside there was a lineup of people waiting to get in. Also, there were all these different departments, like addictions counselling; free clothing; food bank; areas where people were being trained in various skills, such as woodworking, sewing, plumbing, electrical and much more. The amazing thing though was the fact that there were all these skilled professionals training, feeding and clothing these homeless people."

"Wow!" John said. "Was there any more to it—the vision, I mean?"

"Just one more thing, and I feel inside that this is the starting point."

"The starting point for what?"

"For John and Bart's Place—at least that was the name I saw on the side of the building."

John was openly weeping now as the realization of the Lord's words to him so many years ago were now about to become a reality.

"The starting point is to house these people."

"H-how will w-we do that?" John whispered through his tears.

"We will have to go shopping, my friend."

"Shopping? ... For what?"

"Real estate!"

CHAPTER SEVENTEEN

"So have you been thinking about your futures at all?" Katie asked Caroline, Julie and Winter, who were all out for a day of shopping and had stopped for a bite of lunch downtown in the city.

"Actually we are way ahead of you there, Mom," Caroline piped up as she looked at the other girls.

"What do you mean?" Katie asked, surprised at her daughter's words.

"The three of us have been discussing a business venture and were going to ask your advice in time, but seeing that you have brought up the subject, we might as well ask you now."

"Business venture?"

"Yes, Mom, you heard me right."

"Okay, what do you three have cooking in those lovely heads of yours?"

"Well," Julie said this time. "You know that I have my license in real estate and that was what I did in our old location."

"Yes, I know that," Katie said.

"You also know that I have skills in photography," Winter said next.

"Okay, yes."

"And, Mother, you know I love decorating and designing."

"Ooookay, just where is all of this leading, girls?"

All three of the women just looked at each other, nodded their heads and turned to face Katie.

"We are thinking of opening our own real estate office here in the city," Julie said as the others wore excited looks on their faces.

Katie was unsure of what to say. On one hand, she was glad that they all had a sense of direction, but she wasn't too sure of their choice.

"Okay!" was all Katie said.

"What?" Caroline asked her mom. "Aren't you excited for us?"

"I am, yes, but do you think real estate is the way to go?"

"We each possess a quality that would work great in real estate, and we all want to work together in whatever it is that the Lord has for us," Julie said.

"Well, I can see that you have made up your minds, and who am I to stand in your way? I pray that the Lord will be your guide and that you will all uphold good Christian morals along your journey. Do you happen to have a name for your new business venture?"

"Yes, we do, Mom," Caroline said with a smile as she turned to Winter.

"Three Sisters Real Estate!" Winter almost shouted out.

"Sisters?" Katie asked with raised eyebrows.

"Yes, we know we are not legal sisters, but we are sisters in the Lord and that is what really matters to us," Julie said.

"Yes, I can see the Lord in all three of you and in this new step in your life as well."

With that said, congratulations made their way around the table as all four of them stood and hugged each other for a few moments.

"So where do I fit into this plan?" Katie finally asked after they were all seated again.

"I thought you would never ask," Julie said again.

"How do you feel about being a receptionist?"

"Well now, girls," Katie said, "I am flattered that you would offer me such a position, but there are two things I would like to say about this. First, you want a younger person in this position.

You are three young women—no matter what you have to say about that—and you want all young people working in the business with you. Secondly, Earnest and I have plans to travel the world once you are all married and settled into your new roles as married couples and into your careers as well.

"You will do well, I am sure, in whatever endeavour you pursue, but make sure that the Lord is the head of it all and in doing this he will pour out his blessings on you. Marriage alongside a career is not an easy accomplishment, so my advice to you is to make sure that you leave work at work. Do not bring it home, and also make sure that you take time for each other at least once a year, even after the kids come. You will need that time alone together to recharge your marriage, and believe me when I say that I am talking from experience."

With that said, all four of the women stood to leave, but before they even went to pay the bill, they all gathered for a group hug right there in the downtown restaurant.

Bart had missed his opportunity to revisit the racquetball court at his father's former building in the city, but it mattered not to him any longer. He was truly on a mission now with the desire to help the homeless, right there within his very own city.

He had shared with Winter that very evening everything that had happened with him and John, and she was more than excited to hear all the details. She in turn had shared with him what she and the other two girls were thinking of opening within the city, but deep down inside, Winter knew that she would be working with Bart full-time in the future, for that was truly where her heart was.

Bart had changed so much in such a short amount of time, that there were times when Winter wondered if it would truly last, but when she saw the time he was giving John and the time he was spending with the homeless right where they were, she knew that he was definitely moving within the will of God. Her prayers had already all been answered, and she now looked forward to their upcoming marriage and life with her husband and children after that.

"What are you going to call your ministry, hon?" Winter asked Bart as she snuggled up close to him on her sofa.

"We talked about that and came up with the name 'John & Bart's Place.' I didn't want my name to be first, because I don't want the place associated so much with my family's wealth. What I am saying is that if people see my name first, they will just say that it is the Woodsworth's money that made this place happen. Yes, I will use that money, but it is the Lord who is making this place happen, and John and I are just the willing servants."

"Yes. Amen to that," Winter said.

Bart noticed that she was deep in thought about something. "What?" he asked her.

"I think there might be a better name, hon."

"Okay, I am open to suggestions as we are just in the starting stages and nothing is in stone yet."

"How about Bartholomew's Place?"

Bart was instantly silent, which caused Winter to look directly up at him. She could see the tears forming in his eyes.

"Are you okay?" she asked him as she rose and sat on his knees with her arms around his neck so that she could look directly into his face.

"That's it!" he suddenly said.

"What is?"

"The name—Bartholomew's Place. That's the name. The Lord told us both that we would meet because of our mutual name. That is the name that the Lord wants us to use; I am sure of it."

"Earnest, I remember once you telling me that Bart liked to tinker with things, right?" Thomas asked his friend in his office that day.

"Yes, the boy has an uncanny way of looking at things and the skills to fix the problem as well. He never really got the college education his mother and I had hoped for him, but he is not totally without skills," Earnest said across the desk between the two business partners. "Why are you asking?"

"Well, I know that we have a fantastic working staff all around us, who are just as dedicated to our projects as we are, and we now have Franklin working alongside us as well, but we are missing one key skill in all of it."

"And that is?"

"Someone who likes to tinker, think outside of the box and is innovative."

"Bart? Really?" Earnest said, which surprised Thomas to say the least. He thought for sure that he would be thrilled at having both sons work for them.

"I would at least like to talk with him and see if he would at all be interested."

"Do you really think we need a tinkerer, as you put it?"

"Most definitely."

"Why are you so adamant about it?"

"Because, my friend, when I first started out that was the type of person I was, right up until I met you on the Green Heat project."

"Couldn't you just handle that end of it?"

"No, sorry, for two reasons."

"And they are?"

"First, I am way too busy with what I am doing now. Quality control, new materials and new projects have most of my time as it is. Being a tinkerer takes a lot of time just sitting and thinking, and you would also be surprised at how draining that can be on a person. Nope ... we need a young person for this job, and I think that Bart might just be the one we are looking for."

"Okay, well you can ask him, but I know he is really into some downtown project he is working on and I even think he has a partner of sorts."

"Could you please ask him to drop by in the next few days, so I can have a chat with him, just to see if he would at all be interested?"

"Okay, yes, I will see to that tonight when we have supper together."

"Do you like the sound of that, my friend?"

Earnest stopped, like he was listening for something he had missed.

"Uh, I am not sure what it is that I am supposed to be hearing."

Thomas chuckled before speaking. "No, no, I am not talking about a specific sound. What I meant was the words you said about your family having supper together. Did you ever think that would happen again?"

"All I can say is that God is so very good and that I am a very blessed man, even though I never deserved it."

"That is truly one of the amazing things when it comes to God, the fact that he loves us so much that he made a way for us to come into his blessing. He only ever wanted the very best for his children, but humans, being in nature who they are, figure they have it all together without God, so he just patiently waits for us."

By then, Earnest was in tears, his head down in his hands on the edge of Thomas's desk. Being a new Christian, he found that he was always emotional at the slightest little things. He couldn't even watch most movies without having to have a tissue with him.

Thomas just looked at his friend and silently thanked God for Earnest's salvation. Here he was, one of the wealthiest men in the country, in tears just at the thought of having supper with his family.

After a few moments, Earnest looked up and dried his eyes before speaking. "Sorry about that," he said.

"Don't you ever feel sorry around me again. I am just so very happy that you finally came to find the Lord, because you know how hard I tried to lead you in that direction."

"Yes, you are persistent if nothing else," Earnest said with a slight chuckle.

"Well, I try."

"Okay, I will talk to Bart about you wanting to see him. Shall I tell him what it is about?"

"No, please don't. I want to lead him into the thought of possibly working with us after I show him what we are doing and where we are headed first."

"All right. So just where are we headed next?"

"I have something rolling around in my head."

"You always do."

A huge crack of thunder brought Bart to a sudden awakening very early in the morning, and even though he was used to thunderstorms, this one seemed to be louder and more intense than he could remember for quite some time. He rose from his bed and slowly wandered over to his bedroom window in the dark.

Obviously the power must be out, he thought as he stood at the window facing the city and noticed that not a single light was showing. *That's weird*, he thought. *Normally I should be able to see emergency lighting somewhere.*

In the blink of an eye or faster, Bart suddenly found himself seated in a huge easy chair, and as he closed and then opened his eyes again, he realized exactly where he was.

"The white room of darkness?" he said out loud this time.

"Yes, my son," Bart heard in that audible voice he had come to know well these days.

"I ... I kinda thought this part was over?" Bart said, stumbling over his words.

"This is the closure, Bartholomew. When it all started for you,

I showed you something you did not understand and I want to make it clear to you now."

Bart tried to think about how it all started. He remembered the encounter he had had with the stranger in the café back at his father's former office building. From there, his mind wandered to the game that he had played with the stranger and his attempt to physically hurt the stranger, which actually backfired on him. From there, he recounted the pain in his arm, the touch of the stranger's finger on his arm and the pain that would not leave. At that point, Bart remembered passing out and seeing his body from somewhere up above in the racquetball court area. Then Bart recalled a very weird sensation begin to coarse through his body, and he never even had a chance to say a word before he shot up straight through the ceiling, picking up speed as he seemingly flew through floor after floor of the 80-story skyscraper. He could see floors flying by, complete with cubicles, stairways, copy machines, desks and so much more as he continued speeding faster and faster as he rose.

Finally he seemed to slow down as he approached the very top floor of the Woodsworth Industries International building, which held his father's private office, complete with a small gym, steam room, large private washroom, kitchenette and the patio gardens, all of which had been designed by his father alone. Bart then found himself standing on the floor, able to walk and move around even though he knew he wasn't in his own body. As he looked around the huge office with all its ornate objects, fine paintings and expensive archeological objects from various parts of the word, his eyes finally came to rest on the area of the vault with all the pictures and sounds, which were a testament to a father's love for his children.

From there, Bart remembered being on the roof of the 80-story skyscraper where he met someone looking over the ledge. Suddenly he was moving towards the person, but not of his own will, it was as if he were being softly pushed in that direction. Then something caught his attention. It was a smell, a very pleasant smell, like cotton candy, meadow flowers and the first rain of spring all mixed together. Oh how he loved that fragrance and just wanted to breathe it in deeply and forever. Then he was standing right beside the person who was still looking over the edge.

As Bart thought back to that experience, he remembered all the details of the person's attire, which seemed very strange to him. It looked like a coat of many colors but not just ordinary colors. They seemed to be alive and bursting forth, almost florescent, if that was the term to use. More than that though, Bart remembered what looked like feathers mixed in with the colors, and as his eyes made their way upwards, he caught sight of the hair. It was jet-black in color with thick curls, just like Michael's hair, but there was something else there too. He had to lean even closer towards the person as he took in thousands upon thousands of small jewels within the dark curls, almost as if they were a part of the hair itself.

Continuing to think back, Bart also remembered turning to his right side up there on the roof where he saw a sight that frightened him right from the top of his head to the very toes on his feet. He was now looking into the eyes of sheer terror, accompanied by the smell of rotting garbage, mixed with the smell of death, like one smells in a vehicle that has a dead animal in it somewhere, all mixed in with the smells of sulfur, smoke and fire. But it was the eyes that scared him the most, he recalled; they looked like molten metal mixed with red-hot coals.

Bart also remembered suddenly shooting straight up into the air, passing through the clouds and the light of the earth's glow at breakneck speeds. Looking up, he could see the stars coming into view in a brilliance he could never even have imagined. He could see the moon as a huge bright ball of light before his eyes, and off in the distance, beyond that, he could see star clusters of various bright colors, much like what he had just seen in the person's jet-black hair.

He was floating once again in outer space, and as he turned

to look back to where he had just come from, he gasped at the sight of the earth far beneath him; still, he was not afraid and had a strange peace about him. As he looked down on the earth, his eyes suddenly picked up on an object just coming around the far side of the earth, floating it would seem, just as he was. As it got closer and closer, he started to figure out that it was a very large cube, a pure black cube.

"What is that?" Bart remembered asking at the sight of the large black cube. But now he wasn't thinking back as he heard the Lord talk to him in real time.

"Stand up, my son."

Bart did as he was asked.

"Move to the wall directly in front of you."

Bart moved forward in the whiteness that surrounded him. He could not see the wall, but he knew it was there and kept moving with his hands stretched out in front of him until his fingers felt the solid wall. As his hands slid over the wall, they finally came in contact with what felt like a railing at waist height.

This is something new. This wasn't here the last time, Bart thought.

"Yes, you are right. This time, it is here for your benefit," the voice said to him. "What are you standing in right now, my son?" God asked with that smooth, pleasant voice.

"A room somewhere?"

"Grip the rail and hold on."

Bart instantly gripped the railing just as a very weird feeling came over him, and then next thing he knew, he was standing in outer space staring back at the large black cube. He viewed it for what seemed like mere seconds before he was back in the room, still gripping the railing.

"Do you now understand?"

It took a few moments as Bart remembered being in the white room and then outside looking at the cube.

"I-I am in the c-cube?"

"Yes."

"But the cube was black."

"Only on the outside."

Bart was suddenly aware that something was changing when he started to see the whiteness fading. He began to see the corners of this strange room, with walls that looked as if they were made of pure glass, with the exception of the railing that looked as if it were made of finely polished rosewood. But he could not see outside of the cube as the outside of it was still black.

"The blackness was your sin, my son, as it was you who made this room dark."

With that said, Bart could see the darkness dissipating right in front of his eyes until finally he was looking out at the vastness of space.

"Look down."

Bart dropped his head and was surprised to see that the floor too was made of what looked like pure glass, but more than that, he could see the earth in all its glory directly beneath his feet.

"Wow!" he said.

"Thank you."

"I never really saw the earth like that, and even the pictures I have seen from the space station don't do it justice."

"Your planet is the handiwork of my creation, my son, and it is humanity's playground. Now slowly turn around and face the other direction."

Bart did as he was instructed and froze in awe at the sight of billions of stars with explosions of color here and there. His mind could not fathom it all, and he even saw colors that were unexplainable to him.

"This, my son, is my playground, and there is even more beyond that. But it is time for us to part."

"W-will I ever see ... uh ... be with you again?"

"I have always been with you, Bart, and you have already seen me a number of times."

"I-I have?"

Suddenly within the confines of Bart's mind, he could see images of the homeless man, the stranger on the racquetball court, Winter and his mother.

"When you see any of my children, you see me. Now, my child, go forth and accomplish your heart's desire. Show love always, laugh always, feel for those who are hurting, feed the hungry, clothe the naked and visit those who are shut in.

"As my word says: Bear with each other and forgive one another if any of you have a grievance against someone. Forgive as I forgave you. Don't let anyone look down on you because you are young, but set an example for the believers in speech, in conduct, in love, in faith and in purity. And most importantly always remember in your heart that what is impossible with man is possible with me!"

With that, Bart broke down and instantly he was back in his room with a storm raging outside. He lowered his head as his emotions welled up to the surface, and through his tears, he managed to say a few words.

"I want to th-thank you, Lord, for all you have shown me and taught me in the white room of darkness!"

EPILOGUE

Eight years to the day of Earnest Bartholomew Woodsworth's 50th birthday, his family laid him to rest after a three-year battle with leukemia. Even though his family were in mourning, they were happy at the same time, knowing that their father was now with the Lord and that one day they would see him again.

At his funeral, attended by over 800 people, Franklin, Earnest's eldest son, gave the eulogy.

"My father was a man of vision, a pioneer in many fields of invention and innovation, but what he was most in life was a good father and a child of the King of kings," Franklin said, along with many other tributes and praises for a life well-lived.

At the private graveside ceremony, attended only by family members and business partners, Earnest left a family he loved dearly. Left to cherish his memory were his beloved wife, Katie, of 28 years; Franklin and Julie and their two girls; Caroline and Mitch with their daughter and son; and Bartholomew and his wife, Winter, who was with child at the time of Earnest's death.

Bartholomew's son was born one month after the death of his father, and in tribute to the man, they named their first boy Earnest Bartholomew Woodsworth Junior.

The last time that Earnest was able to carry on a conversation with his now-married children, he marveled at and reflected upon their journeys as grown men and women.

Franklin and Thomas, Earnest's former business partner and best friend, went on to form an innovation company of their own. They completed the F3 Dash Commander project for big-rig trucks. They also completed the Green Heat II project, which was making a huge impact all over the world when it came to personal power consumption. This product was in high demand from a number of friendly countries for use in their militaries, along with hikers, campers, wilderness guides and companies working in the frozen north.

They were working on a number of other projects that were a way ahead of their time. One of these projects was a totally new fuel source for automobiles that used none of the current forms of fuel or energy in the automotive sector. Also, they were delving into the world of wooden-steel. This was a new building material that they had accidentally stumbled upon in one of their other project adaptations, as they liked to say—even though they both felt that the technical expertise and chemical combinations were from the Lord.

Franklin's wife, Julie, had gone on to form a very successful real estate business, which grew from one office to three in the span of two years. In the beginning, Caroline and Winter were equal partners in the venture, but over time, they drifted into work with their husbands, while Julie kept up the business. She eventually found two other Christian women to join her company, and to date it was a thriving, very-busy real estate enterprise.

Caroline worked with Julie for three years but began to feel the tug of the Lord leading her into street ministry with her husband, Mitch. After parting ways with Julie, still within the realm of Christian love, Caroline joined her husband's music street ministry within the downtown core of the city. So effective was this ministry in reaching the youth and the lost for Christ through the realm of music that a number of other such ministries were asking Mitch to hold seminars and workshops in their cities and areas of work.

By then, Mitch and Caroline had one daughter in their family, and everywhere that Mom and Dad went, so too did baby Rose. Other than the first six months after birth, baby Rose began to travel with Caroline and Mitch in their work to reach the lost. Even though they could afford a nanny, they chose to have their daughter with them, to be a blessing as well as a future candidate to take over where Mom and Dad left off.

Caroline had one other blessing come into her life one day when working at her desk in the downtown core music ministry office building. As she sat at her desk that day, watching people streaming in and out of the ministry café, Caroline's eye caught a face that she thought she would never see again. There, standing in line to enter the café, was her old best friend Jenn, holding the hands of two young girls who Caroline assumed were her children. Caroline jumped up and rushed down to see her old friend once again.

Jenn was in shock almost as Caroline rushed up to her and swept her up into her arms in a big hug. The two women quickly caught up on lost time with Jenn telling of her failed marriage to a copper processing manager, who lost it all in the recent recession. He had basically kicked her and the girls out as he tried vainly to regain all his monetary gains. Finally when he realized that he would basically have to start over, he placed a revolver in his mouth and took his own life, leaving Jenn and the girls with nowhere to turn. She had heard on the radio about this new café opening downtown that would help out anyone with a need, so she came down to check it out and see if they could help her and the girls in any way.

Over the course of time, Caroline got Jenn a full-time job working in the ministry, and four months after she started work, Caroline had the privilege of leading her former/new best friend to the Lord.

One year after Bart's conversion and salvation, Bartholomew's Place opened its doors for the first time. The downtown former school was renovated with the latest technology, building materials, cooking and serving facilities, bedrooms, gymnasium, counselling rooms, food bank and a host of other outreach ministries. The entire building was brought up to the local and federal codes that included fire exits, sprinkler systems and an inner secure room in the case of weather-related threats or even threats from humans themselves that might require a lockdown situation.

Many times in his ministry to street people and the homeless, Bart used the lessons of the white room to reach out to the lost, explaining to them why it was that God could not look at them as they were. He would tell them that when Christ came into the picture, he was like an all-encompassing whiteness that covered them completely, even though sin was still in the picture like a darkness. So when God looked at them, all he saw was the whiteness of his Son, Jesus, covering the darkness of sin, and through this, God accepted them as his children.

Bartholomew's Place started small, but because of demand, it soon grew from 500 beds to 1500 and then two years later into another building that would allow them to double the number of beds. Within the span of five years, this ministry grew to house 3,000 men and women complete with a huge food bank that covered the needs of at least three-quarters of the city and rural districts as well. The ministry also employed 50 full-time staff, 120 part-time staff and 600 volunteers. In addition to all of this, it also had 80 meal trucks that went out to those who were too far away to get to the downtown ministry, 55 clothing trucks that gathered donated clothing from dump bins located at various locations throughout the city and surrounding districts and 32 food-gathering trucks that brought in donated and bought food items to the downtown ministry location.

When Winter left the real estate business to join Bartholomew's Place, she had a vision of a feeding program that involved well over 5,000 people, so that was where Bart and John placed her. Through the trust fund set up by Earnest and Katie, Winter was able to get the operation up and going within a mere 10 months. When the doors to the new facility opened, they were feeding well-cooked meals with professional chef coordinators who saw to evenly portioned healthy meals to men, women and children alike.

Eventually the feeding program included healthy food preparation classes, for those who wanted to cook more economically for their families, dietitians and a host of other areas that dealt with feeding the family.

Katie and Shelly became even closer friends after the death of Katie's husband, Earnest. Katie had no desire and no need to work as she spent her time with her friends and taking care of the grandchildren as they came along. She greatly missed Earnest but was even more thankful that he finally came around and accepted the Lord into his life at the same time as their son Bart out on the country club's golf course.

She prayed for her children and their families and ministries every day, along with Earnest, knowing that he was now happier than he ever could be with anything earth had to offer. So Katherine Sylvia Woodsworth patiently waited until it was her time to join her husband once more, and then the circle would be complete.

Earnest, Katie, Franklin, Bart and Caroline Woodsworth had endured much in their walk of life, but the most important lesson learned was that no amount of money, gold, fame or even family could ever compare to the riches that await the children of God in heaven!

ALSO BY LORNE SPENCER HRABIA

The Brighton Furlong Trilogy:

Book 1: *21 Drops*
978-1-4866-0445-6

Brighton Furlong is a fast-rising star in the world of architectural design, but he has a problem that keeps him up at night—every night. He has a reoccurring dream with no explainable meaning, along with many other dreams and visions.

In the small town of Mardillon, Brighton meets Lexi, a woman capable of interpreting his nightly dream. Together the two of them delve into the depths of the dream world and discover an amazing pattern and direction that could lead them and the world to eternity.

From small-town coffee shop encounters to a coordinated worldwide terrorist attack, Brighton Furlong and his small band of followers embark on the journey of a lifetime in their quest to find the answer to his visions and more ...

Book 2: *14 Visions*
978-1-4866-0449-4

Brighton Furlong's visions become a reality, as terrifying world events begin to unfold. Like a modern-day Moses, Brighton leads a small but growing group towards their future home in an increasingly hostile time. While the world is held in the grip of uncertainty and fear, God prepares the way for his children, through his servant with a little help from on high.

The adventure continues with spiritual battles, both in the human and heavenly realms, attacks from the enemy and the gathering together of those servants who will fulfill the wheel vision ...

Book 3: *777 Days*
978-1-4866-0453-1

In *777 Days*, Brighton Furlong's adventure comes to a head as the world implodes and people must struggle to survive in a hostile and dangerous environment. The Star Christian Community Complex is filling fast as the Lord leads his children there. Work at the Praise the Lord building is on full swing, its walls hiding its real purpose.

Rumors of war explode into reality all around the globe as Brighton, his Group of Ten, and 3,000 souls go into hiding, living their lives free of the world they once knew. In the midst of limited nuclear war and the collapse of the world system, humanity is thrown into near-extinction for a period of time before the Lord restores his chosen ones for a time of revival unlike anything the world has ever seen.

Gripping stories of survival, attacks, raids, romance and murder are thrown into the mix of *777 Days*, culminating with a glorious reawakening. This awesome ending is sure to capture your imagination and make you ask: what if?

AUTHOR'S NOTE

I have been asked many times where my book ideas come from, and the answer is always the same—my dreams!

It seems that I have been blessed with the ability to remember my dreams in great detail, so much so that my wife often tells others that I wake up in the morning and relate to her a novel I have dreamed.

Every book I have written so far has come from a dream I have had, and I hope it continues for some time. I can remember a dream I had when I was about 10 years old. I can picture it in my mind, remembering the feel of it, the colors and almost the smell if that is really possible.

The White Room of Darkness, like the other books I have written, has partially come from a dream, and then the rest of the book comes from within my mind, which I know is very active in the hours I am awake.

All of my life, I have searched for that niche that we all fit into, and it is writing for me. I love to sit and write a book with my computer, so much so that I could write for hours on end, foregoing even my meals. Writing is the passion that drives me, but the gift of writing stories comes from the Lord, and to him all glory and praise go ...

Printed in the United States.
D. B. (something)

Printed in the United States
By Bookmasters